ERIC MICHAEL VRTIS

This book is for readers.

Please, reader, know that the above's self-evidence is, I hope, the corniest thing in these pages. And know that I really do mean you:

You who are in love, the imperfect kind; you who have considered not a few times whether you might be crazy; you who are afraid of what unimaginable future might follow the dark times of now; you who seek

comfort/escape/meaning/laughter/catharsis/transcendence

here, in books about made-up people in made-up places.

I'd also like to express sincere gratitude to this book's first readers, without whose insight and encouragement I would never have been able to write something I could consider finished:

Dani, Alex, Adam, Kevin, Morgan, Nick, Gordon, and Mike,

and to my parents, for everything else.

Book 1.

i.

Letter to V.

V,

  I knew—we both knew—that it would end eventually. Every love story has an ending. Sometimes two people stick together right up until the very end, but usually they don't. You and I...we simply do not speak the same language. Your words were never enough of an assurance for me, and my casual hand on your skin could never be more than casual. Didn't you always want it to be more than casual? At the time, I just wanted everything to be casual. Now I know better, but now it's too late. Oh well. Like I said, we both knew it. Alas, this is the end. There, I said it. I have my assurance. My closure.

  But what is an end besides a new beginning? I'm sure we are both better off for it. We can begin our new lives apart, as others so happily do together. I'm trying to think back on where our togetherness began. I can't easily recall a place, or a time, for any matter. Maybe it always was. Or like the cliché, "In a different life," or whatever. I guess this thing of ours goes on, past and present.

I asked you once if you were staying. You said it was either that or leaving. Now I know what you meant by that. Never lose your sense of humor, V. Anyway, you stayed and I didn't, and I try not to wish that I had.

I would be happy to hear that you are well -- Lado

ii.

Narrator's Introduction

Who am I to be telling this story? Allow me to start off by saying that I know Lado as well as anyone does. In fact, I probably know Lado better than Lado knows himself. That's not his fault, by the way, because who really knows himself? I know, that sounds like some Confucian bullshit. But seriously, anything you know about yourself you learned from experience, and that, my friend, works retroactively. Sorry to break the news. You may think you know everything, but what happens today and what you, in turn, learn tomorrow could throw all that right out the window.

And as far as 'story' goes, I hope this one is worth telling. Otherwise, I'll be wasting my time and your time alike. I don't want to do that. Honestly, I don't. What I want to do now is ask you a question: What do you make of Lado's letter? Does he seem believable in that letter? Because one thing that I can say about Lado is he's honest. And you can believe him when he writes a letter like that. He meant that when he wrote it. It's about a real person in his life, someone he knew very well, someone he loved. But these days when someone writes something like that we think they're putting on a show, don't we? Because it's so melodramatic and cheesy, like a big fat load of cheese whiz in a movie that you feel guilty for enjoying because it's so shamelessly, indulgently cheesy. We like to see that crap in movies but when people act that way in real life we don't think it's for real. But that's the way Lado lives, using his guts and his instincts and following his heart.

But there's one thing that I just can't seem to figure out. I can't say exactly what it is, either, because I don't know it. Maybe that's why people like me tell stories in the first place, so that people like you can help shine some light on things. But I can say that this thing I don't know for sure is the very thing that compelled Lado to live his life in a way that makes me want to tell a story about him. People will talk about thinking on a certain wavelength, or being wired differently than others. That's mostly what I mean about Lado. He was just different in a way that I can't quite describe in words. I hope that by telling this story I can give you that same impression of him and you will find his story worthwhile. Maybe you'll be able to relate to it or learn from it or even be changed by it, and you will start to understand for yourself why I feel this way.

He surely had goals, and I can say that he spent much of his time searching for the answers to his questions. But he didn't have a destination in mind when he set out on his journey. Like so many other wanderers and adventurers, he set out into the great unknown of the human heart, hoping to arrive at some kind of a destination sooner or later.

As you may or may not know, sometimes there's no coming back to where you came from once you leave, especially when you set out for an unknown place. There's only going forward until you find your destination, and if you do arrive at one, you have to make a pretty big decision: do you stay or do you leave? If you choose to stay there, you'll find that the destination offers a calm relief, serves as a resting place. After all, even a short journey through the unknown can be exhausting enough to choose lasting comfort over continued exploration. Chances are there are other wanderers that have decided to remain there, and you will always find yourself among interesting company as new faces come and go.

The other option is to go off journeying again, unsure whether you'll find another place to rest, whether you'll encounter anyone or anything more interesting than what you knew before. You may never know if it was worth it to get up and go again. It may take months or even years to find anything at all, anything besides blackness and quiet.

But some people are cut out for it, you know, some people belong out there in the unknown. For them it's not a scary place, it's not vast and empty and dark. For these types of lifelong wanderers, the unknown is the harbinger of clarity and understanding, a place not unlike outer space, uninhabitable and cold to most but to others irresistible, warmly lit by the ancient light of a trillion burning stars.

iii.

Mismatched:
A Vignette

Lado woke up at 6 a.m. and his first thoughts were of the night. *How is it that years, a lifetime even, can pass by in a dream?* With his hand he searched the nightstand for his glasses, where they were not. *I must have knocked them off the table in my sleep.* He reached down to the floor and found his glasses next to a mess of books. He sat up and looked around and made a noise. It sounded like the letter *f.* As he exhaled he tasted the alcoholic fumes from inside his chest and his belly as the vapors passed over his tongue and between his lips and out of his mouth.

Ernie needed to tinkle. Lado bundled up and took the dog outside for a long walk through their neighborhood. It was still dark, but people were already going about the early-morning motions that signal the beginning of a new day. At this hour, since it was still too early for the stores to be open, there weren't very many people along the sidewalks or at the storefronts, but that would happen soon enough. A slow procession of cars rolled by in the streets as people came into the city from the suburbs for business of some kind or another. Most of the people who worked in the neighborhood's convenient stores, restaurants fast and slow, boutiques, markets, cafes, and auto shops came on foot or by bicycle from a home nearby. Lado most liked to see commuters riding bicycles.

Lado began to notice the scores of people standing or walking with no destination and no apparent purpose. Lado wasn't sure what these people were doing up so early. *Probably homeless*, he thought, *waking with the first light of the sun.*

Meanwhile, Lado heard the faint rumble of moving trains downtown, across the river, where East Valmesta had already begun to come alive. Soon the horde of the city center work force would turn up having taken a train or a cab or a chauffeur.

The people around him, Lado noticed by studying the eclectic neighborhood he lived in, were most often of a certain lifestyle type that was characterized by their relationship to binary extremes, for example: hyperactivity and languid inertia, gluttony and abstemiousness, munificence and self-interest and so on. Often people's lifestyles took shape based on their profession— businessperson or social worker or service worker—and such people usually interpreted the world around them as a set of symbolic meanings and messages that were constantly used to ascertain their personal sense of value to the world. People who thought highly of themselves wanted to be, and usually were, successful. Successful people showed it in their faces and in their walks and wore their success like a badge, somehow. They could be picked out of a crowd. Other people had no ambition whatsoever and paid no mind to success. But most people Lado knew and met were really just somewhere in between. Lado himself was not overly concerned with making a success of what he saw as his life's work, which was writing. Lado was more intent on writing something with artistic value, something that would last. In

Lado's mind, to do so would affirm what he had long believed to be true: that he was an artist. *Artist*, Lado believed, is a very tough label to rightly obtain, for it suggests not only a level of talent and creativity that Lado wasn't always sure he possessed, but it also suggested a pervasiveness beyond forms, that an artist is an artist whether they're writing an epic poem or styling a person's hair. He couldn't be a real artist, could he?

Regardless, Lado tried to live the life he had come to imagine as the artist's life. After reading the biographies and Wikipedia pages of his idols, learning the virtues and vices of the literati, he had made a number of deliberate lifestyle choices. He would travel when possible, spend time in nature, and try to remain inebriated for extended periods of time if not as a state of permanence. He would wait tables in order to financially support himself during his years of being an unknown, would not sleep and would rather surrender to his muse whenever she called upon him to do her bidding. He would compose impetuous prose and haphazard poetry at the most insane hours. He would forgo eating and smoke cigarettes instead. Not watch TV. Perhaps most importantly he would consider himself a member of a privileged group of similarly inclined solitary expressive types, and he would deliberately avoid contact with others in order to get work done. Other people wouldn't understand him, would not know how to be kind to him. To explain his experiences, his internal sufferings, with them would inevitably lead to confusion and distrust. He would avoid that. The people Lado considered his friends all shared many of these feelings with him. What was important to them was important to him, and so on, and success, when it came, if it came at all, would resemble the happiness he gained through friendship with other artistic types. That is not to say that he didn't long to be recognized by his peers or by the literary elite or by the critics as good. On the contrary, he did.

Lado's observations usually led to insights but never to the establishment of a specific nomenclature to categorize people. In fact, what he came up with was in effect a system of human categorization completely devoid of titular references, a sort of counter-nomenclature, or at least an elected lack of criticism that could be looked upon by others as a self-conscious choice to avoid being judgmental, but it was really just an acting out of Lado's personal belief that people simply were like him or they were not.

Some people will claim that they are good judges of character. Other people will tell you that they aren't, that they are prone to miscalculations and that they will never fully trust anyone again because of the times they have been misled and betrayed in the past. Maybe it's true that some people are and others aren't. Good judges of character, that is. It might be sort of an intuitive thing, and for those things one is at an advantage if one has a strong sense of intuition. As for Lado, sometimes he was impressed by how much he felt he knew a person after a casual encounter, or after a few months of knowing them, but a lot of times he was surprised to find out later that he didn't know them very well at all because they did something that he would never have predicted, or they said one thing and did another with, or without, bad intentions. The people Lado spent time with the most were the ones that he thought he knew the most and had always the best intentions.

As for what people liked to do and how people earned a living and whether they were any good at what they did, sometimes Lado had a general idea based on first impression. Mostly he learned that you simply couldn't tell for sure without getting to know someone. Lado himself was a writer first and a waiter second. Some people thought it was the other way around since he served tables to earn a living for himself and he wrote simply because it felt like the right thing to do, but Lado would disagree. Writing was the most important. He enjoyed the irony of the cliché "don't quit your day job," which he heard often, clichés being clichés because you hear them often, because he wrote during the day and went to work, so to speak, at night.

When Lado got back to his apartment after walking Ernie through the neighborhood, he had two eggs fried over easy and two pieces of toast with butter. After eating, he started to make coffee and he lit a cigarette. He checked his e-mail. Then he showered. That is more or less how Lado began just about every other day, though he didn't usually wake so early. When he finished taking a shower he poured himself a cup of plain coffee and sat down with his laptop near the living room's bay window to write. He looked outside. Turned away from the window, closed his eyes, swallowed. Wiggled into a comfortable seating position, lifted his hands, rested the heels of his palms on the cool surface of the keyboard. His fingers hovered over the keys for a full minute or more. Then he wrote. Times New Roman symbol after Times New Roman symbol. Delete. Delete. More words and delete. That was his process. Select, cut, scroll up, paste, and delete. More words. Writing and always some more of the rewriting for several hours that seemed to pass by in minutes.

Afterward Lado had a small lunch and got ready for work. He shaved and brushed his teeth and swished Listerine around inside his mouth and then he got dressed in all-black clothes with black shoes and a black belt. When he left his apartment, he walked two and a half blocks east toward Richard Boulevard and turned right down an alley between a Trendy Clips and a Sombrero's fast food restaurant. From there he had to pass two dumpsters, one on his right and one on his left, and then a respite for the local homeless that included a charred metal can, several empty 40-oz beer bottles, a few empty bottles of cheap whiskey, a used and tattered copy of *The Adventures of Huckleberry Finn*, some blankets, two shopping carts, three empty plastic gas canisters and a pair of drum sticks, one of which was broken in half. It was a similar scene to the one Lado beheld the day before; the only difference was the drumstick, which before had been intact.

Almost at the end of the alley, on the left side, was the rear entrance to Doraku Sushi restaurant, which had a door that opened into the alley for the employees to enter. When Lado walked inside, the restaurant was almost empty, and Jeon, the manager, was sitting at the bar with his laptop open next to what looked like a vodka and soda or a vodka tonic. There were powdery green stains on his black shirt where he had wiped his hands clean of wasabi, and his hair, which was usually very neatly styled and shiny black, was out of order and unclean. It was clear from the quiet and the overall sense of absence that Jeon was the only other person in the building, which meant he had been doing everything from greeting customers and taking their orders to preparing and serving their meals. *He sent the other servers home early,* Lado thought. Jeon didn't notice Lado approaching the bar from the rear entrance.

"What's up, Jeon?"

Nothing. Lado cleared his throat.

"What are you working on?" Lado looked over Jeon's shoulder and saw that he was entering numbers into a spreadsheet on his computer.

"I'm trying to find a mistake," Jeon said. "But what I find is that there is no mistake. I do the numbers, this is what I get. Negative dollars," he inhaled slowly. "My restaurant is not making any money." He exhaled a deep breath and ran a hand through his hair. "I tell everyone else to go home. But you can stay. Dinnertime we will be busy." Lado immediately felt for Jeon and understood the strain he was under. Renting a commercial property in Valmesta was expensive, even on the west side of the river. Lado, though he didn't know much about running a business, knew that. Valmesta got a bad rap in the media, and people from other cities liked to make fun of how run-down it had gotten since the decline of manufacturing, but outsiders were surprised to find out how much it cost to live there. It wasn't cheap, unless you ventured into the truly downtrodden parts.

Lado could tell Jeon was straining to do the math. He didn't say anything, just nodded and started setting up for dinner service, making sure the tables were clean and the glasses polished.

Jeon was an immigrant from Seoul who had spent many years in Japan learning the art of sushi before moving to the United States for his alleged slice of the American pie. He was a very skilled chef, specializing in Korean-style sashimi and *gimbap* as well as Japanese sushi, but after relocating to the U.S., he adjusted his menu to appeal more fittingly to the less sushi-experienced palates of American mouths. Still, wanting to remain authentic, he kept some of his live fish and raw sashimi dishes on the menu for the more adventurous foodies. Lado, for one, was especially fond of salmon and squid sashimi as Jeon prepared them, and would sometimes stay after work for sashimi and a few rounds of sake. In Lado's opinion, Jeon was a superb chef who fell upon the misfortune of serving a clientele who preferred the comfortable simplicity of a California or a spicy tuna roll over the freshly prepared and delicate sashimi varieties, which were prized commodities in Seoul. Jeon, at that time, had been owner and operator of Doraku Sushi Bar for twelve years, and during that time, he had only served one customer a live sashimi. A live sashimi, by the way, is a fish sliced evenly along the rib cage and plated and served alive, gills flapping, so that the pieces of raw flesh are removed from the fish with chopsticks and eaten unsullied. It is a fresh and artful presentation if it's not a little bit gimmicky, and customers ordered it quite often in Korea. By the same token, never once had a customer ordered a live octopus. In fairness, Jeon told Lado, even in Korea live octopus is considered a bit of an adventurous dish. As one would expect, octopi don't very much like to be shoved into the mouths of large, bipedal land creatures, and justly they put up a good fight, wriggling about and suctioning the inside of their would be devourer's mouth and esophagus. In the U.S., each of the two items, live sashimi and live octopus, were considered either insanely rogue or unethical and inhumane, meaning only some, but a very small few, customers would be interested in trying them. Jeon still kept a live octopus in his restaurant, ready for someone to order the freshest possible tentacled cephalopod, but it had become more of a pet after being in the tank for so long. Jeon was considering taking the poor thing off the menu.

Dinner service was indeed very busy. At times Lado was waiting on eight or nine different parties, most of which included businesspeople who had come in for an after work meal. The business clientele typically ordered a few rounds of sake bombs to go with their food, especially if they were dining with coworkers and not clients. "In Korea," Jeon once told Lado, "everybody go if the boss go. And everybody drink just as much as the boss. If the boss fall over drunk, you fall over drunk." With that sort of cultural understanding, Jeon typically encouraged his business class parties to get as drunk as they wanted to, and to stay for as long as they liked. They didn't just come for the sushi; they came to dine like Korean businessmen. Most of the American businessmen, as it happens, had been to South Korea and had experienced this type of top-down inebriation, and when they brought their assistants and interns to Doraku, they expected them to follow suit when they got drunk. They did.

For Lado this meant a lot of difficult customers, and many of them stayed long, got wasted, mixed up their bills, and didn't tip him as much as they should have. Fortunately, this didn't happen that day.

Most of the other parties were couples or regulars. Lado always liked to watch the couples interact—talking, eating, drinking—when he wasn't busy. When it was just Lado and Jeon, they would sit or stand behind the bar and watch the customers, making guesses as to how the couple had met and how long they had been together, which usually ended when another customer walked in and Jeon had to greet them and pretend like he wasn't just standing behind the bar drinking a beer with Lado.

At eleven o'clock Lado and Jeon locked the doors and finished cleaning up. Lado sat down to do his paperwork. All told, he reported $174.13 in credit card tips. That money was reported income, which would appear on his paycheck after taxes. He also had close to $100 in cash that would be going right into his pocket unreported. When it was good, it was good.

Before they turned off the lights and walked out the door, Jeon invited Lado to stay for a drink, which usually meant three or four. Lado gladly obliged. Lado went behind the bar and reached into the cooler for a bottle of sake. He assessed the coolness of it and decided it should be colder. He scooped some ice into a small bucket and poured a tablespoon or so of salt onto the ice and placed the bottle in the salted ice to chill it quickly. Lado opened two bottles of Sapporo and slid one of them across the bar to Jeon. They clanked the bottles together in a universal gesture of good spirit or good health or good sex or whatever—probably all of the above—and drank.

Jeon went into the kitchen to prepare some salmon sashimi and a seaweed salad, taking the beer with him. Lado drank his beer. Soon Jeon returned and set the food down on the bar. Jeon didn't skimp on the quality when he prepared sashimi for the two of them. Before Lado lay a beautifully sliced filet of wild pacific Chinook salmon, with its rich pink flesh, almost red in color and striped with white fat, which Jeon would swear is the best thing in the world to eat, both for flavor and nutrition. Jeon also brought a salad of seaweeds and some fresh wasabi. By then the sake was well chilled, and Lado opened the bottle and poured it into two small glasses. Lado swished the sake in his mouth to taste it fully before he swallowed it. The liquid was clear and cold, smooth as velvet, and mostly dry, but it became a little sweet as it passed over the back of the tongue. The two men ate in quiet.

After a while, Lado noticed Jeon staring fixedly at a picture hanging on the wall of the restaurant. It was a photograph of a young Jeon standing on a very tall bridge overlooking a waterfall with his arm around another teenage boy. The two boys had the same smile: modest, luminescent, and shrewd. Lado had always assumed it was a photo of Jeon and his brother, but he had never asked Jeon about him. Sensing that Lado was about to ask him what was on his mind, Jeon said, "My brother is missing." He looked away to regain his composure while his eyes welled up with tears. "In South Korea, all men have to go the army for mandatory service. He very good, you know, at being a soldier. He has much responsibility. They make him do things very difficult, very dangerous. He has been two weeks missing."

Lado stopped chewing and stood still. He swallowed his food and washed it down with a generous mouthful of sake. Jeon was still holding back the tears, covering his eyes with his hands. Lado patted Jeon on the shoulder, "I'm sorry, man," a minor affection, and Jeon couldn't resist crying any longer. "I wouldn't worry about it until you know more. No sense being upset." A full minute passed before Jeon could stop himself from crying.

"Perhaps it's nothing," he said at last.

Lado poured his boss another sake and raised his own glass. "To your brother, a courageous soldier and a fine gentleman," he said, and the two men drank.

"I worry because it is just him and me. I send money to my mother once a month. No other money for her if my brother is gone. And if here, Doraku, I don't make money, and my brother can't support her, she need me there to help her. It is very hard make money in this country. In South Korea, we try to be like United States. We want to own business, work in tall buildings, get drunk, make love to our wife. Be better than the other men. We think that's what America is like. Where is my wife? Twelve years I've been here! And no wife. No money to show."

Lado was beginning to feel emotionally beleaguered. He was young, unconcerned with finding a wife and making a lot of money, and he definitely was not expecting to have an intense conversation when he cracked open the two bottles of Sapporo and sat down to drink. He also had $100 cash in his pocket, which could buy a lot of fun after midnight in his part of town, and because he was a little wired from caffeine and the newly consumed alcohol, and because he was a little tensed up from witnessing Jeon's breakdown, he was already devising a plan to blow off some steam.

Lado tried to steer the conversation in a different direction, but when he, say, brought up gossip about coworkers, Jeon replied that he didn't keep up with his employees' personal lives, and that he didn't care. When Lado asked Jeon if he had seen the college basketball game where the one team came back to take the lead and the other team tied it up again in the final moments, only to lose in overtime, Jeon said that he didn't follow sports. When Lado realized there would be no taking Jeon's mind off the subject of his missing brother, he decided to politely excuse himself, thanking Jeon for the food, saying he wished the best for Jeon's brother and that he, Lado, would see Jeon tomorrow.

His mind abuzz with sake and beer, Lado walked the dim, lamp-lit streets. There weren't very many people outside. The weather was not great. Chilly. And there was the smell of impending drizzle in the air. Dampness in Valmesta brought with it the fragrance of fermentation, a sweet, sour must like a moldy peach, a reminder that even the best things, an entire city even, can spoil. On a cold night it wasn't so bad, but during the summertime it could be enough to make one's stomach turn inside out.

Lado walked the few blocks between Doraku and one of his favorite dives, the Fool's Gold Tavern, which had good beer and bourbon prices, a decent jukebox, and an attractive, all-female staff. Well, at least somewhat attractive. Most of the waitresses were young, at least, and encouraged to show off whatever they had to show off. On nights when bars weren't very busy, Lado liked to visit places like that. They gave him someone to hit on without concern for offending a boyfriend or getting rejected. Lado was a shameless patron. Usually the girls humored him as they served him lots of drinks and got him very well drunk, but it was just aimless flirtation.

On the other hand, one particular waitress at the Tavern, Monica, had given Lado her number a few weeks back, and she seemed like she might be interested in becoming more intimately acquainted. She was there that night.

Lado was sitting at the bar rail. He flirted with the bartender, hoping to make Monica jealous. The bartender was the middle-age type who works out all the time and follows dieting trends but also stays up late and drinks a lot. It was impossible for Lado to tell how old she was exactly, especially since he had been drinking. Thirty or fifty or somewhere in there. She was the tavern's matriarch. He told her she had nice hands and asked if he could hold them. He felt them as if determining their quality. "You could totally be a hand model," he said. "No ring?"

"I don't wear it at work," she said. "I get better tips when men think I'm single." At the service end of the bar, Monica stood waiting for some drinks she had rung in, and she observed the back and forth between Lado and the bartender, who was holding her up.

"Whitney, did you see my drink ticket for table twelve?" Monica called out across the bar. The matriarch pulled her hands away from Lado's and made her way over to Monica. She removed the ticket from the printer and read it.

"Do they want salt on the margarita?" she asked.

"No. If I wanted it with salt I would have rang it in that way." Monica walked away into the kitchen. Lado watched the bartender. She rolled her eyes so that only he could see her rolling them. Lado grinned and held up his empty beer bottle. The bartender sauntered over to bring Lado another beer, and then went back to making Monica's drinks.

A half-minute later Monica came out of the kitchen with a basket of fries and a plate of chicken wings. She passed by Lado on her way to a table, and Lado made it a point not to look at her. The next time she walked by Lado spoke.

"You can bring me some food, too. Whenever you get a chance."

"Did you order it?"

Lado studied her. She was annoyed, perhaps jealous of the attention he was giving the bartender. "I was hoping you could just bring it," he said.

"Ask your bartender."

"I'm asking you."

"I'm not your server. I don't think Whitney would appreciate it."

"Whitney's the bartender?"

"Yes."

"I guess I could ask Whitney. But I really like the idea of you bringing it to me."

At that point Lado was sitting on the barstool still facing forward with only his head turned to face Monica, who had moved from behind Lado to be more alongside him. She leaned her elbows on the backs of Lado's chair and the chair next to him. Whitney walked over to check on Lado. He turned to face her.

"Can I order food from you?" he asked.

"What do you want?"

Monica leaned in closer to Lado. He could feel her breast press against his shoulder.

"Chicken wings."

"How many?"

"A dozen."

"Mild, medium or hot?"

"As hot as they come."

"Anything else?"

"Another beer. Thank you. And another shot of Jameson."

Whitney turned to the computer. Lado looked at her ass. It wasn't very much to look at.

Monica said, "See how easy that was?"

"As long as you bring them out."

Whitney placed another beer in front of Lado. He raised the old beer up and finished it in two big gulps and set the empty bottle down. Monica walked away, her hips and ass swaying. Whitney handed Lado a shot glass filled to the brim. He took it right out of her hand and shot it.

"A nice money maker on that one," he said.

"Yea, she's one of our more popular items."

"Can I take her home?"

"I don't give a shit."

"I'm going to invite her over tonight."

"You think you can get it up?"

"Of course I can. Never had that problem before. Have you seen her ass?"

About five minutes later Monica returned with a dozen steaming red chicken wings. The smell of them burned Lado's nose.

"Thank you. I'd better let them cool off."

"I saw what he put on them. They're not going to cool off."

"What are you wearing?"

"Excuse me?"

Lado looked at her chest.

"It's part of the uniform."

"No, I mean under your t-shirt. I'm finding myself very curious as to what kind of undergarments you have on. Especially since I can see the outline of your bra."

"If you're lucky, maybe you'll get to find out."

"If you give me your number, maybe I'll get lucky."

"You have my number."

"Oh, yea." Lado took out his phone and pressed the home button to unlock it. It was not a smart phone; Lado couldn't afford one yet. "Which Monica are you? I have several."

"Shut up."

"When are you off work?"

"Depends. Maybe three."

"I'm texting you right now so you have my number. Call me when you're done."

Monica walked away and Lado bit into a chicken wing. They were very spicy, but Lado played tough. "Whitney, come here. You must try a wing."

"Absolutely not. Are you crazy? Your eyes are watering."

"They are not. Here, try one."

"No, thank you."

"Suit yourself."

After finishing all twelve chicken wings, Lado finished his beer and pulled the cash out of his pocket. He counted three twenty-dollar bills and left them on the bar. On his way out he found Monica by a computer. He put his arm around her waist and whispered in her ear, "I'll see you later."

"Bye," she said, "be safe."

Lado's living room, altogether still and quiet, was spinning. Soon the quiet became a ringing in Lado's ears. To get his mind off things he went to the fridge for a beer and sat down at his laptop to read a poem he had written earlier. When he finished reading it, he realized he didn't like it. It was not art. It was, indeed, rather self-deprecating, self-pitying even. He didn't like that he could feel that way about himself. He started to cry. Would he ever write anything worth calling *art*?

Suddenly he felt tired; he felt his poetry was a tired amalgamation of other poet's old work, like another artist's painting being reprinted, cut into jigsaw pieces, and put back together by another so-called artist to appear mostly just like the original. Lado considered the unlikely but terrifyingly real possibility that, throughout history and by some act of human or universal creation, everything of value had already been made, that everything being made now is just a remake and, as such, is basically artistically valueless, just a waste of time and energy and human potential. Another form of human excrement. Simply put, shit.

Artistically speaking, however, even shit probably has some value. If Duchamp could put his name on a shitter and it appeared in a fine art gallery, then someone else could come along and take a shit in it, and would the gallery not be pleased? That is a harsh criticism, and probably is not true. But, alas, Lado considered: has not art pushed the limit to the extent that any attempt to achieve shock value in lieu of artistic value ultimately results in a brutal calamity of unbearable banality?

His thoughts raced furiously: the great artists have always been brave enough to push societal boundaries, but then suddenly an entire generation, fueled by false bravado and a socially conditioned sense of self-importance, decide that everyone, not just the artist, has a right, even a duty, to push society's boundaries. Teeny bop rebellion disguised as Cultural Revolution. Artists respond by further pushing the boundaries of what is believed to be acceptable, and it's at its most grotesque when concerning politics. Photographic depictions of clerical misdeeds are hung from the spires atop the largest Catholic Church building in America, and the church becomes a shocking artistic statement instead of a place of worship. How fucking *insightful*. A woman's vagina is transfigured into a razor-toothed monster intended to chew up and spit out all penises, horror cinema with pseudo-academic merit by way of radical feminism, so *intelligent*. But really all the film does is desexualize women, and nobody wants that. A newlywed man and man enact their own suicide on stage to a live audience in the name of art, "'til death do us part," how *avant-garde*.

Lado didn't aspire to be shocking. He was far too sensitive and self-conscious. Lado was, in fact, so very self-conscious of his own writing that he was sometimes afraid to say how he really felt about things. He needed to toughen up, develop a thick skin. He tried to avoid cliché. He stopped reading for a year hoping that by not reading he would be free to write uninfluenced by others' ideas. He believed that if he didn't read, then anything he wrote would be exclusively his. His writing suffered as a result of not reading, or at least that's what he thought. Eventually he started reading again.

After reflecting on his poem for a while, and following one tangential, alcohol-fueled thought to the next, Lado opened another beer and sat down by the window looking out into the street. There were a few people walking on either sidewalk, most of them dressed in varying shades of black or grey or navy blue, the men wearing tennis shoes and not wearing hats. Lado was surprised to see them. It must have been three in the morning. Lado thought about women.

He was extraordinarily horny. He imagined the type of woman he most longed for during those moments: young, sexy, easy, uncomplicated. The type that went out looking for a man to go home with, dressed to leave men yearning, hard. He fantasized of aggressive encounters, drunk to excess, freed of inhibition, raw and primal, teeth and flesh, blows and bites nearing blood and pain and violence. Then he thought about what the bartender had said. He probably couldn't even have gotten it up, he was so drunk. The booze-sex paradox: Alcohol increases desire but hinders performance. At what point is the most pleasure to be had?

Lado distanced himself from his reverie. He thought of the women he had loved, really loved and not just fucked. Isn't that what he really wanted? Yes and no. He kept looking outside, at the now almost empty street. A bearded old man, dressed in layers to weather the cold night, smoke rising from his face, the act of lifting and lowering a cigarette to and from his mouth the only thing to do. For Lado no sound but his own ears ringing. Alone, he fell asleep, facing the window.

When he woke up it was afternoon. Ernie got up and nudged Lado's thigh with his snout when he noticed Lado stirring. Lado's neck was stiff. He groaned and stretched and stumbled to the bathroom to take a piss. He didn't feel well. The only way he was going to feel better was by having a drink. There was coffee leftover in his French press from the day before. He poured it into a mug and microwaved it for one minute. He took the mug out of the microwave and breathed the coffee's steam and he started to feel better. He unscrewed the cap off a bottle of Jameson and tipped the bottle and the whisky poured into his mug. He stirred it and took a sizeable gulp.

When he took Ernie outside for a walk, he lit a cigarette and looked at his phone and saw that Monica had called him and left a voicemail at 3:38a.m.

"Hey Lado, it's Monica, I know it's kind of late and you're probably asleep, but I'm just getting off work and I thought maybe you'd want to have a night cap? I could come over or something. Call me or text me. Bye."

The sun shined brightly in Lado's eyes. He felt a headache coming on. He put out his cigarette halfway through, thinking it was the cause. *This isn't a day for being outside*, he thought.

Ernie shit on the sidewalk and Lado wondered whether he should leave it or pick it up. He even looked around to see whether anyone else had seen. There was no one. He decided it would be better to pick it up, but he didn't have a plastic bag to put it in. *There's enough litter in this city for me to find something to pick up dog shit*, he thought, but there wasn't any that he could see. He walked to the end of the block and stood on the corner where the two streets' sidewalks met. The pavement was rising and splitting in places from the growth of tree roots beneath it. Grass grew between the cracks, unmowed, probably almost a foot in length. Down the block a plastic bag blew across the road and met a fence by the old baseball field. Lado started toward the bag quickly, hoping to catch it before it blew away any farther. Behind him, a car was approaching. Before he made it twenty steps, Lado noticed that a car parked along the side of the road had one of its rear windows busted out. The car appeared abandoned. The front tire adjacent to the curb was completely flat and dried out. In the backseat was an assortment of trash and clothes; perhaps someone had lived in the car recently. Lado leaned inside to see, first, whether there was anything he might want, and, second, whether there was anything he could use to pick up Ernie's shit. There was an awful smell, mostly the rot of synthetic upholstery, smoked weed, tobacco, crack, whatever, and a little bit of human excrement. Had it not been for the ventilation provided by the broken window, it would have been enough to make Lado ill. He didn't see anything he wanted, and it wasn't worth rummaging. Lado found a discarded submarine sandwich wrapper that he could use it to pick up Ernie's poop.

Through the windshield of the abandoned car, Lado saw the moving car approaching. Two men were inside. The music got louder as they slowed to a halt beside the parked car, and Lado removed himself from inside when he noticed they were looking at him. Ernie was growing anxious.

"Can we help you?" the driver shouted over the music in a thick Indian accent. Lado was a bit confused by the question.

"Just walking my dog," he said, holding Ernie's leash above the roof of the car so the men could see, "just poking around."

"See anything you like?" the driver asked.

"Actually, I found this," Lado said, holding up the sandwich wrapper. His two hands were up in the air in a *don't shoot* gesture, almost.

"That'll cost you," the driver said. The other man laughed. "Twenty dollars."

Lado wondered whether they were joking. They must have been, but they continued to observe him, the driver stoic, the passenger grinning like a buffoon.

"I'm just fucking with you," the driver shouted, finally breaking the act by smiling. The passenger howled. Either this was the most entertaining thing he had witnessed in a long time, or there was something wrong with him. Lado watched them drive away, the only car on an empty street.

Around the corner, Lado squatted and used the paper to pick up Ernie's shit. It felt warm through the paper. Nearby was a big metal trash can, no bag, no lid, no words or symbols that say "garbage," just a metal vessel the community understood to be for waste and the city, presumably, emptied now and then. Lado dropped the shit in there next to the other decomposing organic matter and a few beer cans that the trash pickers hadn't gotten to yet.

Upstairs in his apartment, Lado thought about what to do with his day. He was utterly hungover and he didn't feel like doing much, but he didn't want to waste away the day sleeping or watching TV. He walked around looking at things. He cleaned some dishes and wiped the kitchen counter, the stove top, the inside of the fridge. Sat down at his computer, browsed the internet, found some porn, masturbated. Ate a bagel with cream cheese. Went into his bedroom, slithered into bed, took a nap.

He didn't wake up again until it was cocktail hour. Ernie needed to go outside again, and Lado obliged him. Back inside Lado made himself a drink and decided he would prepare a dinner, something decent enough to invite guests over for. Pan-fried perch and a mango salad to serve with it, along with some wine. He chilled a bottle of sweet gewürztraminer and a bottle of New Zealand sauvignon blanc. Before he started cooking he sent a text message to a few friends to let them know that he would be cooking dinner and that they were all invited. The message read: "Dinner at my place! 7pm. whitefish and white wine. Bring anything, bring nothing." He sent it to four people altogether.

The four people who received the message were, as one might assume, Lado's friends. They all saw themselves as members of a certain culturally savvy, elite group, even if they were elite only because they viewed themselves that way. Valmesta was the once-great American city that they each adored and that each of them experienced richly in his or her own way, and that the reader already has some understanding of. People were being drawn to the city once again, especially young people. There was history, an elegant downtown, neighborhoods with old homes and cheap rent, a food scene, a techno scene, an indie scene, a hipster scene, any kind of scene, ghettos, rich people, poor people, dangerous people, naïve people, gentrification, urban ruin aka "ruin porn," wild dogs, children that roamed the streets like wild dogs, tourists, plenty of places significant enough to see and get lost in and be swallowed up by.

Most of the people Lado hung around with were in their twenties, and Lado was one of the youngest. But, even though Lado was young, because of his aching determination to maintain the integrity of an artist through the hardships that he was made to endure, his friends looked up to him. For Lado and his friends, it was not always hardships in a material or physical sense, but hardships in an artistic sense, and those hardships that are specific to being a young, un-established artist, that they suffered. And to face those kinds of hardships, they say, one needs to have a certain level of artistic integrity. For example, there is a minimum level of that kind of integrity needed to make certain life decisions. Letting V. go, that took integrity, in Lado's mind at least. Though from the outside the whole ordeal could be made to look pretty pathetic, it was an artistic decision. Realistically, it was better for her that she left. During their time together, Lado had his own personal issues to attend to.

Anyways, they—the members of the group in discussion—each came from a different background, but they shared a common desire to be a part of something unique, and, at the same time, each strived to be apart from that very something that they were invariably a part of. Each had an art, or a passion, and each waited tables or bartended to support that passion.

The friends that Lado invited to his apartment for dinner were listed in his phone under the following names and aliases—Manny the Cat, Miss Ellery, Olivia Ramirez, and Kyle Neighbor. The reader will get to know them all in due time.

Lado sat down at his desk to check his e-mail while he awaited his friends' responses. There was an unread e-mail from a client asking him if he would be able to provide a fresh draft of web copy by the following Wednesday at noon. The project specifics were attached. Most of the assignments Lado had taken on for the client were bullshit, in Lado's opinion. Food writing, web content writing, web marketing copy. It was all bullshit and a waste of his time and creative energy. The reality was that Lado didn't make nearly as much money freelance writing as he did waiting tables. Many of the checks he received in the mail were made out for less than $100 for a morning and afternoon's work. Still, making at least a marginal income via freelance projects made Lado feel more like a real live author, like he was a part of the greater writing world. Anyway, the earnings from two short assignments usually paid his electricity bill, so he kept up with it.

Ellery was the first to respond to his invitation, answering with a text message, saying, "i'm down for sure :)". That meant she was definitely going to be there at or before 7pm because she only said what she meant. Ellery Montgomery Jones was classic American pedigree with a new school twist, and she was probably the hippest of all of Lado's friends. A sort of ultramodern cultural savant. To Ellery it was important for people to do whatever made them feel good, and keeping up with the latest trends in music, art and fashion made her feel superb.

Ellery possessed a visible display of good genes. She was tall and lean but well built, as if she came from a family of athletes but had herself never been one for sport. She had lengthy, lustrous blonde-streaked brown hair, which had a tendency to arrange itself in even waves, a shiny set of white teeth, a rosy hue to her cheeks and a youthful display of freckles, and she always dressed well. She always looked good and brought a positive energy with her, Lado thought, and her feel-good attitude was contagious. It can be said that Lado had a more-than-platonic interest in Ellery and had felt that way for some time, basically since he'd met her, and he'd known her for years. In fact, the sexual tension in him had escalated to a steady and palpable vibrato that he could only assume Ellery was privy to even if she didn't feel the same way herself.

Lado prepared a batter for the perch using flour, cornstarch, cayenne pepper, and a pinch of salt. He opened a cheap beer and took a swig, and then added some of the beer to the dry ingredients. He whisked the batter, and, seeing some lumps, added another ounce or so of beer. He whisked it smooth and put it in the fridge next to the fish.

He did a mental check of everything that he needed to have prepared. So far only Ellery had responded, and he felt a bit nervous, like he was expecting a date. He finished the beer in two large gulps and opened another one. His thoughts began to race. *What if no one else shows up? Should I clean my apartment so she doesn't think I'm a slob? Is my apartment even dirty?*

Ellery probably won't think it's a date, but she might feel like I feel like it's a date, and if she does, what then? Will she think I'm a creep who invited only her, or a loser who can't get anyone else to show up? She'll find an excuse to leave.

Why do I care? I mean, yeah, I like her. She is attractive. And fun. Do I want it to be a date then? If it turns into a date should I make a move, or is that not cool between friends? What if she makes a move...?

Lado went over to the living room and picked up the guitar that he had borrowed from Manny. Manny "The Cat" Montego was a local guitarrista. He owned and operated Manny's Juice Joint on Richard Street and often played with his band, The Cat's Pajamas. Manny replied, "cool brotha, sure thing," but that didn't mean it was a sure thing. In fact, Lado suspected that Manny would not be coming based on his response. It never really made sense to Lado how some people like Manny could say one thing and mean another, but it happened all the time. Just as he could read a person's face to know if they were telling the truth or not, somehow Lado knew when a text message that said one thing actually meant another.

No one else replied to the invitation. Lado made sure not to take his friends' dismissal to heart. He would see them in time.

As the beer made its way through Lado's digestive tract and the alcohol through his bloodstream and he picked at Manny's guitar he felt his nerves settle. Half an hour went by in what seemed like a few minutes. When he noticed the time, he set Manny's guitar gently on the couch, upright, making sure not to place any strain on the neck. He made his way over to the kitchen and took the perch and the batter out of the fridge. He lit the large burner on the stove and placed a sauté pan over the flame. He waited about thirty seconds for the pan to get hot before he added enough oil to the pan to fill it half an inch high. As the oil heated up he added dry flour to the perch and opened another beer, and then he submerged the pieces of fish fully in the batter. He put them in the pan all at once. How they sizzled and cracked.

There was a knock at Lado's door about twenty minutes before seven as Lado was dicing a mango into large cubes. It was unlocked so Ellery let herself in and she entered Lado's apartment with a six-pack of India pale ale under her arm. "Hello, hello, welcome, welcome," Lado said. They moved to embrace each other, but each kept it cool, each concealing any more-than-friends desire they may have had for the other. Ernie appeared most excited of the three and was wagging his tail and barking as he ran into the kitchen.

"How are you?" Lado asked.

"Fabulous. How are you, dear?"

"Fine, thanks. The fish is down, I'm just putting the salad together now."

"It smells delish in here! Look at you, mister chef. Do you need help with anything?"

"No, I think I'm good. Food's almost ready, actually. Just make yourself comfortable."

"Where's the fish?"

"On the stove. In the frying pan."

"And you have wine?"

"In the fridge."

"I'm feeling something sweet."

"There's a gewürztraminer."

"Perfect. Opener?" Ellery took the bottle of sweet out of the fridge.

"Uh, yea. In my room, I think on my desk, should be my wine key."

Ellery went into Lado's room and came back with the wine key.

"You want me to…"

"I got it," she said, and she opened the bottle quickly and poured a tasting amount.

Ellery swirled the wine around the glass and put her nose in it, inhaling deeply. She held the glass up, inviting Lado to breathe it in. "That will be perfect," he said. Ellery tasted it, nodded, and poured both herself and Lado a big glass each.

Lado finished making dinner. Ellery said that she was impressed, and when Lado shrugged it off as if cooking a quality dinner weren't a big deal, Ellery insisted that she meant it, that she really was impressed.

"Will anyone else be joining us?" she asked, and Lado said, "No, I don't think so, it's just going to be you and me. Manny said he would stop by, but you know how he is."

They talked, and ate dinner, and drank wine with the food. And isn't that how it so often goes? He asked her how her day had gone and she was happy to present him, in the form of two CDs, her days work, a collection of brand new songs that she had downloaded earlier that day, compiled into playlists and recorded onto discs. They were sitting on Lado's couch because he didn't have a dinner table, and the informality of the evening called for a comfortable seating arrangement. Listening, exchanging subtle words and gestures, they finished the bottle of wine while the sun went down. Long shadows angled across the living room like phone lines or a spider's web, an uncertain and beautiful scene. Ellery said she had had enough wine and got up and walked over to the fridge for a beer, and Lado watched the gentle sway of her hips, like a ship on the rolling waves of some comfortable, feminine ocean. She ambled through the apartment with her head tilted back so that her hair appeared to be bouncing downward, falling more toward the ground with each step, and from the front her gait would have revealed a chin-up, thin-lipped smile, with her eyes pointed down to the ground, knowing that Lado was watching her. When she opened the door of the fridge she leaned in and felt one of the bottles of beer. It was cold enough so she grabbed two of them. Lado watched her shoulder and back strain slightly from the motion—strong, feline, lean, and graceful.

She returned to the couch, keeping her eyes on Lado. She set the two India pale ales on the table in front of him without saying anything, and he, without saying anything, pried them open with the bottom end of a lighter. He handed Ellery her beverage and she sat cross-legged on the floor and changed the CD while Ernie made his way into her lap. She examined the contents of the coffee table—books, notebooks, pieces of scratch paper that had been written on by hand, birthday cards from various people. Ellery asked Lado whom the cards were from, and to make small conversation Lado explained to Ellery how he had known Erica during college and Iris while on vacation, but he didn't go into much detail to expound upon past love. He explained to Ellery how Daniel was a close friend of his growing up and was also a writer, and how Daniel's parents seemed to love him more than anyone else had ever loved anything. He explained that his friends from college rarely wrote him but that the funny card was from Alan, Lado's roommate from freshman year at state. Ellery wondered whether she too would one day be a figure from Lado's past, sending him birthday cards, but Ellery kept this thought to herself.

There was a piece of mail addressed to a person named Natalie. "Who's Natalie?" Ellery asked Lado.

"Don't know. She must have lived here before me."

Ellery suggested they open it, but Lado thought that opening other people's mail was wrong. It would betray the strange intimacy he felt with the woman who used to live in his home, whom he had never met but somehow felt close to. Instead of opening it, they just talked about what it could be inside the envelope. "What if it's a winning lottery ticket?" Ellery said.

"We'll never know."

"Would you share the money with me?"

"Why should you get any money? It was sent to me."

"No, it was sent to Natalie."

"To my apartment."

"I'm the one who suggested we open it."

"Fifty/fifty."

There was a knock at the door. Lado got up to answer it but the door opened before Lado could get there. The neighbor Kyle walked in. He wasn't wearing shoes. Kyle always met Lado with the same, "Yo what's good, my man?" and this time was no different. So Lado explained, "Everything is good, man, everything is okay. I didn't know you were coming."

"Yeah, well I wasn't sure about it. I just decided. I figured what the hell, I live across the hall, I may as well stop in." Kyle noticed a woman's jacket hanging on the coat rack. "Am I interrupting?"

"Nah, man. Ellery. We're just chilling." Lado led Kyle through the kitchen. There was wine and food still on the table. "Help yourself to whatever's left," Lado said. Kyle said he wasn't hungry. In the living room Ellery was already on her second beer. She stood up to give Kyle a kiss on the cheek and a hug.

"How was your birthday?" Kyle asked Lado.

"Fine."

"What did you do?"

"Manny came over with a cake. Then we went out to the reggae bar. Ellery got us in even though the bar man told us the place was closed."

"A birthday cake?"

Yea, a big chocolate cake. In the shape of a penis. Manny made it himself."

"Was it good?"

Lado and Ellery agreed that the cake was very good. Everyone laughed and took a swig of beer. Kyle apologized for not being able to come out for Lado's birthday but he had been busy writing his dissertation on the evolving strategies of warfare throughout human history. "And how is that going?" Ellery asked.

"It's going well. It's interesting, especially if you look at the bigger picture, what with technological innovation and changing cultural attitudes and what not. But I think I chose too big a subject. There's just too much history there. You would have to dedicate an entire university to the study of humans killing each other for political gain. And I'm beginning to question the importance of obtaining a PhD in the first place."

"Well, if you want to be a university professor and teach history, you need to have a PhD," Ellery said.

Kyle already knew that, and he didn't want to talk about it. He put his hands on his hips akimbo, wiggled his toes and looked about the room to identify where the music was coming from.

"What do you call this?" he asked.

"I think it's called second-guessing your decisions," Ellery said. She was reclining on the floor now, propping herself up on one elbow, and as she lay there she drank from the bottle of beer.

"No, I mean this music. This type of music."

"I don't know. What would you call it?" Ellery said.

"I don't know. Lado?"

"Why does it matter what it's called?" Ellery said. "It sounds like it sounds. It shouldn't matter what it's called."

Lado leaned back into the couch and crossed his legs. He tried to listen to the music and to the conversation at the same time and realized that he couldn't do both, so he stood up and took the empty beer bottles into the kitchen. Kyle and Ellery continued.

"All these songs can't really be called anything. And they don't really sound at all alike from one song to the next. The last one sounded sort of like techno music, but I wouldn't call it techno, and this one reminds me of folk music but I wouldn't call it that because it's a bit less observational and more personal."

"Do you like the songs?"

"I don't know."

"Well I like them."

"What do you call them?"

"'Songs.'"

"But what is music nowadays if you can't even figure out what any of it is? What ever happened to jazz and funk or rock 'n' roll? Not only do people know exactly what you mean when you say 'jazz,' for instance, but the word actually sounds like what the music is. Music today is just clumsy, all over the place. I guess maybe that's why you can't figure out what to call it."

"Music has evolved. Just like war has evolved, Kyle. And technology."

Lado came back to the living room and sat cross-legged on the floor next to Ellery, facing Kyle on the couch.

"What about cool? Musicians, especially jazz musicians, used to be cool as hell. Are there still 'cool' musicians?"

Ellery said, "Well, one could argue that the definition of 'cool' has changed, or evolved, but I think 'cool' is rather specific to a feel and a time period, so I wouldn't be the one to make that argument."

"The music isn't 'cool,'" Lado said.

"Then what is it?"

"I don't know. I guess I put it so bluntly because, in my opinion, 'cool' is a word that should just go back to meaning what it used to mean. And I don't mean the literal definition of 'cool' as leaning towards cold on the temperature reading. I mean 'cool' as in subdued, stoic, dispassionate."

Kyle made an audible exhale.

"Or high on marijuana," Lado said. Ellery laughed. "I'm going for another beer."

"We're out," Ellery said. "I can go out and get some more from Walgreens. Where is it again?"

"It's right at the corner of Richard and Belmont."

"You sure you don't want one of us to come with you?" Kyle said.

"You're going to protect me from the bad guys?" Ellery said. Kyle looked at Lado, who shrugged and sipped his beer.

Ellery found her jacket on the coat rack and as she began to put it on Ernie walked over to her wagging his tail. "It looks like Ernie wants to come," she said.

"Now there's a body guard," Kyle said.

"You can take him."

While Ellery walked down the three flights of stairs and out into the street, Kyle told Lado that he thought Ellery was a hipster. Lado explained to Kyle that Ellery was a good person whether or not Kyle was right in labeling her.

Meanwhile Ellery walked along Evaline street with her hands in the pockets of her jacket, looking around and wondering what it would have been like to walk along the same street a hundred years ago while all of the tall buildings were being built and the only question for the builders was, "How tall can we make them?" She was admiring the city's skyline across the river, dark in the foreground but still illuminated by the just-set sun behind it, held together at the horizon by a rosy pink ribbon of distant sun-blushed sky, and while she was taking it in Lado told Kyle that Ellery might be sensitive and that Kyle shouldn't come at her that way, and especially not to her face. Kyle agreed that the music, indeed, sounded all right. He just didn't always understand it, that's all.

Ellery walked around inside Walgreens until she found the beer section. She grabbed another six-pack, this time of a locally-brewed IPA that she had never tried before. She carried the cardboard carrier by the handle across the store with just her middle and ring fingers, and in the checkout line the cashier said nothing as he scanned the label. Ellery swiped her credit card to check out. Ernie barked and Ellery said she didn't need a bag, thank you, and the cashier said, "Have a good night, miss," and he watched the automatic doors slide open for Ellery and Ellery pass through them.

When Ellery got back to Lado's place Kyle was gone. Ellery didn't seem to notice, and she said, "I got this new kind for us to try," indicating the beer. Lado suggested they go out on the balcony and drink them. They stepped through the glass door-wall and onto the balcony and Lado slid the screen shut behind them. On the balcony were several plants, some for growing herbs and foods and some just for decoration. There were fennel and parsley for seasoning, chamomile and peppermint for tea, baby palm trees and oriental peppers. There was a table surrounded by chairs where Lado and Ellery sat down.

It was dark and had begun to rain, but weather never stopped this part of town from coming alive at night. From where they were sitting they could look down and see the street lamps shining their light on the tops of the umbrellas and the people who walked by underneath. Not everyone had an umbrella. Some people were just wet. But there were black umbrellas and dark blue and some were multi-colored. A few had polka dots or stripes or patterns.

"None of the umbrellas have spirals," Lado pointed out. "Look." Ellery looked down and saw that, indeed, none of the umbrellas had spirals, and she looked back at Lado. A few moments passed and Ellery asked Lado whether he had ever seen a spiral umbrella before.

"I think in a movie," he said.

"In a movie?"

"Yea, I think Danny DeVito—the Penguin—had one in *Batman Returns*."

"Interesting."

"Yea."

"It reminds me of those cartoony spirals that were supposed to hypnotize people in the old movies."

Seconds passed. Lado's mind wandered; a line from a Neruda poem he had read earlier that day came back to him. "Have you ever been hypnotized?" Ellery said, bringing Lado's attention back.

"No, I haven't." Lado replied. He had never been hypnotized in the way that he knew Ellery meant. "But I saw a guy get hypnotized once. In a bar. He was part of a small audience who all got it but it really only worked on the one guy. The hypnotist asked everyone to close their eyes and he did this thing where he counted backwards and then said something like, 'Voila! You are now under my spell!' When they all opened their eyes they thought it was a joke, they weren't at all hypnotized, but the one guy really was hypnotized and everyone knew it right away. Especially the hypnotist, who went right up to him and told him to put his hand on the bar, and the kid did, and then the hypnotist told him he couldn't take his hand off the bar until the hypnotist told him to. He sat there for over an hour, with his hand on the bar. He didn't understand why he couldn't take his hand off the bar, but he certainly couldn't."

"Did you know him?"

"No, I didn't know him. I went up to him, though, and I said something like, 'You're just hypnotized, man. That guy over there, he has you under his spell.' He said he didn't believe in spells and I said, 'Then why do you have your hand stuck to the bar?' Eventually I just bought the guy a drink and left him there. But when I came back the next day he wasn't there anymore, so the hypnotist must have lifted his spell."

Ellery laughed. "Maybe he was just friends with the hypnotist and together they conned the whole bar. Didn't you think of that?"

"No."

"Well it must have been pretty convincing. Either that or you are gullible. You don't think that's real, do you?"

"Of course it is. You'd believe it if you saw it."

"But you have never been hypnotized so how can you know for sure that it works? You know it wouldn't be that difficult of a trick to pull off. Especially at a bar full of drunk people like you."

"I wasn't drunk."

"Bullshit you weren't drunk."

"Perhaps I was a little fixed." Lado looked inside through the glass and saw Ernie on his hind paws trying to reach the food on the kitchen counter. "I've never been under a spell like that, if that's what you mean. But you must know the mind can play all sorts of funny tricks on you at times, and if someone really good knows how to manipulate that…"

"Let's go do it." Ellery said.

A moment passed. A car drove by in the street below. The sound of water splashing onto the curb.

"I mean let's go hypnotize some peeps. Or one of us will pretend to do it and the other one of us will have to be hypnotized. Definitely you. I'm going to be Isabella, the world's most marvelous hypnotist. You can be anyone. Francisco, or Francis. Or maybe just Frank."

"I'll be George."

"Be Roy, like Roy Orbison. Or Siegfried and Roy. And I'll be the marvelous Isabella."

"I don't want to be that Roy. Didn't Roy get brutally mauled by a tiger?"

"I think that was Siegfried."

"I'm pretty sure it was Roy."

They talked like this for a while and then went inside and turned off all the lights and put on one of the premium movie channels. Lado was beginning to fall asleep on the couch when Ellery asked him to take her to bed. She said it was too cold in the living room, on the couch next to the window, and that they should be together in the bedroom.

The following afternoon was a Saturday afternoon. Lado went to Manny's Juice Joint to see Manny. Saturday afternoons Lado often found himself there, at Manny's place. They would talk about the latest news and hearsay. Lado saw Manny as a mentor of sorts, and to Manny, Lado was a younger version of himself whose friendship kept Manny connected to his past. Besides, Manny was the type who could easily become disconnected from the world outside of Manny's Juice Joint if he didn't maintain friendships with people like Lado. Today they were talking about an article that Lado had read in *The New Yorker* about the blurring boundary between independent and mainstream filmmaking. Lado was offering his own thoughts on the matter, and Manny was listening to Lado while hand-rolling a cigarette."

So many of the movies that come out of Hollywood are all about instant gratification, you know what I mean? No matter what genre...comedy, action, drama. The characters almost always find themselves in these, these difficult and seemingly insurmountable circumstances. And then, I don't know, for the movie viewer I guess two hours or so pass by and the characters overcome. People walk out of the movie theater or they get up off their couch and think they can accomplish anything. Then when they get back out in real life they expect things to happen that way, you follow?"

Manny licked his cigarette, rolled it tight, and struck a match. He had a tendency to look away while Lado was speaking to him and then look back up at Lado to speak. "Maybe that's what people are looking for, man, something to make them believe in the impossible. Movies are good for that," he said.

Lado agreed. Movies were good for that. "But don't you think it happens enough already, people expecting too much? I mean, people expect everything, they all think they're on the verge of living the Hollywood lifestyle. People want cars. People want property. For what?"A moment passed as Manny puffed his cigarette intently, enjoying the smoke, and let Lado catch his breath. "These days what does it mean for someone to have all those things? It means at some point consciously or unconsciously they made the decision to put that shit first. That's called materialism. People feel entitled to whatever it is they feel entitled to. And is that a good thing? It means everyone *thinks* they're happy, everyone gets what they've been led to believe is rightfully theirs. But is that what it's really about? After all, there's no intrigue there, there's no romance to it.

"People want Hollywood love. Hollywood love doesn't exist in the real world. There's romance out there, in everything, if you know what to look for."

Manny smiled and blew smoke out of his nose. "What's wrong with that, man? Happiness comes in many forms. Maybe some people find happiness at places like Wal-Mart. They come for a form of spiritual cleansing, leave feeling fresh and rejuvenated. Happy. Happiness is a feeling." He took a long, slow drag on his cigarette. Manny's cigarettes burned like cigars. If you pulled too hard you'd get burned. "What's important is that it be authentic."

"Mind if I roll a cigarette?" Lado asked Manny. Manny took out his papers and his pouch of tobacco and set them on the table.

Lado began to roll a cigarette while in his mind he compared the pleasure of retail therapy to the experience of seeing a simple, but entertaining, Hollywood movie at a theatre. "That happiness, where does it go? Because I don't think it lasts, Manny, I just don't think that kind of happiness lasts. You have to find another movie, so to speak. And in order for people to gain that happiness in their boring, routine lives, they create problems that aren't really there, the same way that conflict is written into a movie script, problems that can be overcome in order to avoid the real ones that really exist. But that's a bad habit to get into, because what happens to the real problems in the world that we have to work hard to fix? They are kept at a distance, Manny, because the made up ones are just so much quicker to solve."

"So you're saying that movie watching and shoe shopping are ways to cope with the modern world by avoiding its more serious problems?" Manny put his cigarette out in the ashtray on the table. "I think you need to get laid, hombre." Manny believed that things were simpler than Lado was making them out to be. After all, Manny was a musician. He believed in the guitar. He believed in the progression of A to E-minor and a good key change. He valued friendship and idle conversation. He believed that if he could make people close their eyes, sing and dance, or come together under one roof and share an experience, he was doing the best he could. Even so, he enjoyed talking with Lado.

Lado looked toward the stage, where technicians were setting up for Manny's show. He was thinking that fiction—literature, film, graphic novels—needed a new approach. He believed that each person has his own existential dilemma and that stories should address it head on. What people needed were depictions of the real, stories showing that in real life it's better not to expect too much, that there is an austere beauty to be found in the tale of zero gratification. Had he come to despair in his own life? Maybe Manny was right. Lado just needed to get laid.

Manny stood up and made a move toward the stage. "Hey, sorry I skipped out last night. Gloria called me. A man has to have a hobby. I can't play guitar all the time." He winked. Not everyone can truly pull off a wink, but Manny could. "How was the turnout?"

"Ellery and I got drunk. She stayed the night." To this Manny raised an eyebrow. "Nothing happened," Lado assured him. Manny shrugged and approached the stage.

While they played Lado sat among the crowd. He had heard the songs before. He diverted himself occasionally from the music by looking around the room at all of the people. Manny's guitar playing captured the attention of most of the people in the room, and they sat at their tables with their seats situated so that it was easy to face the stage and watch Manny play. At times the performance was emotionally moving and Lado could see it on the people's faces. That was the surest way to tell whether Manny was playing a good set. It wasn't important to Lado and it wasn't important to most of the people in the audience whether Manny hit all the right notes during a solo or whether the saxophone playing was of just the right pitch. Some people in the audience maybe noticed those things, the critics. Lado could tell who they were because instead of showing some level of involvement with the music the critics would from time to time screw up their face as if a smelly and poorly-dressed stranger had just walked into the King's Court. Lado couldn't really identify the small details of a performance that caused the critics to disdain. He could, however, allow himself to be moved by the music and by the people's faces as they too were moved.

The next day, let's see, it would have been a Sunday now. Lado was at the Kingston Café. On Sundays he liked to sleep in and stay in bed until long after the sun had come up. It was nearly noon. He looked at his coffee and breathed the steam. He felt old. Suddenly a man came through the door of the café. The man stumbled on the steps and nearly fell to the ground. When he regained his balance he looked up and reached into his pockets, which were empty, and the man grew confused. He looked to the cashier and then turned to look at Lado. He appeared to mumble something, paused before making the final turn, and then walked out the door into the late morning light. Lado watched all of this, puzzled and somewhat amused. He finished the poem he had been working on since the night before.

Later the man re-entered the café through the interior side door that connected the coffee shop to an adjoining bookstore. He walked over to the cashier and ordered a coffee and a pastry. When he received his purchased items from the cashier, he walked out the doorway of the café that he had entered through the first time. Lado wondered whether the man intended to return to the bookstore, and, if he did, why he did not just go through the adjoining doorway to get there. Lado stood up and approached the cash register. "Did that man pay for his coffee?" he asked.

"No, it's all right though. He comes in all the time."

"I come here all the time, too, and I pay for my coffee."

"Well, I don't think that man has very much money."

"I'll pay for it," Lado said. "How much was it?"

"Don't worry about it. I mean, the owner knows about it and he said when that man comes in not to worry about it. As long as he doesn't order anything crazy, lake cappuccinos and stuff."

"Five bucks sound good?"

"I mean, if it would make you feel better."

"It would," Lado said, and he took five singles out of his pocket and handed them to the young cashier.

"Thanks. You didn't have to, you know." She made change for the purchase. Two dollars and seventy-five cents. Lado placed the change in the tip jar.

Just then he got a text from Ellery. "What made you think it was a good idea to start feeding the rumor mill about me staying the night at your place?" Lado's immediate reaction was confusion. At first impression, Ellery seemed pissed off. It took him a moment of playing out all possible scenarios in his head before he realized she must have been joking. As it's been said before, it was a funny thing with text messages; one learned how to pick up on things that might seem impossible to pick up on—sarcasm, irony, and other forms of humor—in a text message.

Still, he was a little concerned about what information had made its way back to Ellery in order for her to feel the need to kid him about it. He replied, "What? What did you hear?"

"Oh you know Lado thinks he's such a big stud and has girls over and Ellery spent the night and blah, blah blah…"

"Haha I have a reputation to uphold."

"Haven't you ever heard don't kiss and tell?"

"There was no telling of kissing."

"I think tales of wining and dining are suggestive enough."

"Yea but I kept it PG," Lado typed and sent. Then he sent another, "Just for the record the only person I talked to was Manny and I told him you stayed over but nothing happened."

After he sent this last text, Lado tried calling Manny, but Manny didn't answer. He sent Ellery another text. "I hope you don't think I would actually do that." He sat there for a while and looked out the window, thinking. He wondered whether Ellery actually had some resentment for the fact that he had said anything at all.

His phone rang. It was Manny. Lado stood up and walked outside, holding up a finger to signal the cashier that he would be right back. "Manny."

"Lado, my man…"

"Dude, did you tell Ellery I told you I fucked her?"

"What? No. What? I thought you said you didn't fuck her?"

"I did! I mean I didn't fuck her, yeah, I told you she spent the night because she was drunk but that we didn't fuck, but just now she texts me and she's basically like, 'Why'd you tell people we fucked?'"

"Man, I don't know. I didn't tell anybody that."

"Well, did you talk to anyone about it? I mean, I think Ellery was just joking, but that's still kind of messed up because I never said that."

"No. I saw Paul O'keefe in here last night. He was with Olivia and that new guy Olivia is running with, what's his name…"

"Does it matter?"

Manny laughed. "Judging by her track record? No," he said.

"I'm only asking because I haven't even talked to anybody besides you, and I don't want Ellery getting the wrong impression," Lado said.

"They just asked me if I went to your apartment the night before last, and I said no. No because I was busy with a girl. About you and Ellery, I just said it was just the two of you and Ellery spent the night there with you."

"Kyle was there, too."

"Kyle spent the night with you, too?"

"No, no he just stopped by. Ellery spent the night."

"That's what I said."

"That's all you said? They didn't ask any questions?"

"That's all I said, and they didn't say nothing, just kinda looked at each other, Olivia and O'keefe. Olivia's guy doesn't know Ellery. Or you. You met him?"

"No."

"I don't know, man, maybe they assumed that something happened because she spent the night. I mean, O'keefe and Ellery...maybe he's jealous or something, jumping to conclusions about what he don't know." Lado didn't say anything. "Lado?"

"Yeah, I'm here." Lado let out a deep sigh. "Well, fuck. All right. Thanks Manny. I mean, I didn't think you would start a rumor..." Manny started to laugh. "What's funny?" Lado asked.

"But you called me and asked me about it."

He was right. Lado, realizing the phone call alone was a bit of an accusation, felt sorry. "I'm sorry, man. I really am." Lado and Manny were quiet for a moment. Lado contemplated telling Manny in confidence that he felt Ellery might be the one he wanted to settle down for, that he could see himself getting along with her family, traversing the various roads and alleyways of life together and even being old with her, that the last thing he wanted was for her to think less of him. But all he said was this: "I care about her, Manny. I just don't want to mess up that friendship." They talked for a brief moment about what Lado should do, and then they wrapped up the conversation in standard telephone fashion.

Lado decided he could use a drink. Anywhere would do. He put his laptop to sleep and packed it away in his messenger bag, slung the strap over his shoulder. He bussed his table and took his coffee mug over to the barista and left. The young girl watched Lado walk out the door, and when he was gone she walked over to the table where he had been sitting and wiped it with a sanitized rag, even though it appeared clean.

The girl returned to the counter and took Lado's empty coffee mug to the dishwasher, and as she did so she smelled it, as she very much enjoyed the aroma of coffee and was beginning to fancy herself a connoisseur. She was also fond of smelling the used glassware of men she found interesting. Upon inhaling she noticed another smell that she wasn't accustomed to smelling in coffee, but it was an odor she recalled her father having on him sometimes when he would embrace her at, say, a family Christmas party, which was always a bit awkward because her father, normally, wasn't very affectionate. Or, when he would occasionally come home late from work and kiss her on the forehead, sometimes she would smell that smell.

Out on the street, even for Lado, who enjoyed the sun, it was very bright. He squinted narrowly to keep the sun out of his eyes, glancing up and down the street, considering his options for an afternoon drink. One block west was the corner of Edwin and Belmont, and from there, down the street was The Playground, where he was friendly with the wait staff and he knew he could have at least one drink on the house.

He sat down at the bar and ordered a Pabst Blue Ribbon and a shot of Jameson, setting his messenger bag down on the adjacent stool. The bartender, Lou, brought the drinks over and Lado took the shot right away, chasing it down with beer.

Soon he was on his second round. He texted Olivia and asked her whether she was busy. She was on her way to work, she said, but had an hour to spare. Could she meet him at The Playground? he wondered. On the other end of the line, Olivia would have been seen half-dressed, fixing her hair up into a food-service-appropriate bun, making a scrunched up, disapproving face at the prospect of stopping in at The Playground before a shift. She didn't much care for rancid dives, especially not right after a shower and on her way to work. However, she didn't want to be rude about it. She politely reminded Lado that work for her meant a 15-minute bike ride south to the Arbor Borough district, where the restaurant where she served overlooked Belle Park. It didn't make much sense for her to go out of her way to meet

Lado for only a short time. Lado read this and quickly decided that, based on the urgency of the matter, he would be willing to meet Olivia much closer to where she worked. They decided to meet up in Belle Park in half an hour. Lado ordered another shot, took it, chased it with the rest of his beer—this one his third—and asked Lou if he could cash out. "These ones are on us," Lou said.

Lado walked the half hour to Belle Park. Olivia was fully dressed in cocktail blacks. They found a place to sit down. The sun was low in the sky. Upon sitting down Lado realized that he felt much warmer while walking, and despite the alcohol, with such a light jacket on he very much felt the cold, sitting there on a park bench. He offered Olivia a cigarette, and she accepted. He put a cigarette between his own lips, lit Olivia's first, and his second.

Lado and Olivia had gotten to know each other years ago. Initially their interest in each other was a mutual attraction that never quite realized itself in any sexual act, though they had slept together on a number of occasions, most often drunk and passing out in one or the other's bed for the sake of comfort. Olivia was small and attractive, with bright green eyes that provided a very interesting contrast to her otherwise dark features. She had black hair and auburn skin, a beauty mark on her right cheek and one of those smiles that is slightly higher on one side of the face than on the other. She had grown up in a household dominated by a father who more or less favored his four sons, who were excellent athletes in their respective sports, and all older than Olivia. She was the baby. Her mother was a prescription drug abuser, an altogether emotionally absent figure. In some ways Olivia, having spent her youth in alternating states of solitary reverie and fervent household upkeep, had undergone some of her most important personal growth and development since she had moved out on her own. In that way, Lado felt that Olivia had grown up right in front of him, and he had learned much of what he knew about women through intimate conversations with her.

"Paul and I talked about it," Olivia said when Lado finally got around to asking Olivia whether she had said anything to Ellery. The reader will remember O'keefe being referred to in the conversation between Lado and Manny only a few pages ago. That is Paul. Paul O'keefe. O'keefe was always kind of a shit in Lado's mind, and he refused to call him by his first name.

"You believe me that we didn't sleep together, right? And that I never said that we did?"

"Well, yea, I believe you. I mean it seems like something that could happen, and I'll admit Paul and I bounced around the possibility that you did. Ellery is very attractive."

"That doesn't mean we had sex, though. Or even that I think of her that way," Lado said.

"You really didn't?" Olivia couldn't help but smile a little.

"No. I just really value her friendship, and I like her a lot as a person. I wouldn't want anything to get in the way of that," he said.

Olivia paused, took a deep breath. "I didn't want him to, I told him it wasn't really his business and that he didn't even know the facts. But Paul and Ellery are friends. You know that, right? He talked to her."

"Do you know what he said?"

"No. But he seemed to be getting agitated while he and I talked about it."

"Do you think he's jealous?"

"If nothing happened, what's there for him to be jealous about?"

"To me, it seems like he had to have more of a reason to talk to Ellery about it than he just cares about her."

"We didn't really *talk about it* talk about it. I can't say if he feels that way. I mean, it wouldn't surprise me. Who wouldn't want her?"

Lado looked away, breathed in the smoke from his cigarette and then watched how the smoke he exhaled became clean, warm breath and steam. A car drove by in the distance with one of its rear windows broken out and replaced with plastic fixed into the window frame with duct tape. Lado looked at it closely, thinking it looked a lot like the car he had seen a few days prior during his walk with Ernie. He decided it wasn't the same one. That other one would have been a doozy to get running again.

"Maybe you should talk to him."

"It's not him I'm worried about. It's Ellery."

"It sounds like you really care what she thinks about you."

"Well her messages were a bit cryptic, like I'm pretty sure she's not mad, but I don't know."

Olivia took out her cell phone to look at the time. "Listen, I have to go to work. I'm almost late. Good talk. Let's get together again soon, okay?" Olivia stood up. Before she walked away she said, with genuine concern in her voice, "It seems like you're making this into a bigger deal than it is. I'm sure she'll text you back and everything will be good," and Lado watched her go.

He smoked another cigarette. Twilight set in as the sun sank beneath the horizon. What could he do? He felt cold and depressed. It had been a long winter. He pulled out his phone to text O'keefe. "Did you tell Ellery I'm going around telling people that she and I had sex?" he typed into the screen. He read over the message, decided not to send it. It would sound too anxious and severe. Lado wanted to play it cool, but, to be sure, he was in a bit of a panic. Anytime a girl he wanted took such a long time in responding to a text message, he became nervous. *What if she doesn't like me?* he would think. *Is she mad at me? Does she even care? Is she with some other guy?* It was these uneasy thoughts, subliminal worries occasionally growing so forceful upon his psyche as to swim through his mind at greyhound speed, nipping at his ego, that he tried in vain to flush back down into his subconscious by drinking.

The text message he eventually sent O'keefe read, "Hey man. Just wondering what you said to Ellery. Just don't want any rumors getting tossed around." He decided to walk over to Manny's Juice Joint, which was only a handful of blocks west of Belle Park, where he would await O'keefe's reply.

Before Lado walked a block O'keefe had responded. "Nothing really, I just told her what people are saying about you two."

"Haha dude no one is saying anything," Lado replied, walking and texting at the same time. He always thought this was harder than it sounds. It was really easy to run into things, especially since he rarely walked in perfectly straight lines. One time Lado saw a guy texting walk right off a curb and into traffic and get hit by a taxi. He stuck around only long enough to make sure an ambulance arrived and took the guy away. Lado never looked into the matter, only presumed the man dead.

He stopped walking to compose another message. "I for one am not going around telling people things I only denied it actually the one time I was asked about it." In Lado's mind, O'keefe owed him an apology, and he was ready to receive it. Lado didn't want an argument. But O'keefe went on, and soon after Lado continued walking, he received another message: "I'm just trying to look after her. She's vulnerable."

Lado's jaw dropped, and he read the text message again. He couldn't believe the audacity, the condescension. *Vulnerable?* he thought. *Are you fucking kidding me?* If anyone knew Ellery, it was Lado. In his mind, she was his girl.

Lado shoved his phone in his pocket. That would be the end of it. When he arrived at Manny's his buzz was wearing off. Manny was behind the bar, polishing beer glasses. Lado asked him for a beer and a shot. Manny served them up without ringing them in.

Lado's anxiety was beginning to show. He had been running his hands through his hair and he had a weary look to him. He smelled of alcohol and tobacco smoke. "What the fuck?" he asked Manny.

"I was about to ask you the same question," Manny said.

The following day Lado was prostrate on the hardwood floor of his apartment. Sunlight from a partly cloudy afternoon reddened the backs of his eyelids and woke him up. He opened his eyes, blinked a few times. A headache, and then the urge to vomit. Lado wriggled his way onto all fours and stood up. Making a move toward the bathroom, he made it partway, stopped, and retched in the kitchen sink. Afterward, he collected himself. He looked around, trying to piece together the night before. He had blacked out at Manny's, and he didn't know what happened after his second beer there, which was probably something like his twelfth drink of that day. Who knows how much he drank all told. He found four empty beer bottles in the living room and kitchen, as well as a half-empty pint of Jameson that he didn't remember buying or drinking from. Just then he saw some handwritten notebook pages on the floor, torn from their spiral binding and assembled into a haphazard and rudimentary book, title page and all.

Lado began to read the book, wondering why it was handwritten and not typed. He rarely wrote by hand. He continued reading, actually enjoying it. Because he didn't remember writing it, Lado felt like he was reading someone else's story, though the handwriting was certainly his. Like all good literature, it was funny and poignant, tender and intense, and dealt at times with the fear of death.

Lado's laptop was not at his writing desk, so he began looking around for his messenger bag. He wanted to type the story and do a rewrite of it. He imagined sending the story to dozens of publishers, all of whom would be competing for the privilege of publishing it. But he didn't see his messenger bag anywhere. Not in the living room, not on the kitchen table, not in his bedroom. Confusion set in, followed by panic. He couldn't remember where he had it last.

Lado retrieved his cell phone and started calling people. First he called Manny and Olivia, then The Playground and The Kingston Café. Olivia said she didn't remember seeing Lado with a bag at Belle Park. The Café hadn't found anything that anyone left behind. Manny, who didn't answer at first, called Lado back, saying he didn't remember seeing Lado with a bag either. Lado tried The Playground several times but never got an answer, the phone just kept ringing. Maybe they weren't open yet, though that was unlikely because it was past two in the afternoon. Perhaps they weren't in the habit of answering the phone.

Lado got dressed quickly and went outside. The Playground was just a short walk from his apartment. When he got there he asked the bartender on duty whether anyone had found a bag with a laptop in it the day before.

"Yeah, actually. Yesterday afternoon. Ryan is in the back office looking through the laptop."

"Who is Ryan?"

"Ryan is one of our servers."

"Why is he looking through my laptop?"

"Ryan is a she."

"Why is anybody looking through my laptop?"

"Well we thought you would have come back, like, last night. Or this morning. Since no one came for it, we figured maybe if we looked at it maybe we could figure out whose it was."

"Where's the office?" Lado asked.

The bartender showed Lado to the office. "Ryan, it's this guy's shit," he said, and left. Ryan immediately struck Lado as being plainly, and naturally, appealing: healthy radiant skin, long brown hair, graceful posture, very little makeup. "I thought it must be yours," she said, peering up at him. Her eyes were a green he didn't quite remember seeing in anyone else, something like algae, an outward vividness that signaled inner energy, mystery, and depth. "You come in here a lot. You're the writer guy. Or you're trying to be, right?"

"What are you looking at? You didn't read my writing, did you?" he said to her as he made a move to see the screen over her shoulder. She closed out of whatever file or window she had been looking at.

"Well, yeah, duh."

"I try to keep that stuff private,"

"What else was there for me to look at? There's not much else on here. I was just trying to help," she said. "I've seen you in here before. And I've heard about you. How do you say your name?"

"It's pronounced like 'lotto.' Listen, I just came to pick it up. In fact I have some work to do, so if you don't mind..." He paused and evaluated his hangover. His head throbbed. Under normal circumstances he wouldn't walk away from a chance encounter with an interesting girl, but there, in the office, he felt likely to vomit again. But hadn't he thrown it all up already? The worst that could happen, he decided, is that he would dry heave. "...what did you think, though, of my work? Are you a reader?"

"I only read a little bit. I liked it, though. You have some talent."

"You think you can judge literary talent even though you don't read much?"

"Well," Ryan argued, "I think that talent, to some degree, is a quality free of attachment to any sort of skill or hobby. Don't you? What I mean is to have talent is to have the choice of where to direct it."

"I don't know if I believe that. I think I was kind of born with this drive. One of those 'gift and a curse' situations," Lado said. Ryan held his gaze, not saying anything, but not showing a lack of interest. Lado continued, "I'm not sure I chose this direction. I think it chose me."

"Of course. It's your calling, the calling to be a writer," Ryan said.

Lado detected a bit of sarcasm. "A desperate desire to share my thoughts with other people. I'm sure all the greats felt it. You're looking at a future great *auteur*." As Lado said this he imagined other such greats as having been in similar situations, defending their work, their calling, engaging in witty banter with an attractive acquaintance, probably motivated almost one hundred percent by the desire to have sex with said acquaintance, all the while on the verge of retching or dry heaving in twice said acquaintance's face. It probably wasn't so unlikely, he thought. He threw out some names that came to mind. "Hemingway, Joyce, Carver, Bukowski. If not gentlemen all, then great, *driven* authors, each and every one," he finished.

"Yes, I'm sure they all felt it. I didn't hear you mention any women, though. Rather chauvinistic of you, don't you think?"

Lado did not want to admit that the authors he had mentioned came to mind because of their drinking habits foremost of their literary talent. Couldn't he have thought of some women drunks? He tried. *Sylvia Plath, Dorothy Parker, Anne Sexton...*

Every one he thought of was a poet, and not a novelist. Was there something to that?

"I don't mean to offend. I'm not a misogynist."

"I didn't say you were a 'misogynist'," Ryan said.

Lado peeked out into the dining room. There were a few groups of people walking in, sitting down at tables and in booths. Overweight men with loud voices. Most of them appeared already partly drunk. "Am I going to get you into trouble back here? The bartender looks pissed. I should be going anyway. I have things to do."

"Oh, well, that's unfortunate. I was just starting to enjoy our conversation. You know, you're not at all what I expected you to be like."

Lado didn't know what to make of this. He didn't say anything.

"You could have a drink and wait for my shift to end and we could go get something to eat," Ryan continued.

"We could, yes. But I'm not sure if I'd want to. I feel terrible, honestly, and I have some writing to do. Besides I think maybe you're coming on strong. I thought maybe I could discreetly find out when you work and pop in periodically in a borderline stalking manner, but do so in just the right way that it would appear to be a matter of coincidence. You would, inevitably, conclude that the stars were aligned for us to be together, and we could then proceed to hangout outside of this hole-in-the-wall pub.

"But, then again, since you have other, less roundabout methods in mind, I think I may have to reconsider my original plan."

"Well while you sit here and make up your mind, I'm going to go see if those kind gentleman would like something to drink." Ryan stood up. She was wearing a shirt of a light, loose-fitting satin material that gave Lado the pleasure of imagining, in detail, the shape of her torso. Ryan possessed, Lado could surmise, medium-sized, firm tits with nipples that pointed slightly up and to the side when resting. Her stomach was not hard and not totally flat but smooth and soft. Somewhere in his mind, for a brief moment, he remembered the peach fuzz around the navel of another girl he'd known. As Ryan walked past him he picked up a mildly scented perfume that he maybe did or maybe did not remember from anywhere else, he wasn't sure, and he smelled a bit of Ryan naturally, as she had been working and perhaps perspiring slightly. Her smell was electrifying.

A strong jolt of testosterone entered into his bloodstream. His headache was suddenly gone, replaced by a thirst for beer and an appetite for sex. He watched Ryan approach the table of men. To go with her loose-fitting shirt she wore a tight-fitting pair of skinny jeans with a high waist. *They must be tailor fitted,* Lado thought, *the way they fit her ass.* Her hair was long and came down to the midway point of her back. It appeared not to have been washed in a day or two, and it had a slight oily sheen to it. Probably smelled good. Lado imagined holding a tuft of it in his hand and, closing his eyes, taking in a big whiff, both of them naked on the floor of his bedroom, drunk from orgasm, purified by the steam of their own lovemaking. He allowed this fantasy to linger.

"I've decided I had better take you up on your offer," Lado said to Ryan as she came back over to the service side of the bar, which was near to the office, "I need to eat something. What time will you be getting off? The sooner the better."

"Well, if we get this little push, I'll probably stick around and make some extra money. Maybe around six? The night crew should be here by then. What time is it now?" It was quarter to four. "Sit at the bar and have a drink. Rob will take care of you."

So the bartender's name was Rob. Lado would try to remember. He didn't like Rob. Lou was a lot better, and treated Lado appropriately as an industry man.

Lado told Ryan that he would have to do something else besides sit at the bar and wait for her, that he really needed to write otherwise he would feel guilty for having wasted the day. He shut down his laptop and packed it away. She asked for his phone number and gave him a pen. Lado wrote his number on a bar napkin and asked that she text him right away so that he would have hers. She didn't have her phone with her; it was behind the bar. Lado slung his bag over his shoulder and followed her. She picked up her phone and held it next to the piece of paper with Lado's number on it, and touched the screen of her phone to enter the number and dial it. A comfortable silence, a glance and a bashful smile. Seconds later Lado's phone began to vibrate in his pocket. He mocked sexual arousal. She rolled her eyes and grabbed a tray full of beer and walked over to the table of men and began, Lado presumed, to flirt with them as she set the beers down in front of them and was smiling, saying things that Lado couldn't hear in a quiet and feminine voice that was overpowered by the booming laughter coming from the mouths of the grown lushes. All of the men appeared to have a great deal of drinking experience in general. Red noses, large round bellies. And they seemed to be the type to frequent The Playground. Lado didn't like them.

So often it is a server's duty to entertain certain ideas with customers. It is, at the very least, to a server's monetary advantage to flirt gracefully, but in general, it's considered unprofessional to follow through. Lado, being employed in the service industry, understood this. He was, in fact, a customer here at The Playground. But, again, in large part because he worked in the industry and understood the situation as such, he had a certain right to take advantage of all of the attractive opportunities that presented themselves in the form of hot waitresses and bartenders. It is an incestuous social group.

Lado walked out of the bar and gave Ryan a smile and a nod on his way out. She waved and mouthed the word "bye," and Lado made for his apartment quickly, where Ernie was hungry and Lado fed him. He then reassembled his mess of handwritten pages from the night before and set up at his desk to transcribe his story. He did this for two hours, stopping briefly to take Ernie outside, to go and grab a beer from the fridge. To grab another beer from the fridge. To smoke a cigarette. To take a piss. In the bathroom, he looked at himself in the mirror and felt that much-talked-about feeling of almost not recognizing yourself as yourself. His hair was a mess, his face was unwashed, and his facial hair situation made him look like a bum, he thought. His glasses were filthy, had not been cleaned in days. His undershirt, which he had slept in and, apparently, vomited on a little, was appalling. He was glad he had covered it up when he went to get his bag and met Ryan. Somewhere in his brain the words "I'm an alcoholic," rang out. He ignored them and went out on the back porch to listen to the trains rumble past while he smoked another cigarette. Then he went back to work.

When he finished writing he took a shower. He didn't shave. In his bathrobe he lay on the bed and fell asleep.

He woke up to the sound of his phone vibrating on his dresser. It was Ryan. "Well, hello, there, stud," she said. Lado liked the sound of her voice on the telephone. He snapped out of his haze. "Hey. You off work?"

"Yea, those fucking douche bags camped out forever and didn't even leave me twenty percent. Sorry it took me so long to get out of there. You haven't eaten yet, have you?" Lado took the phone away from his ear to look at the time on his screen. Eight seventeen. He had been asleep almost two hours.

"No, I haven't, actually. I've been quite busy with working and what not and I haven't even thought about it yet. You know, if you're leaving work now you can come by my place for a second as I get ready and we'll figure out some place to go. What do you have in mind for food?"

"I don't really care. But I don't eat meat. So they have to have good vegetarian options. No bullshit either."

"One four three Kingston Avenue, number three. Third level."

Five minutes later, Ryan arrived and Lado buzzed her up. He was just finishing getting dressed. Inside, Lado introduced Ryan to Ernie, who circled his visitor, sniffing her. In what seemed like a form of approval, he let out a small bark, stuck his tongue out, and waved his tail enthusiastically; meanwhile, Ryan commented on how cute he was. Lado made sure Ernie had enough water in his water bowl, and, since Ernie was afraid of the dark and tended to disrupt the *feng shui* of his environment through various acts of destruction when the lights were out and his master was away, Lado kept a lamp on in the living room. Lado didn't show Ryan around his apartment much. He put on his coat and they were on their way.

Ryan and Lado walked the slow walk of talking and getting to know each other and not really having anywhere to go. Not the first date walk, which is a little more intense, with heads turned to face one another and purposeful, forced smiles, but much more casual, with each pair of eyes taking in its own perceived beauty of the world they beheld. Somewhere along the way, both Lado and Ryan had decided that Valmesta had a lot of beauty in it, and it wasn't about knowing where to look. It was about seeing the beauty in what was in plain sight. To an outsider, it may have been hard to see an abandoned home, with paint chipped away, the grass in the yard overgrown and gone to seed, the garage caved in on itself next to an old Chevy convertible half-hidden beneath a tarp representing the owner's almost-but-not-quite-abandoned dream to get it running again, to walk past an empty lot where there used to be a house but it burned down in a fraud scandal and was now vacant and for sale ten years, where there was the triple homicide just two years ago that everyone in the neighborhood didn't speak of anymore, to see the blight and the madness and the frustration and the insane resilience of the people who refused to leave the place they called home, and call it beautiful. But not to people like Lado and Ryan, who lived it and saw it from the inside and appreciated the richness of the imagery and the lives within.

During their conversation, they avoided first date topic clichés like siblings and level of education and current profession. People who really wanted to get to know each other didn't care about such trivial things. It would be later that Lado learned that Ryan's background and upbringing were quite different from his own, and that, despite her appreciation of the grittier surroundings she and Lado found themselves in that night, she was still an outsider.

Ryan did seem pretty interested in Lado's writing, which Lado wasn't always enthusiastic about discussing, even though writing did have a very slight rock star appeal to it. At the very least writing was something that other people liked to talk about, probably because they didn't understand why anyone would be crazy enough to want to do it. Writing was mysterious, almost magical. And if he could use it to get laid, he certainly would.

"What's your thing? I mean, I have to assume waitressing is the same for you as it is for me."

"Oh, you're a waitress, too?" Ryan said.

"You know what I mean."

"I would like to open a flower shop," she said.

"I think that would really suit you."

They ate at a Mediterranean deli. It was one of Ryan's favorite places to eat. They shared an appetizer platter of falafel, grape leaves, hummus, and tabbouli, all of which Ryan squeezed a lemon over top of and some of the juice squirted in Lado's eye. It stung, but they laughed about it. After the appetizers Lado ate a chicken kabob with lemon and oregano and Ryan had vegetables and rice pilaf with a spicy tomato sauce. Lado enjoyed it and told Ryan that it would become a regular stop on his quick eats circuit. The only problem with the place, Lado said, was that it didn't have any booze.

The two of them left and hit up a string of bars, meeting other people, buying one another shots and getting altogether quite drunk. Neither of them felt the cold that the clear night brought with it. They were nearby the river that ran through the center of town, and they ventured into Belle Park, where Lado had been earlier, and walked along the Industrial Bridge, which took them over the river and into downtown.

Downtown seemed like a whole different world, taxis flying by, people very much dressed up, coming from the entertainment district where they were probably at an expensive show. Diamonds sparkling in the ears of women who kept warm in fur coats, while the men who accompanied them shined in their expensive suits and held the door as the women got in and out of the taxis. They cast sidelong glances at Lado and Ryan, not sure what to make of them. Lado felt uneasy, but Ryan seemed unaffected. She seemed, in a way, to come alive under the bright lights, amid the noise and bustle of downtown city life. Lado felt the stares of older, wealthier men, and he began to realize that some of them were looking at Ryan. He realized just then that her appeal was a universal one, that almost every straight man or lesbian with any amount of sexual vigor would be desirous of her. Ryan seemed to return some of the looks. Lado wasn't sure what was going on. When Ryan suggested they find a place to have a drink, Lado admitted he felt uncomfortable east of the river and that he didn't want to upset their otherwise harmonious, booze-filled evening together by remaining downtown, spending too much money, and getting Lado kicked out of bars. After a while, they decided to head back to the bridge to West Valmesta.

Approaching the bridge from the eastern side of the river, Lado saw his neighborhood, his stomping grounds, in an unfamiliar way. The buildings were short and dark. From this side of the river his world appeared impoverished and mean. He liked it that way. He smiled as they walked onto the bridge, sensing that Ryan, in this moment, understood him.

By the time they got to the other side of the bridge, Lado was at ease. He asked Ryan if she wanted to see where he worked, and she said yes. Doraku wouldn't be open, of course—it was almost two a.m.—but he had a key and would be able to show her around. When they arrived at the back door, however, Lado found that his key wasn't right. At first he suspected that he had drunkenly tried the wrong key, and for a moment he felt embarrassed, but when he looked closely at all his keys he realized he had the right one. *Why won't it work?* he wondered. Ryan looked at him, puzzled, amused, and perhaps even a little anxious.

"This is strange," Lado said. He strained his eyes to try to look in through the glass door. From the rear it didn't appear any different than it normally did, though it was normally of very minimal appearance and décor. He took Ryan around to the front of the building in order to try the main entrance. Lado could not have been ready for what he was about to discover. The locks had indeed been changed. From the front doors and in full view through the windows, Lado could see that the little decoration Jeon had erected over the years was no longer there. There was, taped to the window on the inside of the front door, a note:

To my customers,

I must thank you for your business over the years. It is with sadness that I inform you all that Doraku is now closed. I will be returning to Seoul to be with my family at this time.

To my employees,

Your most recent paychecks will be arriving by mail in the next few days. I have enjoyed working with you all and getting to know you, and my years in this country I will look back on very fondly. It is a sad time for my family and me and I thank those of you who were there for me.

All of the best wishes,
Jeon

The full emotional effect of this—of losing his job so swiftly and abruptly, of Jeon moving away without a real good bye, of what would be done with this space that was Doraku—would not sink in until much later. Ryan stood there, looking back and forth from the letter to Lado's expressionless face. Lado adjusted his glasses and ran his hand through his hair. Ryan put her arm around his shoulder, and Lado returned the gesture. Each of them with their sense of balance impaired, they wobbled on their feet. Neither of them said anything for a while and Lado wondered whether he was going to cry.

"I'm kind of drunk. Will you take me back to your place?" Ryan asked Lado.

Back at Lado's apartment they found Ernie fast asleep. Even though Ernie wasn't known for being a great guard dog, Lado was surprised they didn't wake him.

Lado reached into the kitchen cabinet quietly and pulled down two drinking glasses and set them on the counter, pouring Ryan and himself each a glass of water. He offered Ryan a cocktail, but she declined. She said "no" in the mysterious yet absolute way that meant she had something different entirely on her mind. A devious little smile spread across her face. Lado asked if she wanted to see the library in his bedroom. He took her there without a word and shut the door behind them, not turning on the light. There was a streetlamp outside Lado's rear window that provided them with enough light to undress each other, which can be a challenge for an inebriated pair of lovers, and they began to kiss each other, tenderly at first, and then more passionately. Lado felt her tits and soon his dick was hard and Ryan reached for it and tugged it gently. Lado laid Ryan on her back on the bed and used his tongue to get her wet and he felt her to make sure she was wet enough. Ryan told Lado she didn't like condoms, and Lado agreed but wondered whether he should use one just to be safe. She asked him whether he had ever had an STD. He hadn't, to his knowledge, but he hadn't been tested recently, either. They decided to fuck without a condom because it felt better that way. When the time came Lado asked Ryan whether he should pull out, and Ryan said, "No, come in me." Being drunk, Lado took a long time to come, even though the encounter was a surprise and a thrill and they were doing it raw. Ryan came first, in one small wave and then in a second, larger, louder orgasm. Soon after, Lado came. They stayed together for several minutes, no words, no motion, just rest and bliss and intoxication. This was the most satisfying way to end it. They could not be anxious or unhappy in this moment. Some time passed before Lado pulled out. Some of his come gushed onto the sheets. He would have to wash them. Ryan didn't notice. She may have been asleep already.

Lado heard Ernie groaning on the other side of the bedroom door. Lado got up to open it. Ernie seemed tired, like he had been sleeping and, to his chagrin, was awoken by the sounds coming from the bedroom, at which point the poor fellow realized he needed to pee. *At least he was polite enough to wait until we were through*, Lado mused.

Lado put a robe and slippers on and put Ernie on a leash and took him out on the front balcony, where Ernie peed on a potted plant and Lado had a cigarette. Back inside, Lado washed up before disrobing and getting back into bed.

He woke up naked with the sun shining on him. Ryan was wearing her clothes from the night before. "May I use your toothbrush?" she asked Lado as she finished tying her shoes and got up to go to the bathroom. Lado looked for his phone, but he couldn't find it. He was still drunk. He asked Ryan for the time. "Just past eight," Ryan said. She returned to the bedroom and brushed her teeth while she continued to look for something. "Where are my panties?" she asked. Lado looked at her. The fact that she wasn't wearing underwear turned him on. He asked her to get naked and get back under the covers, but she rolled her eyes at him. Foamy white toothpaste dribbled onto Ryan's chin. Lado got up and reached under Ryan's clothes and began to touch her skin gently with his fingertips, but she grabbed his arm and pushed him away. Lado wondered whether he was dreaming. This was not the same woman as before. Lado looked around at his surroundings, eventually concluding that it was not a dream.

Ryan went back to the bathroom and spit out the toothpaste. When she came back she told Lado that she had to meet her fiancé at the airport at eleven and that she had to take a taxi there if she were going to make it in time. But first she had to get cleaned up and wash the sex and the hangover off of her.

Lado tried to think of something to say, anything that wouldn't sound stupid. "You can use my shower," he said. "I should have a clean towel somewhere."

"That's all right." She needed to get home, to forget about this, to be in the right state of mind to meet her fiancé. Lado got up again to embrace Ryan and she averted her eyes away from his penis. She didn't want to think about what happened. Lado wondered whether he should feel bad, but he didn't feel like he had done anything wrong. He didn't feel bad, just, he decided, just awkward. "Wait a second," he said, "I'll put on some clothes, walk you to the door."

"That's all right." They looked at each other, both unsure of the amount of physical or verbal affection they should show one another. They decided that no affection was appropriate. She forced a smile, then turned and found her way out of Lado's apartment. Lado heard the door close. He poured and chugged a glass of water, and then he lay back down on the bed, and, trying not to think too much, he managed to fall back asleep.

A little before noon, Ernie was barking, probably simultaneously hungry and needing to evacuate his lower digestive tract. Lado got dressed and took him for a walk and smoked a cigarette. He was surprised that he wasn't hungover. The reality of the previous night's events began to sink in. Jeon was gone. Lado was unemployed. He just fucked a virtual stranger who was engaged to be married. He came in her. He probably spent way too much money at the bars. It all made him start thinking about real-life things— how much money was in his bank account, how his brother, whom he hadn't spoken to in years, was doing, to what pole or tree or fence was his bicycle locked.

What more is there to say about it? Lado's life was like this. The ups and downs of being a young drunk, smart enough to know what he was doing but too proud to think he was wrong for doing it. Would he ever learn? His upbringing was a tempestuous, unstable failure, but he was gifted and he went to college, thinking he was fixed. Only to what, wait tables? Drink whiskey every morning? If only he could understand what really became of his father, maybe he would better understand the beast that was his birthright.

And every day he tried to write something that wasn't shit, thinking that it was so important that he do so. For years he had woken up each day and his first instinct was that he must write. Mostly what he did was party and try to get laid, even claiming to be a more distinguished writer than he really was in order to impress people. What the hell. Was being a young man an adequate justification for it? He hadn't gotten much done, and he felt guilty for wasting time. He didn't know how he was going to support himself. He had almost nothing in the fridge besides beer and Styrofoam containers of leftover food that he usually fed to Ernie. He should have been even more depressed than he was.

He thought about Ellery. Lately his thoughts always came back to her. Lado liked the way Ellery saw him; that is, she saw him the way he wanted to be seen by others, but that most others didn't see him. She made him feel more like himself.

Lado tried calling her, but there was no answer. He decided to go on a walk to clear his head. He splashed some cold water on his face and used the water to slick his hair back, and he found a pack of cigarettes on the bedside table.

On his way out the door, he tried calling Ellery again, but it just continued to ring. Oddly, in the hallway, he could hear the sound of a phone vibrating. It was as if on a table, on the other side of the thin wall of Kyle's apartment, Ellery's phone rang. *Coincidence*, Lado thought, but then: *Could it actually be Ellery's phone?* He hung up and inched closer to Kyle's door. The vibrating stopped. Faintly, he heard a giggle and a soft moan. *No way*, he thought, but his mind had already begun to race. He thought back to the night, not so long ago, when he sat on the floor of his apartment with Ellery while a barefoot Kyle rambled on about this and that. Looking back, through the lens of retrospect, those bare feet offended Lado. *No fucking way...*

Outside, cigarette after cigarette, Lado's thoughts continued to wander. *I can't be sure it's her. I really don't want it to be her. There's no way she would do that. She and I have a thing. Don't we have a thing? I guess I never confirmed with her that we have a thing, but I'm pretty sure she feels the same way that we have a thing. This all sucks. Fuck.*

Somewhat attractive girl over there, walking her dog. I'd do her. Who's that guy she's hugging? He looks like an asshole. Probably a young girl still in her asshole-dating phase. She'll grow up.

What is it with girls? Kyle? Come on, Ellery, you're better than that. I'm better than him.

Then again, I don't even know for sure if it's her. It could not be her. It could just be a coincidence that someone else's phone—Kyle's, even, or some other girl's—was ringing at that same moment that I was calling Ellery's. I mean, if Ellery was at Kyle's place, wouldn't she have at least stopped in to say hi to me?

Would that have made this revelation any easier to swallow?

Actually, wait. I don't even know if what I'm thinking is true.

I need to find out for sure.

Twenty minutes passed like this, the engine generating Lado's anxious thoughts like a dragster at the starting line, fuel burning, wheels spinning and crinkling, rubber burning down, smoke rising, and the dragster not really going anywhere, but only fishtailing side to side. Meanwhile, tobacco burned like brush fire. It was another fifteen minutes before he got back, and, taking the stairs two at a time up to Kyle's doorway, he called Ellery for the third time. He listened for a vibration, a conversation, anything, but there was no sound.

Just Ellery's voice on the other end. "Hey, man," she said.

"Ellery. Hey. Where are you?"

"Uh, what?" She sounded tired and spaced out.

He quickly thought of an explanation for calling her, pretending to have a reason for asking her where she was. "I was just out for a walk and I thought I saw you. No?"

"Maybe. I was out for a bit. I'm home now."

"Gotcha. I just thought I saw you and I thought about you and I figured, I should call Ellery." Lado forced a laugh.

"That's nice of you. How have you been?"

"Good, good, just busy with writing and stuff. You?"

"I've been fine. I miss you. Sorry I never responded to your text messages, I've been meaning to."

"You weren't really mad at me, were you?"

"No, I was joking. I mean, gossip is a fact of life."

"Truth."

"What are you doing? Have you eaten?"

"Not today, no."

"I want breakfast."

"Okay."

"And I could use a mimosa."

"Manny's has the best mimosas. They always use fresh squeezed."

"I can meet you there in half an hour. I just need to freshen up."

Lado was there before Ellery. He sat down at the bar and ordered a beer. He looked for Manny, but he didn't see him. "Is Manny around?" Lado asked the bartender. The bartender shook his head. "Not today." The bartender placed a purple paper napkin on the bar in front of Lado and set the beer down on it. Lado took a swig and set the beer back down on the actual surface of the bar and not on the napkin. He didn't like to lift up a beer bottle with a napkin stuck to the bottom of it.

Lado heard the door open behind him and the sunlight gushed in, swathing Lado in its radiating warmth. In the mirror behind the bar he saw Ellery enter. His heart began to beat rapidly. *She has looked good every moment of every day her whole life*, he decided then.

He spun around on his bar stool and stepped down to give Ellery a hug. She sat down and, already having the bartender's attention, ordered a mimosa. "Oh, man," she said, tasting it. "This is good."

They talked, catching up, as people say, sharing little stories and anecdotes of things that had happened since they'd last seen each other. Lado struggled to keep the conversation friendly despite the nagging question he was planning to ask. Of course, Lado told Ellery nothing of his last night's affair with Ryan.

Eventually the question became too big and too powerful a thing to keep at the rear of his consciousness, and Lado blurted it out. "So were you at Kyle's this morning?"

To Ellery, this question felt out of the blue and crude. "Kyle's?" she said. Ellery had a bewildered look to her. Normally, it was no difficulty for Ellery to be at ease in Lado's company, but she was visibly uncomfortable. She stiffened and sipped her mimosa, and Lado watched her. She appeared to drink more out of nervousness than out of desire.

"Yeah, my neighbor."

"What would make you think that?"

"Well, I was thinking about you earlier. Actually, I've been thinking about you a lot lately, and I decided to call you this morning, so I called you, but you didn't answer. I tried you again on my way out to have a cigarette, and I could hear a phone vibrating in Kyle's apartment. I thought, 'What a coincidence! Here I am trying to reach Ellery, and she's just across the hall.' I thought about knocking and asking for you, but then I realized it was probably just that, a coincidence. But then I thought about it some more, and I thought, maybe you really were there."

Ellery laughed. She was trying to lighten the atmosphere, but Lado could tell she was offended by the forwardness of his inquiry.

Still he pressed on. "So?" he said. "Were you there this morning or no?"

"Why do you ask?" she said.

"I just want to know." It was beginning to seem more and more likely to Lado that what he suspected was true. He tried, in vain, to maintain a look of stoic composure, but he, too, was growing upset.

"You definitely don't need to know, but yes, I was," Ellery said.

"How did that happen?"

"How did what happen?"

"How did you end up sleeping with him?"

"Dude, you need to respect my privacy a little bit."

"So you did sleep with him."

"Whatever, yeah."

"How could you do that?"

"What do you mean, how could I?"

"I mean how did that happen?"

"I don't know. It just happened. What are you getting at here?"

"Wow."

"Oh, come on. Don't do this right now. You know how it is. Kyle asked me to hang out, I said sure, one thing led to another...and it just happened. I didn't plan on it. It was really casual."

"I didn't think you were like that."

"Excuse me?"

Lado looked out the window.

"Like what, exactly?"

"Like the type of person who just does that. You barely know him."

"You don't know that. You barely know me."

"Ellery, yes I do."

Ellery sipped her mimosa with difficulty. Her hand was trembling, her lips quivered, and she let out a sigh. She tried to hide the tears in her eyes, and she dabbed at them with her shirtsleeve.

"Ellery, stop doing this."

"I'm not doing anything."

"You're making me uncomfortable with your crying."

Ellery turned back to face him, no longer ashamed of being distressed. "I thought you'd be happy for me. I thought you liked him."

"He's fine, but that's not the point. I like *you*. I wanted you."

"Why are you telling me this right now?"

"Because I want you to know that you made a mistake."

"You're being an asshole."

"I still can't even figure out how that would have happened."

"It doesn't matter."

"I wanted you."

"Well even if you still wanted me, now I think you're a jerk."

"At least I'm not a slut."

"Okay, you know what. I'm leaving now."

Ellery wiped the corners of her eyes once more to dry them. She looked at Lado squarely. What was it about him that inspired such jealousy? She had been blindsided.

That very moment Ellery vowed to never again allow herself to be vulnerable around Lado. "If you have anything else to say to me, say it now."

Ellery took up her bag and stood up off the barstool. She waited a moment for a response, but Lado never gave one.

"You're something else, man. Do you know that? Do you even realize how much of an asshole you are?"

Lado drank his beer.

"Don't call me, don't text me, don't talk to me if you see me out somewhere. I don't need friends like you," Ellery said, and left.

There were the stains of Ellery's lipstick on the champagne flute and the mimosa that she didn't finish. Lado picked up the flute and studied the lip mark. He drank the drink in one big gulp. He got the bartenders attention and ordered a shot and another beer.

Was Lado heartbroken? I guess it's tough to say; heartbreak isn't easy to understand. He didn't think he was ever in love with Ellery. They had never really expressed romantic love in any demonstrable way. Sure there were the furtive, momentary connections that made the heart race slightly and the pupils dilate, but nothing had been realized, nothing of the little daily nuances of kindness or generosity that over time add up to a voluptuous and complex web of relation and reliance and brain chemistry that we have come to understand as love. No steamy make out after a fight, no slow dance at a wedding reception. Just true, honest companionship and the pleasure of being near.

Yet Lado felt something that night, listening to mix tapes of music he had never heard before, savoring the floral, bitterly resinous India pale ale and the subtle vibration of magnetic proximity. What he had experienced with Ellery was something different from the norm, something uniquely special and thus too precious and too fragile to handle rashly and without thought of consequence.

But alas, he had done just that, and now he didn't know what to make of his own behavior or of his being dumbstruck by what had come out of his own mouth. Of course he knew he was being an asshole, but he couldn't help feeling rejected, even betrayed, and angered by what Ellery had done. Even more to his dismay, he couldn't stop himself, in that moment, just minutes earlier, when he uttered that most intolerable word. He had done so with such malice, and yet, there was nothing else he could have said honestly in that moment, such was his desire to inflict pain on her, to deliver her retribution.

Nonetheless, the following day Lado felt it necessary to compose a letter to Ellery, perhaps as a final effort to share himself with her.

iv.

Letter to Ellery

Hello Ellery,

> *Two days ago, I didn't think I would be writing you a letter like this. I don't want this to be a farewell, although you may read it that way if you like. I'm leaving it up to you.*

> *I think you and I are kindred spirits. I always felt at ease with you. If you don't write me back I will take it as a sign that you don't care to remain friends with me. That's okay, I guess. I'll live.*

> *You know, I've come to the conclusion that nothing is written. There is no plan to this thing we call life, and we do our best to make of it what we like and succeed or fail to varying degrees, and then we move on. No one ever really gets it right. I don't believe in God, in any sort of afterlife, and I certainly don't live by any upright code of morals. But I've always felt, from an early age, that there's something important about being here, that the things we do and who we*

decide to spend time with are significant in some way that we'll never really be able to understand.

Lot's of things have happened to me, and at times I've gotten very discouraged. There's a lot that can happen to bring you down. But somehow, no matter how much I learn about people, I still manage to maintain the belief that some things matter just because they do. Between the beginning and the end of each and every one of our unimportant little lives, there's a lot of things that seem like they don't mean much but somehow amount to something that is just plain meaningful. Think of how much the things we do affect the world around us. Human existence is infinitely complex, with the unimaginably intricate and beautiful connections we make with one another. The decisions we make and how we choose to respond to the events in our lives determines how and how much our lives have meaning.

The hardest part is trying to ascertain which of the little things matter and which don't. Knowing whether or not something matters enough is to know the difference between someone you try your best to hang on to and someone you have to just let go.

Ours is a fragile existence.

Lado.

V.

Intermezzo

By now the reader may have begun to wonder about the legitimacy of Lado's approach to his craft. The reader has every right to be so inquisitive. "Was his writing any good?" is a likely question.

The process of writing is a difficult one to understand, and impossible to analyze. For an observer to see a writer in the act of writing, and in that state of dream, is impossible. Writing is done alone or not at all.

Therefore, it is impossible to study the writing process because the mere presence of an observer or an examiner renders the state unattainable. The truth is a writer can live by whatever means necessary or available, but his work remains separate from his life story. It is but a mere dream. Another likely question is: Why did he have such a persistent notion that he could have any success as a writer? It is very difficult to find success in the economic market of the present day. Lado knew this. Still, he kept on working at it. Unlike the first question, the answer to this question may be known by understanding Lado as a person, and this story exists in order to render feasible that understanding.

One day, Lado was bicycling through the neighborhood where he spent most of his youth. He had left the neighborhood years prior to attend college, but, after graduating, having nowhere better to go, he had returned. He stopped at the gas station on a street corner in his former environs, as if by old habit.

The mini-mart was bigger than Lado remembered it. Business had expanded. (How not, with such a rapidly growing number of motorists out there?) The store had increased its inventory vastly to cater to a wider clientele, including an array of marijuana growing equipment in the back corner of the store, called the "Hydroponic Center." Lado noticed there was a bulletproof plexiglass barrier, which had never been there before, between the checkout line and the cashier.

Lado got in line to pay cash for the iced tea he held in his hand. He was in line behind two adults and a child. First was a middle-aged man who appeared to be a long-time drug user. What he purchased and how he talked and how his damaged nervous system contorted his body during the exchange are unimportant details of the story, but what is important is what the middle-aged and heavyset man behind him said to his young son of, maybe, ten years after the addict walked out through the store's propped door. He said, in a loud voice, as if to make sure his son could hear, but also in a mock-proud way, so that the addict, just a few paces away, could maybe also hear and maybe feel sorry for what he had been doing to himself all this time using drugs, "You see, son? You see how these people live? Do you see what you have to be grateful for? I work hard to give you a seven-thousand square foot home far away from here so that you don't have to see these things everyday."

The cashier—a young Lebanese man roughly Lado's age—observed the scene calmly while he rang the customers up, and then they left. Lado had a ten-dollar bill in his hand and he walked up to the counter and slid his money under the bulletproof glass while he ordered a hard pack of cigarettes. Neither party made any indication that they had so much as heard the heavyset man speak.

Inside, Lado raged.

Here now a moment of reflection. Here now let us divest ourselves of this cloak.

Book 2.

i.

If Only to Better Understand the Man

I don't remember when I used my passport last, or where it is now, or whether I still have it in my possession at all. If I were able to find it, it would show my full Czech name: Ladislav Teodor Martin Ruzicka. The full name one would read on my identification and official documents here in the States is a slightly anglicized version of it: Ladis Theodor Rose. For as long as I can remember, though, I've gone by Lado. It works for me. I'm an American, and I don't want my name to be difficult.

I was four years old when I came here with my aunt and uncle, Klara and René, who raised me, and my older brother Alexei. My aunt and uncle were old, or at least I remember them as old. Anyway, they were older than my parents were when they died, and have since passed away, and my brother and I haven't spoken in years. He is somewhat of an entrepreneur of various criminal enterprises and has been locked up a few times for different offenses. I would come to find out later that during the time that the events of this story were taking place, Alexei was incarcerated in a state prison somewhere very far away from where I was living for carrying a weapon he did not have a permit for. I'm sure there were other laws broken in his wake.

He used to send me letters occasionally. Right now, he may still be in jail or he could be out by now, anywhere doing anything illegal. I'm not sure, but I would bet they couldn't fix him in there. In all honesty, I don't really care to keep up with it, though there was once a time when we were both young and we relied on each other and were close. Probably I relied on him more than he on me.

Klara and René took care of us for barely two years before they died, Uncle René of throat cancer and Aunt Klara of heartsickness, probably, and after that Alexei and I lived in various group homes. He was much bigger than I was and was fit and healthy. I was rather small as a boy and often sick. I remember two times when a bully harassed me, trying to cause trouble, and next thing I knew the boy was on his back, crying, with blood gushing from his nose, and Alexei was being pulled off of him by an authority. After those two incidents, bullies generally left me alone.

Alexei was good to me and was loyal and he looked after me until I was seventeen—he would have been around nineteen then—and we decided that we had had enough of living in group homes. By that time I had nearly graduated from high school and Alexei had long since stopped going, so it didn't make much sense for us to stay in homes.

Alexei recognized that we were on different paths. He was smart and good to me about it. Around the same time he was beginning to discover the means of income that would eventually land him in prison, he was also acting as a sort of guidance counselor for me. He made sure I got good marks, which, for me, didn't exactly require much effort, and insisted that I applied for admission to the state university, where I was accepted and where I would begin the following fall semester with scholarship assistance, financial aid, and student loans. Alexei told me it would one day be worth it. So far, in some ways it has been and in other ways it has not been very much worth it.

We separated around then but we still saw each other from time to time. Until I went away to college I was basically homeless, and so was Alexei, but we were in the same neighborhood and we would run into each other occasionally. Alexei had plenty of money and was very good at whatever it was he was doing, and he usually stayed with one of the women at the neighborhood brothel. He took me there once, and that was how I had sex for the first time. Or maybe it was Allison Krakow from school, I can't remember. They happened basically at the same time. Anyway, I didn't like being with a hooker and afterward I decided I would never sleep with one again.

I started drinking right around that time. The first time I got drunk I drank a forty-ounce of malt liquor and took shots of cognac. Of course, it's ridiculous to take shots of cognac, but at that time I didn't know any better. I kept my drinking secret, otherwise I would have gotten the guys I stayed with in trouble and I would have been probably kicked out onto the street.

I stayed mostly with the family of a kid I had met in school. His name was Billy Clark, or Clarkson, or something like that. Call them the Clarks. They were on the wealthy side of things, old manufacturing money. Mr. Clark probably saw taking me in as charity. While I didn't like the feeling I got when I sensed other people feeling bad for me, that first winter on my own it got pretty cold and I didn't have much of a choice. I would have frozen on the street.

Mr. Clark was a hunter, and a serious man. In their house they had a locked cabinet containing Mr. Clark's guns and knives. The oldest boy knew where the key was hidden, and one time he opened the cabinet to show off its contents to Billy and me. The older boy was haughty about the whole thing and he wasn't careful enough to put the key away in secret, and I saw where he put it. One day, after winter had run its course and I was no longer staying at the Clarks's, I snuck in through the basement doorwall in the back of the house and found the key right where the boy had left it.

I took my time feeling all the weapons. I was very fascinated. It gave me a primitive pleasure to handle deadly weapons, and the sound made by the blade of a really sharp buck knife when I picked it with my thumb—that *shiiiink* of wrought and insanely sharp steel reverberating, slicing through the air—got my adrenaline going. It appealed to the part of me that had been passed down in the Y chromosome through millions of years of evolution and has the potential to turn most seventeen- and eighteen-year-old males of the *Homo sapiens* species into brutal young warriors. I used reason and process of elimination, combined with visceral longing, to determine which weapon I would take with me. The rifle and shotgun were both out of the question for obvious logistical reasons, and a handgun was unnecessary, way too risky to carry, and would lead to severe penalty if ever I was caught with it.

There were several knives. Some smaller, flip-open types. One knife that I imagined would be used for cleaning a fish or a rabbit, and a similar looking but larger knife that looked like it could be used to clean a bigger animal. Some of them looked like military-issue. All of them sharp as hell. It was the Buck knife that really got my attention. A true beauty. The blade was seven inches long, curving up to a point on its front end, with one and a half or two inches of sharp edge on its back end. I imagine that, if I had to, I could stick it into somebody and, depending on the angle and the location of the blow, either press down or pull up and do some pretty serious damage either way. The knife had been enclosed in a thick leather sheath that could be wrapped around the shin and concealed above the ankle, and that's where I wore it.

Carrying my Buck knife helped me to not feel weak and entirely vulnerable, which was my natural state, even though I had grown to be much bigger than a lot of my peers. If I were eating like I should have been at the time, I probably would have filled my frame well—my father was built and Alexei is stocky, so it's in my blood—but I wasn't eating much.

I spent a lot of my time around the western fringe of Valmesta, living as a vagabond by the abandoned rail way station. The station was near Industrial Park, and the rails going to and from the station weren't being used anymore. There was still a lone train on the rails. Why it wasn't removed from the rails, I will never know. Perhaps the city was condoning homelessness, or at least trying to isolate it to the area around The Valmesta Station, since the station and the trains were the primary respite for the city's bums.

The station itself was for the hardcore, the severely insane, traumatized, dismembered, sick, addicted. A twenty-story monolith of signature Valmestan gothic architecture, complete with two hundred abandoned and empty offices, the Valmesta Station had become a mere skeleton of what it once was: a glorious, buzzing hub of industry and commerce during the industrial expansion of the American Midwest. That golden age was long gone. I don't think the Valmesta Station has been used since the nineteen sixties. During the time I spent in the general vicinity of the station, it was occupied by only the most destitute of Valmesta's homeless.

I wasn't as naïve as most other kids my age, but I was still naïve. Soon after departing on my own I found myself in the area around the periphery of the Industrial Park district. The station and the surrounding area were both unfamiliar to me, away from schools, and, for the most part, away from any businesses and homes that I would have ever been to. I found my way there as my wandering radiated outward from the weak, beating heart of West Valmesta into the cold and dark regions reserved for the bums, the dregs of our impoverished society. I was one of them.

From the outside, the Valmesta Station looked empty, but inside, throughout the main corridor of the station, there were hundreds of people. I scanned the room to take it all in. They were everywhere, swarming the main corridor and tucked into the various terminals. I looked up at the majestic ceiling—a true architectural achievement—and wondered whether the designer had ever imagined this room being inhabited in such a manner as this. All these observations in a matter of seconds.

Suddenly the stench of human decay overwhelmed me. It was a layered stench, rich and complex and absolutely appalling. I almost choked on that first full breath. Piss, shit, vomit, booze, body odor, must. Rot and decay and, probably, death in abundance. I tried to resign myself to it the same way one would resign himself to losing an arm or a leg. It sucks, but get used to it. This is who you are now.

I looked around. There were sleeping bags, tables and chairs, card games, drinking, gambling. There were people buying, selling and trading, using drugs. I began to walk around, zigzagging through the crowd, people lying, sleeping, passed out, talking to themselves. It struck me at one point as I looked down at a woman lying on her side on a sleeping bag with two young children nestled against her that this was all she had. This was it. Together the three of them would have fit onto a love seat, but this was all they had. A sleeping bag and each other amidst the stink and the rot.

Throughout my life I had grown accustomed to pretending to fit in. I had never really fit in anywhere, so I pretended to, hoping it would make things easier. While I did not fit in there, in the train station, I didn't want to let on that I was an outsider. I moved through the muck of human bodies. At once a man called out to me. Of course he didn't know my name, but he began speaking, and in the way that one knows such things I knew that he was speaking to me. He told me to come closer. I hesitated. He assured me it was okay and that I should come closer. I leaned into my first step towards him. It was the only step I took, but it seemed to close the distance between us so that we were alone together among the crowd. There in the shadows the man whispered in my ear. I left the station immediately, never to return.

But I stayed close, for that summer at least. A couple hundred yards down the track was a deserted train, left to rust and to the elements. I came upon it that day as I left the station. Over the years the flora had engulfed the old boxcars. No one even knew the train existed but the few stragglers who had happened upon it over the years, and the people who lived there were younger and healthier than the people in the station and more able to weather the elements of living, for the most part, outdoors in a climate that brought with it the four seasons. In some ways it was a good time living in that hobo bastion. It was a truly free place. In other ways, it was a waking nightmare.

There I spent my summer. No electricity, no water. Nothing even of the rustic beginnings of a civilized life. Just youth and survival and abandonment to a wayward existence.

The college years were a major turning point for me. I learned how to take care of myself and provide for myself basic things like food and shelter, how to socialize, and how to act in different situations. It certainly wasn't easy. I was as much an outsider on campus as I was in the train station, and the notion of getting meal credits on my dorm room ID card was foreign to the point of being disorienting to me at first.

I began to understand basic needs and how to meet them, how to classify wants as luxuries opposed to needs, how to obtain that that I wanted. In short, I began to learn the important things you learn but they don't teach you.

By this time I was quite tall and I was finally filling out in the way that young men do, eating the meals that were provided by my dormitory. As a student, I enjoyed being at the center of classroom discussions and study groups. I began to realize for the first time that I was gifted and that I could use my gifts to my advantage. The obvious, primary advantage was that I could obtain good marks in my classes and win the favor of my professors, whom I could solicit for an academic reference later on if necessary.

The less obvious, perhaps less easily-exploited advantage was the attention I received from female classmates. I quickly realized that, in a university setting, intelligence is the ultimate sex appeal, and I quickly discovered ways to exploit my intellectual gifts for the purpose of courting mates. Girls were more motivated than the boys, I noticed, and were always willing to put in some extra time studying course material. I began inviting girls over to my dorm to study, which is a very safe and cozy reason to meet up with an eighteen-year-old boy like myself at that time. Of course, sometimes those study sessions would eventually lead to sex, and how could they not? Other times, my study partner would leave on platonic terms, only to later send me a drunken text message in the middle of the night asking whether I wanted to meet up.

I obtained a job at a dorm room cafeteria. I took a full course load. I worked hard, and I enjoyed the gratification of good hard work. On the weekends I rewarded myself by getting drunk and trying different drugs and having sex indiscriminately, which is pretty much what everyone else was doing at the time.

At the end of my freshman year I felt on top of the world, newly cultured and enlightened. That summer I hung around campus. I moved into an apartment that I subleased from a sophomore I had met, working part-time and partying the rest of the time. I felt the privilege of being an educated man. For the first time I was getting somewhere in the world, or so I thought. I began to look down on others less educated than myself, argue with them and make them look stupid, although now, if I could see myself during moments like that, I would think that the eighteen-year-old Lado was the stupid one.

Life was a whirlwind. I'll give an example. One day I stopped by my French instructor's office to discuss a paper I had written. Her name was Jessica, and the students in her class called her by her first name because she was a teacher's assistant, not a real professor. When I entered her office I found her immensely focused on work, and it was very sexy to see her that way. We hardly discussed my paper at all. She confirmed, albeit very subtly, my suspicion that she had an ulterior motive for inviting me to her office. She unzipped her jeans and put my hand in her pants and made me feel her and asked me to make her come. While I was doing it to her with my hand my phone vibrated in my pocket, and I ignored it, naturally. After she came she blew me. Some of my semen wound up on Jessica's shirt, which distressed her greatly because she had a class to teach in twenty minutes. My phone vibrated again.

When I left her office I saw two missed calls from an acquaintance named Paul, a coworker at the cafeteria. He and I had been partying together in our spare time. Basically he told me that a girl I had sex with was pregnant, and, as rumor had it, it was mine. I kind of freaked out and my stomach dropped, and I thought I might be sick. I became so nervous and scared that over the next few days I pulled out a noticeable amount of hair. I decided not to contact the girl, Kristen, a decision that I don't regret *per se*, but that I feel ashamed about. I came to find out later through a third party that she had aborted the unborn child.

Soon after that I fell into a deep, utter depression. It hadn't been so much a slip and fall as a gradual descent. In between the work hard slash play harder binges my lifestyle at that time entailed, I would sleep all the time and stay in the dark under the covers and think about what my funeral would be like and things like that. I was altogether depressed, yet from the outside you wouldn't have noticed. I will admit that I was self-medicating at that time, mostly with alcohol and marijuana but at times with prescription anti-depressants and anti-anxiety meds. I smoked cigarettes all the time, thinking the nicotine was helping to keep my mind sharp. I fucked wildly, but the girls that I had sex with I never ended up feeling any real connection with. (Inversely, the girls that I may have connected with I could never seem to get into bed. What I had come to understand as the means of seducing a lover didn't seem to work on the girls I actually wanted to be with. The girls I was laying were not the girls I wanted to lay, which is a fitting analogy for how I was living my life.)

I wondered whether I was gay, even going so far as to force myself to imagine what it would be like to be with a man. I could never seem to enjoy the thought of it, so I decided I couldn't be gay even if I made the conscious decision to try it.

I was confused and utterly depressed.

It was around that time that the girl, whom I refer to as V, broke my heart, or so I've always been convinced. In reality she didn't really do anything at all and I was just really immature and stupid. I was fucked up and acting out. Maybe I even thought that I was in love with her; but I never was. I know that now that I know what love is really like, I think. What's definitely true is that what V. and I had together was not healthy. Maybe she just wanted to fuck, to "slum," so to speak, with a troubled but intriguing, seemingly sensitive man, which I was at that time. I can understand the temptation in that. I think it's only natural to be attracted to people that are different and exotic. It keeps the gene pool diverse, opens the floodgates of genetic variance. I've read about this. For women, there are even correlations between sexual mate preference and the different phases of the menstrual cycle. For example, when a woman is ovulating she is more likely to be attracted to strong-jawed men, especially if they have a powerful social position, i.e. are very wealthy and in control of their respective environments. That way, if they get knocked up, their babies will likely be strong and healthy, viable offspring, and, as long as the guy who spawned the baby isn't a prick who walks out on his kid, they'll have resources, i.e., in contemporary culture, money. However, at other times during the menstrual cycle, a women is likely to be attracted to empathetic and caring men, those who would stick around and take care of and share resources with the woman's child in the case that the strong-jawed prick walks out. The reason the empathetic, caring man sticks around is because in a primitive society there would be no reason for him to suspect it wasn't his baby, because he, too, would have been having sex with the mother of the child during those times of the cycle when the woman wasn't fertile. Meanwhile, the Alpha is out getting his hump on with another ovulating female. I can't prove any of this, but it's interesting, and, in a way, it explains some things, like a prevalent genetic predisposition toward infidelity among pair-bound mates. I guess, for a guy, the best way is to be big and strong but also sensitive and caring, in order to entertain the most options.

Forgive my digression, as I don't believe it's relevant to the story. To be that age—I was nineteen—and coming to understand so many new things about the way the people of the world think and behave, and what motivates them, and their values and what they are capable of, all the while understanding very little of oneself, calling into question the ideas and beliefs one was brought up with from a young age, not understanding the meaning of existence, questioning whether living is even worthwhile at all, is not at all a comfortable thing. It can be very disconcerting. For myself, and for some of the friends I made during that time, friends who were experiencing similar states of confusion and angst, it was a bit of a crisis of self-understanding. It was about trying to formulate a grownup worldview, based on facts and the university education we were working to obtain, without becoming a scathing nihilist, which I didn't really see the point in either.

By junior year I had gained a lot of weight, probably twenty-five or thirty pounds on top of what I weighed at eighteen. Where before I was the popular life of the party, I had become, in my own eyes, a joke. Girls could sense it, and they didn't want to sleep with me anymore. Of course, I was still a young man—still am now, for that matter—and I had a great many powerful urges, and to have them and have them satisfied and then become unsatisfied wasn't helping me escape my depressed state. The situation with V was humiliating and was at the center of it, though I don't want to get into the telling of that whole story. That's not what this is about.

The point of all this is the writing, my love of language, an enchantment with beautiful arrangements of words, and the desire to write so beautifully. The desire to tell stories has been with me all my life, but at that time, as I began to read classics of literature in school and read Salinger and Hemingway outside of class, my love of writing was maturing almost into an obsession. At least into a bona fide commitment to the life and the craft, a commitment that bewildered those with whom I shared the secret of my passion. I couldn't ignore it. If I wasn't writing, or reading, or thinking about writing or reading, it lingered in my subconscious as a magnetic desire to be near to books, to have my fingertips tapping away at a keyboard, to see an empty page grow full in front of me. The drive to write had replaced my drive to have sex, though I believe that they are intertwined as one universal creative drive that encompasses the artist's longing to create something that lasts and the lover's desire to create life through procreation. Or to escape, if only for a moment, the awareness that one is alive and exists, the awareness whose mirror is the awareness of death. The successful fulfillment of either of the two drives leads to supreme pleasure and provides temporary respite from life and its everyday worries, and even alleviates anxiety over the impending death we will all face.

It was because I was depressed and so preoccupied with death that I used writing as an escape. When I was writing, I was at least neutral if not happy. I found delight in plot twists and beauty in poetics. Admittedly, at the time, my aesthetic was rather undeveloped and I overemphasized style as opposed to content and structure. My writing from that time, apart from a few exceptions, was not very good. Or at least I don't enjoy reading it. Maybe others one day will.

I took some writing classes. Some of them were more valuable than others. Good instructors can help a writer identify ways to improve his or her writing, but with something like writing, I believe that it's important not to let an instructor's personal ideas on writing influence your work. (If one is going to allow one's work to be directly influenced, let it be by the work of one's heroes—the work!— not the lessons left behind.) Feedback is valuable, but ultimately the writer is the master of his own artistic destiny. I can imagine it's rather difficult for an instructor to teach writing because it's so very subjective. The little tidbits that say what is good fiction as opposed to what is bad fiction and the definite dos and don'ts of writing can be taught in a few hours and be applied to any work of fiction. It's practice and doing it that really drives the lessons home. As for poetry, who knows? Poetry might actually be one of those things that simply can't be taught. It's more like an instinct than anything else, and the craftsmanship of a poet depends entirely on his or her own determination to write better and better poetry. There is no formula, only truth and untruth.

Once I began to crawl my way out of those lowest depths of my psychic gloom, I realized that to write is the most important thing for me. Everything else orbits that center and is less important. It became my constant focus and, as I've already said, my obsession. I'm content with that. It's been a thing that a lot of other people I talk to find hard to understand. "Why would you want to do that? Is that what you really want to do? You have so much potential. You could do anything." I can see that, for an observer, it would make more sense for me to pursue a more practical course. By that I mean, from an outside standpoint, it would make more sense to spend my time and direct my brain toward tasks that are more lucrative or more obviously beneficial to society. Counselors and advisors played devil's advocate with me, and on some level I believed them because I was young and I didn't know any better. To this day the notion that I can be successful at my passion has never completely settled as a resolution.

I spent the remainder of my college years going through the motions and just waiting for the time to pass and for me to be finished and have a degree. I felt as if I had outgrown student life, or at least I had enjoyed the experience enough in the first two years that I didn't need to keep going like that. When it was done I graduated with a 3.95 GPA, a bachelors degree in English, high honors. I didn't have any family at the graduation ceremony, and if I remember correctly, I had been up the night before drinking and writing and I was pretty hungover. Actually, I retract that claim. I remember now. I had woken up and felt a desperate need to have a drink in order to relieve a hangover, so I drank a vodka with orange juice, and I was, effectively, drunk at the ceremony.

I came back home to Valmesta, and for the few days I was apartment hunting I stayed at a hostel with some of my things until I could move the rest of my belongings into the flat apartment in Industrial Park that I live in now. I didn't have a job lined up after graduating. As a liberal arts major, there aren't many jobs I qualify for, and to be honest I barely bothered to look. I thought for a while on what to do. Some girls I knew in college supported themselves by waitressing and bartending, and they always told me they made a lot of money waiting tables. I had also heard a lot about actors having to support themselves as servers up until they got their big break. I thought, *if I'm going to try to make a living as a creative writer, it might be a good idea to get some experience in the service industry.* The service industry isn't going anywhere, and waiting tables is a good way to make some quick money. I did some work here and there as a freelance writer as well, mostly writing for fly-by-night online marketing companies, which wasn't difficult for me, but it took all the fun out of writing, and it turned out to be not nearly as lucrative as waiting tables. Freelance writing is, to me, essentially whoring. It makes something that is normally very fun and even exhilarating and turns it boring and meaningless aside from the function it serves to earn money, and the amount of money is not adequate compensation for the time and the creative-juice-zapping nature of the work involved. I walked away from a contract renewal after a year of that sort of work to be a full-time server.

That wasn't so long ago. I had been living in my apartment in Industrial Park for a few weeks, writing here and there but mostly looking for a restaurant job. I had a little bit of money saved up from working in the university printing shop, so I wasn't in a big rush, but I didn't want to wait too long either and have my savings totally run out. After having a college-sized sampling of upper class privilege, I wanted to stay above water, financially speaking. I would spend my morning writing and tending to my e-mail and social media, and then, in the afternoon, I would have lunch at different restaurants in my neighborhood to survey possible job opportunities. I believe the reader already understands that my neighborhood is across the river from downtown Valmesta. Mostly it is a residential neighborhood where the middle and lower classes dwell. There are quite a few restaurants speckled throughout, some of them high-end, what with property and rent being relatively cheap in West Valmesta. A lot of the people around my age that live in my neighborhood work in the service industry to support themselves, either on the west side or downtown on the east.

It was while having a sushi lunch at Doraku that I met Jeon. The food was good and the atmosphere was minimal, definitely trendy enough, and there were maybe a dozen people eating at the restaurant aside from myself. My server was a young Korean guy. At the end of the meal I inquired with him as to whether the manager was available. A minute later Jeon came over to my table. Jeon spoke good English. I asked Jeon if the twelve to fifteen people was typical for this time of day, and he said it was sometimes more busy. I noticed that Jeon was doing a lot of the work himself, greeting guests, seating the floor, and even bussing tables and taking some drink orders. I respected a hardworking manager. He had one server on the floor in addition to the one who had been waiting on me, but my impression was that Doraku was understaffed. I asked Jeon if he was hiring, and he answered my question by asking me who was looking. I told him I was looking and eventually admitted that I didn't have any restaurant experience, but I was a good learner. He smiled when I said that, and looked away. Then he looked back at me and told me to come back with my resume.

I came back the following afternoon around two o'clock, thinking that the busy lunch hour would already be over. I was more or less correct, and I had time to sit down and interview with Jeon. We got along well enough, and I had little difficulty convincing him that I would be capable of learning the ins and outs of the type of service he expected at Doraku. I already owned a pair of black jeans, which Jeon explained would be acceptable for the uniform. The dress code was basically anything black. I told Jeon I had tattoos on my right arm and asked him if he would want me to cover them up with long sleeves. He said it wouldn't be a problem and he didn't ask to see it. From the interview I went straight to a thrift store and picked out a few different black shirts that I could wear.

The next day I reported for duty so to speak at eleven in the morning. I was glad that I didn't have to be at work any earlier than that. I was not accustomed to being very active in the mornings. Doraku was only a couple of blocks away from my place, on Richard Boulevard. It had a nice view of the river and the Columbia Avenue Bridge, which was the nearest drivable bridge to East Valmesta and downtown. When I arrived at Doraku there was an extra server there to train me, four of us there altogether. I got the impression if it weren't for me needing training, he wouldn't have had to be there, and he didn't seem happy to be. All the other servers, it can be noted, were Korean. Their way of talking fascinated me because, while it was undoubtedly Korean, to my ear it sounded infused with New York neighborhood slang, like they had each lived in Queens for some time before making their way to Valmesta. They could have all been related to one another. At the very least they had known each other for a long time, I knew that by the way they interacted. Aside from talking with guests and giving me instructions, all they ever spoke was Korean. They were a close-knit bunch, and I found myself, once again, an outsider.

The type of service didn't involve much back and forth, mostly just order taking and running around. Therefore, my training was straightforward and fairly easy. How to grab an ice bucket and where to find the ice to fill it. How and where to put the dirty and used dishes and silverware and how to run them through the dishwasher. Where the dry goods were kept. How to use the point of sale computers. How the tables were supposed to be reset for the next round of customers. As far as the nuances of how to make customers happy, how to entertain them and be there when they needed me without intruding on their conversations, I tried to observe the other servers, who, understandably, weren't exactly the best models. Their manner of serving involved very little emotional effort and was more or less the type of service you would expect at a Coney Island. That is not to undermine Coney Island waitresses, because what they do is hard work. Anyway, serving at Doraku wasn't as emotionally demanding as serving at a higher-end place, which I would discover later.

I found that I had a knack for being a good server. Of course, it helps that I put forth the effort to learn it and be good at it. Serving is a skill that requires patience, communication, and the ability to multitask. At the time I took it as seriously as I did my writing because I considered restaurant work an integral part of my professional development. It was something I had to do to survive, and I had to survive to get my writing done.

Valmesta is a gritty town, full of survivors. I had the right attitude to become a good server. In some ways, even, it was rather fun in the beginning. Everything was new, and I got to see everything that went into making that experience. It was like a peek behind the magician's curtain. And just like learning anything else new, there was satisfaction in it.

I learned quickly that it's important to have some routine for getting into character. Good serving is a performance, if not a performance *art*. For me, slicking my hair back is part of it. It's something like a ritual that puts me in a certain state of mind. Once I'm in that state of mind, I begin the self-talk to reinforce it. I tell myself that I am full of energy, that I'm a fun person, that I'm a great server, and that there is never too difficult a customer or too crowded a restaurant. It sounds silly, but you have to get your mood elevated. And from there I go on to layer my character with accessories. A bowtie, a handkerchief, hipster glasses, anything to get into the character that the audience wants and expects. It's like method acting.

"The fact that people trust you with their food should be a source of pride," I tell my character. "Be proud of the food you're serving, be confident that what you're doing has value. If a guest doesn't believe that what you're doing has value, then they're wrong and it doesn't matter what they think. Those aren't the type of diners you look forward to. Look forward to the good ones, the ones who are excited to be in the restaurant, grateful to have you as their server, the ones who love to drink and eat food and savor it. Maybe your next table will be one of the good ones. By the way, what's available on tap? Is anything 86'ed? Wash your hands again. Always make the hard work look easy. People who are good at what they do make what they do appear effortless."

The reader may wonder: "Really, what's so hard about waiting tables?"

The plain and simple answer is that most of the job isn't hard. The hard part is dealing with people, as people generally tend not to put their best self forward upon walking into a restaurant, and it's the very fact that people don't realize that they are the exclusive reason that their server's job is difficult that their server's job is difficult. Perhaps I can explain this better as the story goes on.

Some guests, for instance, have no sense of humor at all, and no matter what you do as a server you probably won't see those kinds of people so much as crack a smile. That's okay. It doesn't mean they are unhappy, it just means they don't express appreciation for good food and service by smiling and outwardly enjoying themselves. For these people, give good service and hope for a good tip. You'll usually get it.

Then there are the types of guests who appear and act almost identically to the abovementioned type, but instead they are actually unhappy about something.

Sometimes it's something you did that set them off, or the way you talk, or something you're wearing, who knows. People are bizarre creatures, and if you're quirks don't align with theirs you might rub them the wrong way. But it's hard to tell who's who, who is actually mad and who is just a deadpan face, and that's what I'm getting at, I guess. Dealing with strangers is difficult.

Some people just plain don't tip, which is maddening. How can anyone not understand that not tipping is not okay?

There is also a thing called "verbal tipping," which happens a decent amount. Usually verbal tips come from the type of customers who are very vocal about enjoying their time—"this dragon roll is amazing," or "oh my god this is the best mai tai I think I've ever had!" Be careful with these people. I try not to show appreciation for their feedback. Instead, I carry on as if I would expect nothing less from the chef or the bartender, or, if they're praising my service, myself. The kiss of death comes at the vey end of a meal when someone says, "Thank you for your service, you were wonderful, very fun and engaging…" so on and so forth. When I hear something like that, I typically receive, at best, a fifteen percent tip. In the customer's mind, they've already given their tip, and I've heard it and received it.

I will say that waiting tables takes up a lot of the time that I might otherwise spend with people who work a more normal schedule. I work mainly nights now with occasional morning and afternoon shifts mixed in. Always I work Friday and Saturday nights. In the restaurant industry, some of the busiest and best moneymaking days are weekends and holidays, so I tend to work those, too. For the last few years, in addition to working ninety-five percent of weekend nights, I've worked every Christmas, Christmas Eve, Easter, New Years Eve, New Years Day, and Thanksgiving. My only complaint is that it's hard work and it's tiring and it makes it even more difficult to strike a work slash life balance.

At the end of the day, I'm not religious, and I don't really have any family to spend the holidays with, so I may as well make money during the holidays.

Luckily for me, I find restaurant workers, for the most part, at least a little bit interesting if not downright great company. While I was working at Doraku, I met many people who worked in other restaurants who would come in to Doraku on their night off to have sushi and drinks. I would go out for drinks with them, connect with them through social media, and keep in touch with them. Voila, a restaurant industry network was built. Now many of them have left to go work at different restaurants, and my network has become even more expansive. That's another thing about the industry. Turnover happens fast. People leave for a change of scenery or what they think will be greener pastures, so to speak. But everyone seems to know each other.

It also seems that everyone is sleeping together, or that everyone in a restaurant is, at any given time, sleeping with someone else, or multiple someone elses, at that restaurant or at another restaurant. When you think about it, it makes perfect sense. Many servers and bartenders are good looking and a majority are regular drinkers with, thus, regularly-lowered inhibitions, and, like I said, there isn't much opportunity for a life outside of the restaurant except hanging out with other restaurant people. I can't even begin to tell you how many girls I've slept with, either girls that I worked with or girls I met outside of work, by going out and mingling with other industry people. Well, I guess I could begin to tell you, but I'll let my abovementioned hyperbole speak to that effect. Best to avoid bragging.

Even while I was just starting out at Doraku, the life of a restaurant worker had already caught hold of me. It wasn't always a bad thing, and in some ways I enjoyed it. It was rather nice for me to have my mornings free so that I could write. For years writing in my free time has been an important part of my life, and being able to do it in the daytime makes it feel almost more important, as if writing is my day job. The first thing I have to think about in the morning is what to write about, how to write it, what new character or plot twist to introduce to the story. If I'm feeling a bit scattered, I'll write freely or compose a poem. I'm not always happy with the results, and sometimes I have to go back and rewrite things, but that's a good thing. It allows me to treat it like a job, which is how I'll have to be if I'm going to be a professional writer.

After writing all day, some days I am mentally tired, although most often I find writing most invigorating and stimulating, and when I'm done I'm usually in a good mood, but, as I've said, I treat it like a job and sometimes it's very difficult and will sap some of my mental energy. Furthermore, when it's not going well, look out. I can be a mean bugger.

I usually drink coffee while I write, and I'll have an energy drink of some kind before serving to sharpen myself up. It's fairly common for service workers, especially certain kinds in particular but anyone serving high volumes of people, to feel the need to sharpen up. Some people prefer cocaine or some other kind of upper, energy drinks, whatever. I mean, you have to move fast and lots of people need a lot of attention. Cocaine improves focus, if only temporarily. Energy drinks usually do the trick for me. They sharpen me up and make other people more interesting. And when the people are interesting, or fun, then the job is a lot easier, and sometimes amusing.

Otherwise it can be the most miserable job imaginable. In a restaurant, people are literally helpless. It's like all of a sudden, after walking into a restaurant, adult humans turn into toddlers. They can't even figure out how to get to the restroom. They need constant coddling and taking care of.

For serving, alcohol makes other people more interesting as well, but sometimes it makes other parts of the job, like moving quickly and remembering details, more difficult. I suppose it's reasonable to assume that the consumption of different substances, including caffeine, nicotine, alcohol, cocaine, prescription pills and other various medications, and even marijuana, is quite high among service workers on the job relative to other types of workers. But it only makes sense. It's not so much an emotional or psychological thing as it is a means of performance enhancement, *a la* steroids in baseball. I guess the thought is: If I get sharpened up on energy drinks before I get on the floor, then I'll move twice as fast as Square Steve and make twice as much money than him, too. I'll also probably be more quick-witted and fun to be around than Square Steve and, thusly, I'll make more money. Not to mention the hottest female bartender, having primarily coworkers as available sex partners, will see me as the most quick-witted and fun to be around and, financially-speaking, the highest-status employee on the floor, and she will probably want to sleep with me, as opposed to Square Steve, designating me the much-coveted alpha-male-of-my-little-social-group status.

I could go on and on. It so happens that the experience of working in restaurants is pretty important to this story, and integral to my development as a person and a writer. The closing of Doraku Sushi saddened me in no small way. I grew to like Jeon quite a bit, and I liked being around the other wait staff, even though there was an obvious communication barrier. Most of my coworkers at Doraku were actually really fun to be around. I got the feeling that if I could speak Korean and partake in their joke telling and shenanigans, I would have really enjoyed their company. Perhaps I would have made friends. I don't know the whereabouts of any of them now. Jeon, I do know, is back home in Seoul indefinitely. I think about him often.

Pretty soon I'm going to get back to the telling of this story. I'm sure the reader would rather me continue to that end than to keep rambling about "my life story" or being a server or what not.

The truth is, I thought this story, or at least this part of this story, would be better if I told it my way. The part of the story that follows is a part, I believe, the reader needs to read in my own words. I am Lado. The other narrator is not. I don't see why he, or she, should have ultimate say in how my story reads. As far as the actual events of what happened up to this point, yes, he or she did a fine job of telling it. I'm okay with that first part. But it made me look a certain way and I'm just not so sure I like the way it made me look. Right now, I imagine the reader doesn't like me very much. That's understandable, I guess. However, I don't care as much about whether the reader does or doesn't like me as I do about my story being honest and being a story worth reading. Anyway, I've taken the matter into my own hands. I've already given the reader a hell of a lot more back-story than the other storyteller did.

It's true that I was thinking about Ellery a lot after we had our falling out, enough to write her a letter, but it was out of honest concern for her feelings. That, and I was worried about my own reputation being damaged by people finding out how poorly I reacted and how awful I treated her, or, worse, that I don't respect women or their privacy at all, which would probably ensure I never got laid in the metro-Valmesta area ever again. To succeed in the current sexual-political climate of your average American metropolis, one has to have the right balance of good and bad public image. Since college, I've been aware of this fact and excellent at maintaining such a balance. For example, a male must be perceived as mysterious and just bad enough to be perhaps slightly dangerous, but good and domestic enough that, when it comes down to it, a female is not afraid to actually get into bed with him. And when that happens, it's good to be bad, and downright dirty, and open up the girl's mind to all kinds of filthy pleasures that she never even imagined before. But never, *ever* is it okay to divulge the details of a woman's relations, whether with oneself or with another person, within even the smallest social group. Even worse if you pass judgment on her by calling her names. There is nothing a woman is more afraid of than defamation, and, therefore, nothing a man should be more wary of than being a defamer of women. It's cruel, impolite and absolutely unmanly, and it does as much harm to a man's reputation as it does to the woman who is defamed, perhaps more. I've always made it a point not to kiss and tell. However—and this is a big however—this is a story, and I refuse to hold anything back. It has to be completely honest if it is to be any good at all. As for Ellery, to hell with her, that's what I say. We're not good for each other as friends or anything else.

Because I had discovered that Ryan, the waitress from The Playground, was engaged, and because soon after that I had just had possibly the most nauseating and shameful interaction with anyone at any time in my life, ever, my head was spinning. It spun for days. I was also, probably for the reasons above, on an epic binge, alternating between blacked-out rages every night and riding the night-after-drinking struggle bus every morning, and then almost immediately drinking again to help get rid of my hangover, occasionally trying to write something that didn't suck.

I didn't really think I would ever be hearing from Ryan again, by phone or by text, though it was certainly possible that I would see her again at The Playground or elsewhere, in which case I would be completely casual and friendly about it, and I would try to avoid saying or doing anything that would amplify the awkwardness of the situation because, as almost everyone knows, those kinds of situations can get uncomfortable very fast. I would even say that I expected to see her around; Valmesta is one of those big cities that can easily be made to feel small by the frequency with which I run into people I know. What I did not expect was to receive a text message from her shortly after I dropped Ellery's letter into a Post Office box.

Ryan explained to me via text that her fiancé, Steve, was in a strange mood when she picked him up from the airport. She said something didn't feel right. Right off the bat I thought that she was just being paranoid, thinking that Steve somehow already knew that she had cheated on him with me. I imagine there are many complicated emotions that accompany being unfaithful. Personally, I wouldn't know, because I've never cheated. But that's not because I would never cheat or because I'm an especially righteous, honest partner. It's just that I've never really been in a real relationship, and, therefore, I have never had anyone to cheat on. But I'm sure there's an element of remorse involved for most people, as well as a fear of being found out, a fear of losing something that has always been thought of as important. I may have even felt some guilt about it if I had known she was engaged before it happened. Instead, I didn't think much of it. I told myself there was no way I could have known. Ryan texted me again, confirming my suspicion that she was being paranoid. "Are you *sure* you don't have any STIs?" I reiterated to her that I had been tested and the results were negative on all accounts, but that I hadn't necessarily been tested recently.

I believe it was the following day, which would have been a Monday, that I decided to try to look for a new job. I thought to myself how strange it was to feel my job and my means of survival swept out from under my feet. Having done nothing but perform well, I had lost my job. However, another nice thing about being a server is that a lot of places are looking at any given time. Also, the more people you know, the more likely you are to find work easily because most places are happy to hire referrals, and like I've already said, I had a solid network.

The first person I decided to reach out to was an old friend named Jack Malone. I wish it wasn't the case that Jack was the first one I contacted, because I think it would be a better or at least more believable part of the story if there were more to it than that, but that's how it happened.

Jack and I were friends in high school, the type of friends who developed a bond over doing things like throwing eggs at moving cars, getting drunk off stolen liquor, and trying to pop teenage cherries. We were both smart and cunning with a wild side and a tendency toward trouble. When we were younger we really brought it out of each other. We had a lot in common then, though I hadn't seen him in years. I knew he was working in a place downtown, on the other side of the river. I sent him a text and asked him how he was doing.

He said things were going really well. He was sleeping with his boss. That really got my attention. If he gave me a strong referral I should have no problem getting hired. I asked him what he did there. He explained that, technically, he was a food runner and a server's assistant. During any given shift those were his official duties. But I got the feeling there was something more to it, as if he had a lot more sway than he let on. He changed the subject, asked me how I was. I didn't have a job, I said, because the sushi place where I had been working was closed. Right away he said he could get me a job at Birch. That must have been the name of the place. I Google searched "birch restaurant" and found the website: birchamericanbrasserie.com. I had never worked in a Brasserie style restaurant, but I was sure I could learn. I made the courteous attempt to show that I wasn't contacting Jack just so that he could get me a job, though I have to believe Jack knew. He told me to come by the following morning and ask for Clara. She would be there at ten, he said.

Now, I was never very fond of going into downtown. I didn't like the big crowds of people and all the traffic and don't walk signs. I absolutely preferred my side of town. I was comfortable there. People were down to earth, working class. I got along with them. Things were spread out, dark, and slightly run down. It suited my aesthetic sensibility. However, on that day I gave myself a little pep talk. I told myself that if I closed myself off to the type of people that lived, worked, and dined downtown, people very different from me, then I wasn't as open-minded as I thought I was. I told myself that I was a kickass server and that any restaurant would be happy to have me as a part of their staff. I told myself I would ace the interview and get the job. I told myself that it was all just gathering material for my writing.

I chose a route to the restaurant and left my apartment at quarter to ten, planning to arrive at ten thirty. Before I left, I made sure my dog Ernie had relieved himself and that he had enough food and water to last until nighttime. With my messenger bag over my shoulder, and in it my laptop, a pack of cigarettes, a pint of Jameson, and a few copies of my resume, I walked down the stairs and outside onto the street. It was nice outside, sunny and cool. The birds were chirping. The type of early springtime day where you are excited to see just how warm it gets. *It could be sixty degrees by this afternoon*, I thought to myself. I felt invigorated by the weather. I was wearing a decent button down collared shirt and a Lacoste bomber jacket that had belonged to my uncle and that I had been wearing for about ten years. It fit me well.

When I arrived at the destination my routing system had directed me to, I was confused by the apparent nonexistence of a restaurant. The directions had led me to a hotel, it seemed. It was a swanky hotel, rising twenty stories upward into the powder blue springtime Valmesta sky, located on the corner of New Millennium Boulevard and Milton Street. The outside of the building, cold concrete and new age gothic-style arched windows, gave the impression of being an old but well-maintained accommodation, one that had charged customers a pretty penny for many decades. There were some town cars parked out front and a valet standing on the bottom of the steps that led up to the front door of the hotel. I kept on walking, turned down an alley and pulled out my pack of cigarettes. I saw the Jameson in my bag and I thought about taking a pull, as I was a little nervous about the interview. I decided against it and just lit up a cigarette instead. I looked at my phone and re-mapped "Birch" and my GPS indicated that I was standing just around the corner from the address. I walked back around the corner and up to the valet, who gave me a look of condescending helpfulness. His nametag identified him as "Rob," the valet for The Brownstone Plaza hotel. I explained to him that I had an interview at Birch American Brasserie and that I was having trouble finding it. He smiled with the same hybrid look of condescension and helpfulness and explained that Birch was located inside the hotel and that I could enter through the main entrance of the hotel, at which point the restaurant entrance would be located on my right, or I could go in through the main restaurant entrance on the north—he pointed—side of the building. I decided Rob was a bit of an asshole. I didn't want to deal with any more of the hotel people. I went around to the other side of the building. There I saw the marquee and the doorway just below it.

When I walked in there was a hostess standing to my right. The ambiance struck me immediately. It seemed very hip, with deliberate color choices and a good amount of natural light coming in from skylight windows overhead. Behind the host desk, also to the right, was what looked like a deli. There was a refrigerated display of different meats and sausages, advertised as house made, and locally made cheeses. Behind the counter was a prep cook slicing prosciutto.

The hostess greeted me. I said I had an interview with Clara. The girl smiled and informed me that she hadn't seen Clara yet and that I could have a seat while she went and looked for her. She said all this and seemed a bit rude while she said it, like I was wasting her time. She took me over to the bar slash lounge area, which was adjacent to the deli, and she asked me if I wanted anything to drink. I thought about whether I wanted coffee, and decided against it for fear it would make me more anxious, and I said maybe a water would do. She fixed me a water with ice and brought it over, then turned and walked away toward a door leading to the hallway and the offices. I watched her walk. *She is cute*, I thought. *I would like to fuck her*, I thought next, though not exactly in those words. Not in words at all, for that matter, more accurately as images appearing in my mind's eye: what she would look like, from behind, bent over a barstool, with her skirt hiked up to her waist, what visual delights her bareness would reveal.

I looked around. I decided it was indeed a hip place. The general vibe was casual, but one had to assume the food would be really good. I don't know how to explain that. It's like the feeling you get when you meet a certain kind of person and you just have a feeling that they're not going to try to bullshit you, that they'll be honest and they're going to deliver the goods they're advertising. I was suddenly excited, being there. It gave me the feeling of being in a real French restaurant, with small, close together tables and a feeling of being almost outside. Not that I had ever been to France, but I had imagined it before with fascination.

The hostess came back and told me Clara wasn't there, that she should be there any minute. I'll try calling her, she said. I took my phone out to check the time. It was past ten thirty. I was sort of surprised that Clara wasn't there yet. *Wasn't she supposed to be here at ten?* I thought she would be professional enough to be on time if she managed a place like this.

Fifteen minutes went by and nothing. I noticed there were two servers moving around. It looked like they were breaking down breakfast and setting up for lunch. One of them was a tall, heavy, angry looking woman a little older than I. She came over to the bar to drop off some glassware and gave me a mean look. I held her gaze and returned it. I was glad when she disappeared from view. I got up and walked over to the host stand and explained to the hostess that I was acquainted with Jack. Did she know him? She warmed up to me for the first time. Of course she knew him. She asked me if Jack and I hung out. I said we go way back. Suddenly she was being nice to me, almost flirtatious. It made me wonder about Jack. Simply mentioning his name had changed the girl's whole attitude. I would find out later her name was Jennifer and that she had been there since the place opened a year ago, that she had a boyfriend that lived far away in a warmer climate. Just then my phone started to vibrate. I waited to see if it would vibrate again. If it did it was a phone call. If not, it was just a text, and therefore not as urgent. I liked that about texts. They could never be truly urgent. Anyone with an urgent message would not try to relay the message via text. My phone did not vibrate again.

After a few minutes of small talk with Jennifer, the door opened from the employee hallway. I heard voices before I could see their faces. I recognized one of them immediately as Jack's. Jack finished saying something and a girl, whom I presumed to be Clara, was laughing. They came through the doorway and saw me sitting at the small table. I stood up to greet Jack. He had grown into quite a handsome man. He was medium height, a little shorter than I am, maybe five foot nine. He had a bright, sincere smile, nice cheekbones and a strong, masculine jaw and chin. He looked good in his clothes, black slacks, a white t-shirt with a faded denim jacket over it, even though it was obvious he was not trying to dress up in anyway. It could have been a scene from a movie when a character first steps onto the screen, the way he looked. Like Marlon Brando in *A Streetcar Named Desire*.

I didn't quite know how to greet Jack, but he made it easy for us both and just gave me a hug, and as he pulled away he squeezed my shoulders, commenting on how I had filled out, but that I had filled out in a good way. Jack, I would learn, was the type of friend who made you feel good about yourself. He introduced me to Clara right away to avoid any awkwardness. He had a great air about him; I couldn't imagine him working in a kitchen. He could have been a Fortune Five Hundred CEO. Neither Jack nor Clara gave any indication to feeling bad for being late. They had apparently come to work together.

I was rather surprised when Jack took off his jacket and set it on the back of the chair. I wasn't expecting him to be a part of the interview. When he took his jacket off I realized he had a nice musculature that appeared natural, as if he didn't have to workout to stay fit. Clara was very attractive herself. The fact that Jack was sleeping with her made me less likely to pay attention to it, but she did have what I imagined to be nice curves beneath a tight fitting button down blue shirt and a black pencil skirt. She said she would go get the paperwork, and as she walked away I listened to the sound of her heels clacking and I heard her say hello to Jennifer.

Jack asked me what I had been up to. "I heard you're an artist now? A writer is it?" He seemed genuinely interested, and at the same time aware that it might not be something I really wanted to talk about in detail. I said that I was working on a collection of stories and some poems, and he politely said that he would be eager to read them when they were finished. "Besides that," I said, "I've just been working." I explained to him briefly about graduating college and moving home to Valmesta and getting a job at Doraku, which closed all of a sudden when the owner moved home to South Korea. Jack asked me if I had any other experience in restaurants besides my relatively short-lived gig at Doraku, and of course I said no, but he said it really wouldn't be a problem for me to get a job at Birch, what with him referring me and me being smart and capable enough. Jack asked me where I was living, and I told him over in West Valmesta in Industrial Park. He lived in a place his family owned in midtown, on the East side of the river. I mentioned that I knew where it was but that I wasn't all that familiar with the area. "But," he said, "I spend a lot of time at Clara's place."

Clara came back with some papers. She sat down at the table with us and began to look through them. "We're not going to need this one," she said, "or this." She set the papers aside and held on to two items of paperwork. "Here. Just fill these two out. And you're good to go." As it happens it was the easiest interview I ever had. "Jack says you're good people, you got the job. Can you pass a drug test?" I thought for a second, trying to remember the last time I had ingested any substances that would show up on a drug test. It had been a while, at least a few weeks since the last time I smoked weed. "Yes, sure. Well does it detect alcohol?"

"No," Clara said. "Why, are you drunk?"

"No, of course not. I mean no but I had some drinks last night."

"He'll be fine." Jack said, "Won't he?"

"Sure. He'll be fine. Just take this swab and put it in your mouth." Clara unwrapped a sterile cotton swab and handed it to me. "Put it under your tongue while you fill that stuff out. When you're done writing, you'll be good to go."

Altogether it took me about five minutes to complete the paperwork while I kept the bitter swab under my tongue. I put the paperwork in order, and Clara told me I could take the swab out of my mouth. She gave me a sterile plastic container to put it in that would be sent off to a lab. She looked over my minimal application materials. "You put down that you can start immediately," she read, "Can you start right now?" She was kidding, but I humored her, told her I could start immediately after I had a cigarette.

"Come in tomorrow. Do you have blacks?"

"Yes, my last job I wore all black."

"Come in tomorrow at four for the night shift. Black everything. Did you see the employee entrance at the back of the building?" I nodded, even though I hadn't seen it. "Come in through the employee entrance and find me in my office. I'll give you an apron when you get here and Jack will show you around. The basics are pretty simple but I bet you'll need some time to get the menu down before I can put you on the floor."

Clara was acting very professional to me directly, but I got the impression that the circumstances of my hiring were rather unprofessional. I didn't care. Birch seemed like the type of place where I could make good money. Clara left us and went back through the hallway into her office, or so I assumed. I shot the shit with Jack for a few minutes before he said he had to get to work. On my way out I said goodbye to Jennifer, who was sitting at the hostess stand reading a Kindle. She smiled at me, lowering her chin and tilting her head forward so her eyes got really big, and she gave me the fuck-me eyes. She wasn't all that sexy, but she was trying, and I knew the option was there if I wanted to go for it.

Outside, I lit up a cigarette. It was prime daylight, slightly warm. I rolled up my sleeves and wished I had sunglasses, or that I could wear sunglasses instead of my regular glasses. Even if I had a pair of shades, unless they were prescription I wouldn't be able to wear them instead of my everyday glasses. I'm too strongly nearsighted; I can't see more than six inches in front of my face without corrective lenses. I would run into things. Trip and fall, probably. I'm not kidding.

I took a nice, long drag on my cigarette. Things like interviews and first dates, those slightly high-pressure meetings in which I knew I was being evaluated, have always made me nervous. Typically, prior to first dates, I have a few drinks to loosen up. That always works for me, and women aren't usually put off by it if they notice it. Everyone knows an alcoholic, though, and there's definitely the girl whose cousin, or uncle, or whatever, was an alcoholic, and so she doesn't want to date someone who drinks, but even then I could still pull off a lay. Interviews were different, unfortunately. In no way is drinking before an interview acceptable from a manager's perspective.

On my way out I passed the hotel entrance and walked toward the alley I was in earlier. The valet glared at me, the fucker. As I passed him I exhaled smoke toward him, trying to make it appear incidental. "Got the job," I said, "see you around." I turned down the alley and pulled out my pint of Jameson. I unscrewed the cap and gulped it once. It burned a little. The first one always burned. Before I finished my cigarette I had some more, this time it was more of a small scoop than a gulp. I came back out of the alleyway and went the opposite way I had come from. I didn't want to see the valet again. I might have punched him.

I took my phone out to check the time and saw that it was just shy of noon, and I had an unread text message from Ryan. She said I should come in to see her at The Playground. She was working the afternoon lunch shift and she would be there until around five or six depending on when she was cut.

I thought about this for a second. I could always write, which is to say that at any time of any day I could have that as a primary or secondary priority. I could always reprioritize later. That is, writing could wait. At least I thought so then.

I had a thirst for beer, although looking back, I think there was something else motivating me besides that. I decided to pop in at my apartment and change clothes before heading over there. I took Ernie outside on the balcony and petted him and wrestled with him and spent twenty or so minutes showing my love and appreciation for his companionship in this way. I could tell he didn't have to shit, but he tinkled a little on my patio tree the way I had trained him to do. He really is a great pup. I looked at him; some of his hairs had grown over his eyes. I thought he could use a good grooming and I made a mental note to myself that I would make an appointment for him soon. I brought Ernie back inside and walked to the living room where I sat down on the couch and turned on the television. It was on the country music station.

I tried to remember what I was watching last that would have been on the country music station, and I couldn't. I couldn't remember when I last had the television on, for that matter. I flipped through some channels that I usually liked. A chocolate and coconut pastry competition, which must have been the end of an episode, a great white shark, women's college basketball. I turned the television off and looked out the window. I thought about Ellery and felt ashamed of myself. I didn't like it, and I quickly forced myself to think about something else.

I patted Ernie and told him I'd be back in a little while. I always thought he understood me when I said things like that. I put a cigarette in between my lips and went to grab my jacket, but I remembered how warm it was outside and decided I would probably not need one. In a cigarette's length time I was at The Playground.

When I walked in, I scanned the scene for Ryan. It was dark inside. Darkness during prime daylight was quintessential to the dive bar aesthetic. By making you feel like it was nighttime, and by casting shadows over your face, The Dive allows for shame-free midday drinking. Most of the people at a place and time like that weren't drinking for the fun of it.

There were a few older men sitting at the bar, some appeared as old as seventy. I wondered whether this was The Playground's regular afternoon crowd on a weekday. Ryan was standing behind the bar with her arms crossed and her back to the door. She turned to look at me when I came in. I saw her squint her eyes against the sunlight that came through the door with me. Meanwhile, my eyes adjusted to the darkness—a moment of shock and adjustment followed by re-acquaintance and comfort. By the time I settled into a barstool, my pupils were properly dilated and her arms were uncrossed. She had turned to face me with a slight smile. "What are you drinking?" she asked.

"Well, I've been going with whiskey but I think I'll switch to beer." I think she thought I was joking about drinking whiskey, and she laughed. "What do you have on draft?" I asked, straining my eyes in an effort to make out the labels on the tap handles. She rattled off a list of six or so domestic, widely distributed and, in my opinion, shitty beers. I didn't really care for any of them. I contemplated just having another Jameson, but thought better of it. It was still early. I asked whether she had Guinness Draught cans, and she did. I liked those enough.

Ryan bent over and reached under the bar for a can of Guinness and a pint glass. I watched her pour it. Some people will do it where they take the Guinness can and turn it upside down in the pint glass and let it fill up, slowly removing the can from the pint glass at the same rate as the glass fills up with the beer. That's not the proper way to do it, and I watched Ryan pour it, wondering if she would do it that way. I think she sensed my watching and she smiled confidently. She didn't do it that way but instead poured it slowly and gently along the inside of the glass until it was about a third of the way full, and then finished it off by pouring the rest of the beer into the liquid. That was the way to do it with Guinness. Most beers are the same but depending on the body and fineness of the mousse, they differ slightly.

I wondered how this first face-to-face would go after our little affair, thinking it might go badly. At least I had a full beer.

Ryan apologized for not explaining to me sooner that she was engaged. She said she was sorry if she put me in an awkward position. I told her it wasn't a big deal, that it didn't hurt my feelings or bother me personally, but that I was concerned for her well-being. She said she was fine, she didn't think, after all, that her fiancé, Steve, knew anything, he was probably just tired from traveling and that's why he was acting strangely when she picked him up from the airport. I caught myself thinking I kind of wished he knew. As is very common in my experience, I was considerably more attracted to Ryan after I had been with her. Little things about her that I may have overlooked at first became sexy in the way familiar things about a person do. I drank my beer. She was wearing a white tank top. I watched her body fold at her waist as she repeatedly bent over and then stood up, and with her lean arms she popped some beers open and slid them across the bar to the men.

Ryan came back over to my end of the bar. I noticed the other men, most of them past middle age, watching her, and I wondered what they were thinking. Did they still have it in them to think like I did? Did they casually look upon a beautiful young girl and not feel any call to action? Or, if they did feel it, were they envious of me because she was showing a greater interest in me than in them? She said she was sorry, and I told her she didn't have anything to be sorry for. But as she reached both hands up to her ears and gently tucked her hair behind them, I sensed her guilt.

I didn't want to be insensitive by asking questions about her relationship, which was none of my business, but I wondered about her fiancé Steve. I was of the opinion that if someone were willing to actually follow through with being unfaithful, then they were not completely satisfied with their current partner. I didn't come to that conclusion retroactively in order to justify my behavior; I honestly felt that way. The way I saw it, she could deny what happened, go on being with the guy and eventually she would marry him, and either he would shape up and make it right with his wife or she would be unhappy for the rest of her life or until she divorced the bastard. Or she could tell him about it, but that would jeopardize their relationship and, maybe, she really did love him and didn't want to lose him. I didn't know. I had only just gotten to know her a few days ago.

Without getting too personal, I managed to ask questions that she would feel comfortable enough answering so that I would get a feel for Steve. He was brought up in one of the many prominent, old money Valmesta area families and had recently started going out of town on frequent trips pertaining to the family business. I wondered why she was bartending in a dive like The Playground if she was marrying a guy with a lot of money. Of course, I didn't ask her that. Ryan explained that he had cheated on her once early on, years ago, and that they had broken up for a few weeks then, but had gotten back together. She said he seemed really sincerely sorry about it, and, at the time, he said he wouldn't be able to live without her, so she took him back. She told me she had always had trust issues with him since. She was suspicious about whom he was seeing and what he was doing when he went out of town, but Steve was really protective of his right to privacy. "What, you don't trust me?" he would ask her as he snatched his phone away from her. Steve seemed like a real douche bag to me, the way Ryan described him.

"But then he'll turn around and ask me who I'm texting or who I'm getting lunch with or why I come home at six o'clock sometimes when my scheduled shift ends at five. He's a total hypocrite about it."

"It seems to me that's the classic archetype of the unfaithful party in a relationship. He doesn't trust you because he himself isn't trustworthy."

"You would know?"

"I'm just saying."

"Well, then, I sleep with someone else while he's out of town." She said this as if I weren't the person she had slept with, as if I didn't already know, as if it were a form of confession. I knew right then that her relationship with Steve was over. I had already had sex with her, and now she was confiding in me. I guess her very first text message after Steve came back was a sign of that, and so was everything that led us from that moment until the one I've just described, but I didn't realize it until she said those words.

That night, after I had come home from the bar and spent some time writing, and after Ryan's shift ended, she called me and told me she wanted to see me again. It was the second time in one day that she wanted to see me. I asked her whether she remembered where my apartment was, and she responded, "yes" with a smiley face. Oh god, I thought, oh no. I felt a pang of the kind of guilt that sort of feels good. It feels good to satisfy desire, and perhaps that is even more so the case when it is a desire that makes you feel guilty just for having it. It is the temptation of the forbidden fruit that inspires this feeling most strongly.

I tried to reframe the situation so that I wouldn't feel so ashamed of the blatant violation of guy code I was about to carry out. Indeed, after the encounter with Ryan earlier, I was convinced that Steve deserved it. It's possible that I could have circumvented guilt, but I kind of liked it. It enhanced the pleasure.

Ryan came over and I had a bottle of wine open that I poured for her. It was a Cabernet Sauvignon and Garnacha blend from Spain. Ryan told me she liked Spanish wine. She also mentioned that she had family living there and that she had never been to visit them. She wanted to visit them, I could tell. She wanted to get away from Valmesta. Everyone from Valmesta wanted to get away, to some degree, at some point. The city had its way of bringing you down to its level. Ryan, however, in that moment, seemed happy there, in my apartment with a glass of wine.

I had classical music playing in the background because I had been writing. It is the only music I can tolerate while I work; there can't be words. Everything else I find distracting. I kept the room dimly lit and we sat down on the couch with our wine and talked. One of Chopin's nocturnes played in the background as Ernie leaped onto the couch with us. Ryan laughed. She was a little nervous, but it wasn't because of her being with me or being in the space. I think she was nervous about what was going on outside of it and she was looking to me for comfort. Why on Earth she saw me that way I didn't understand then, and I still don't, but it made me feel good to be wanted that way. She was turned to look at me and had her elbow up on the back of the couch, using her hand to prop up her head. I had always thought this to be a very romantic position. She was opening herself up to me. I mirrored her, but instead of propping myself up with my hand I extended my arm toward her. I wasn't going to be the one to make the move this time, were there any moves to be made. I would look like a villain. I enjoyed the tension of our physical bodies being close together as we exchanged long glances and short sentences. I can't remember what was said. It wasn't long until she was on top of me. The tension had cracked and it was all arms and legs and her long hair on my small two-person couch. I leaned back onto the arm and reached up for her breasts, giving them a gentle squeeze, and by that point my heart was rapidly pumping warm blood through my body, to the ends of my fingers, all the better to feel Ryan's skin. Her breasts were surprisingly warm, I noticed, when I reached under her shirt. I undid her bra, took it out from under her shirt, and felt her tits again. Her nipples grew hard between my thumb and forefinger, and her hair hung all around my head like a little tent, and inside it was just our two faces. She pulled away to look into my eyes and she smiled. It was a true smile of real affection and not the beguiling smile of a mistress. I recognized it for what it was and I savored the depth of the moment before we continued. I could smell the greasy, stale aroma of a dive bar on her clothes, which inspired me to push her shirt up over her head and take it off. Her hands and her hair went up and her tits came out and I had the best view of them from below with her head tilted back, her hands in the air, and her back arched. I felt her smooth belly and slid my hand down the front of her jeans. I undid her belt with the other hand as the first hand made its way to her vagina. It was with the familiarity of having made love to Ryan before, but with the passion of new love that I felt her wetness and then put my fingers in her mouth so that she could taste it. She held my hand in hers as she licked and sucked my fingers and then she stood up and undressed fully, bending over to remove her jeans and her thong underwear. I took my shirt off while she, moaning, touched herself, and then I undid my own pants while she put her one foot up on the arm of the couch and put her vagina onto my mouth. By this time my dick was as hard as it's ever been. I liked the way she tasted and after she rode my face and my mouth she licked the juice off of me while she lowered herself on to me and began to ride. I had her tits in my mouth as she went up and down and it didn't take long until we came together.

Ryan lay on my chest while I was still inside of her. We lay there in silence as we looked out my window onto the lamp lit night. Everything was quiet.

She asked me if she could use my shower. At first this surprised me greatly, but after I thought about it, it made sense. I said sure. She stood up slowly, and then I got up. We stood there both naked for a moment and had a look at one another in the light from the outside lamps.

I showed Ryan to the linen closet and found her a clean towel and a washcloth. She said she didn't need a washcloth and she took the towel with her into the bathroom. I asked her if I could pee first and she told me just to pee while she was in the shower, she didn't mind, just don't flush. I watched her get in the shower and close the curtain on herself, and while I peed the ass-out, weak stream pee of a recently-came half-boner, I kept peeking at her silhouette through the curtain. Her head was bent back and she was lathering her hair. I wanted to get in the shower with her, but I thought better of it. Her space was her space.

I put on new clothes and went out into the living room. I picked Ryan's clothes up off the floor and arranged them neatly on the couch. I went over to change the music, turning off the Chopin playlist, and began looking through a pile of CDs. I saw the one Ellery had made for me not two weeks prior, and I set it aside. I decided not to play any music. I looked over into the corner of the room and saw Ernie on the floor resting his head between his forepaws. His eyes were looking up at me. I wondered whether he had watched the whole thing and would it bother me to know that he had been watching? It wouldn't, I decided.

Soon the sound of the shower was gone and I heard the sound of my blow dryer. I had almost forgotten I had a blow dryer I used it so seldom. Ryan emerged with a towel wrapped around her torso. I could tell she was in a hurry to leave, but she didn't have the look of shame that she left with the time before. It was what it was. Without a word she took her clothes back into the bathroom and got dressed, and when she came back out she looked almost exactly as she would have looked two hours before, but fresher and brighter. Revitalized.

"What did you tell Steve?" I asked her.

"That I was getting a drink with one of the girls from work and that I'd be back around ten." She seemed to have no fear of Steve discovering the truth. I was rather surprised by her lack of concern.

"It's not like he and I were planning on getting frisky or anything. That hardly ever happens now that he's been going on these business trips. He always just says, 'I'm tired,' and wants to go to sleep."

"Listen," I said, "I know you two aren't on the best terms right now, but…"

"Lado," she cut me off, "Stop. I'm not expecting anything. I don't know what's going to happen, but I'm not happy with him. That's all there is to it. I have to go though, if I stay longer he might actually start to get suspicious."

I nodded. For a moment it felt like neither of us knew what to do. I regretted bringing up the subject. I decided to kiss her. Fuck it, I thought. Why not kiss her. She's a beautiful girl and I just had sex with her. So I kissed her. At first it was a little smooch, nothing to get all excited about. But then she kissed me back and put her tongue in my mouth, and we had a fiery make out session before she walked out the door. She told me she would call or text me soon, and as she said so she bent down to pet Ernie, who had gotten up and trotted over to say goodbye.

The next day I arrived at Birch at four o'clock for training. I had ridden my bike there since it was a nice day. I think it was a Wednesday, and a good day to start training because it wouldn't be too busy. It took me some time to find the employee entrance, but eventually I found it and went in that way. Once inside, I noticed the hallway had posters and even a banner on the tile floor that had some sort of corporate motto printed on it. It shocked me. Already I was being bombarded with the message to have pride in the corporation I worked for. Until that point it hadn't really sunk in, or maybe I wasn't at all aware, that I would be working for a restaurant and hospitality *corporation*. The notion of a downtown life sent a chill down my spine. How was I to deal with these people? They and I would not understand each other.

I wandered around, reading the bulletin and studying my new environment, slowly making my way towards what I assumed would be the offices or the back entranceway to the kitchen. I found Clara in her office. She was on the phone. "Hold on a minute," she said into the receiver. And then to me, "Jack is around someplace. Probably in the kitchen. He can get you situated. Here's an apron," and she tossed me an apron and swiveled away in her chair and went back to talking on the phone. "Sorry about that," she went on.

I looked at the apron. It had the Birch American Brasserie logo on the pocket. *This is much different from Doraku*, I thought. I walked around a corner and found the kitchen, where I saw Jack standing at the hot line. He was "running the wheel," as we say, also called expediting. He pulled the order tickets from the printer as they came out of the machine, keeping the yellow copy and hanging it up on his side of the line and giving the white copy to the lead cook on the other side of the line, who would coordinate the plating of the dishes with the other cooks, all of whom were working the different stations, i.e. sauté, grill, fryer, and pantry. I would find out later that there was a market station where fresh cheeses and charcuterie meats were to be plated.

Jack showed me around the kitchen. He was very patient. He explained to me what things were called and he had me taste some of the "mother sauces" that were warm in the wells and would be cooked down and finished to order. There wasn't much food being made at the time, just some sandwiches. A chicken club, a burger. Dinner service wouldn't start until five thirty. "It may end up being a very busy night," he said. "We have two big parties on the books and the hotel is at eighty percent." I asked him what he meant by "big" parties. He said there were a twenty-four-top and a sixteen-top at six thirty and seven, respectively. I looked at the hot line and tried to imagine all the food for that many people coming out of this one window.

Jack introduced me to the cooks as we walked through the kitchen. First, the sauté cook, then the fry cook, and lastly the grill cook. He mentioned to all of them that he and I knew each other from way back when. I got the feeling that I had already earned their respect just by being a friend of Jack.

As the reader already knows there were Jack, Clara, and Jennifer, but of course there were many other people working in the restaurant. There are a lot of things to be done and a lot of people running around trying to do them. Altogether, there were, maybe, sixty employees at Birch between the front of the house and the back of the house. The kitchen at Birch also catered to a banquet hall in the hotel, so there was a whole group of banquet servers that I never got to know very well, in addition to the prep cooks who specialized mainly in the banquet catering aspect of the kitchen's work. Some people worked only a few shifts per week, but it wasn't uncommon for others to work upwards of sixty hours weekly. Sixty hours per week may not seem like an exceptional amount, but when you're spending it on your feet and, in the case of front of the house staff, dealing with customers, restaurant work can be particularly grueling both mentally and physically.

However, on my first day there, I met some interesting people. People worth mentioning here. There was Jeremy, the other front of the house manager and the lower-ranking manager at the time, who seemed to be doing most of the actual managing while Clara was serving as more of a figurehead. Jeremy was from New York City, where apparently he had worked in some of the City's better-known steak houses as a bartender and a server and eventually as a manager. Why he had moved to Valmesta from New York was a mystery to me. Jeremy preferred to be on the floor and in the kitchen as opposed to in the office. Jack introduced me to him as he was showing me the plating specification for a burger. I thought it should be pretty easy to plate a burger, but Jack described the specifications with utmost importance, as if to err in that regard would get me fired. Jeremy was equally serious and he talked a lot and asked a lot of questions.

I met a server named George who was Greek and whose surname was Fotopoulos. Some of the other servers who knew him well called him Papa-Dapoulous affectionately, and all the serving staff seemed to like him. George trained me that night after Jack had shown me around the place. George took serving very seriously and seemed to command a good deal of respect from the managers and the kitchen staff, which impressed me, considering the kitchen staff seemed to look down on or resent just about everyone else in the front of the house. It's a common restaurant dynamic for the back of the house to resent the front of the house, and it might have to do with the fact that servers typically make a lot more money than the cooks and, even in some cases, the kitchen managers and chefs. (Not that all servers are pulling in crazy money. I'd estimate that an average server at an average restaurant makes somewhere between ten and fifteen dollars an hour in tips, which amounts to, maybe, thirty thousand a year, sometimes all cash tips depending on where you work. If you count strippers and bartenders, the average income for tipped employees might go up a bit, but food service professionals don't make crazy money in all cases. Ask your server, though, next time you're out, and my guess is they'll tell you their current job pays better than the other jobs they qualify for. At Birch, that was certainly the case for me. With a liberal arts degree, my starting pay at a museum or a marketing firm or what have you would have been about sixty percent of what I made as a server.)

Kitchen employees, however, are paid hourly. The cooks at Birch were paid something between eight and twelve dollars an hour, depending on experience, and the lower-ranking chefs something more like fifteen. Their managers are usually the higher-ranking chefs, who are paid salary and oversee food preparation and whose responsibility it is to make sure the costing is right for food and labor. The front of the house managers take care of their own labor costs, which are two sixty-five an hour per server and around five fifty an hour per busser, and the beverage costs. Of course, I didn't start to learn how all of that worked on my first night.

As soon as Jack introduced me to George I realized he was gay. There was no uncertainty about it, nor was there any effort on his part to keep that side of his personality undisclosed. I admired that about him. No bullshit and plenty of confidence. We got along well. Looking back I think I modeled myself after his style of serving, which was concerned foremost with making sure his guests were happy and comfortable. He was very caring and affectionate toward the people he was serving. Other servers told me George was good at "reading" tables, which was true. Within a few seconds of speaking with his guests he could determine what their needs were, both immediate and for the remainder of their meal. It was important, George said, to try to understand the context of the gathering and, as a server, mirror your emotional frequency based on your guests. It would take time to develop, and once I had developed it, it would take more time still to get to a point where I could do that with multiple groups at once, going from table to table, from one emotional frequency to another like a chameleon. I watched George do this effortlessly, and then go back into the kitchen and, with an air of confidence and respect, communicate the guests' needs to the kitchen manager when necessary.

Everyone in a managerial role took the guests' needs very seriously. I learned that right away. I guess when people are willing to pay good money for a meal they want their needs to be taken seriously, and from an operational standpoint, it's good to go along with that notion. In a way it was hard for me to understand that at first, having never been one to go out to expensive dinners. I still prefer the casual dining experience to a stuffy dinner table ornamented with French wine and obscure food preparations. I enjoy good wine, and I love good food. I have a discerning palate. But, personally, I don't like to be coddled like an infant, the way a lot of people did at Birch. I never could quite understand them.

At one point during the night I saw Jennifer near the hostess stand. She gave me a smile and the sex eyes again, but something about her rubbed me wrong. I went over and said hello. She told me she was getting ready to take a break. "I'm on a double," she said, "I usually work weekend nights and weekday mornings, but tonight I'm picking up for Brea." Just then one of the waitresses walked over. She came from behind me and as I saw Jennifer look at her I turned to look as well and there she was. Her beauty took me by surprise. Her hair was dark like in a comic book, an almost liquid, inky black, and her skin had a dark olive hue. Her whole appearance was dark. Brown eyes and deeply colored lips. When she opened her mouth to speak I noticed the pink of her tongue by contrast. She asked what the books looked like for the evening. Jennifer was visibly uncomfortable in her presence. The waitress' dark splendor captured my gaze like a black hole and none of my attention, for that moment, escaped it. Jennifer submitted to her. "A couple of big parties," Jennifer said, "Barry has one and you have the other. You'll be setting up in the seventies," she said, indicating the seventh row of tables from the door. "Maria," Jennifer said, admitting defeat, "this is Lado. It's his first day of training." I noticed as Jennifer said this she cast her eyes downward in what appeared to be an attempt to evaluate herself. She looked at her tits and adjusted her blouse.

"Who are you training with?" the girl named Maria asked me.

"I'm training with George," I said. I noticed Jennifer making note of it on the evening's floor plan. "I'm Lado, nice to meet you," I said and I took Maria's hand.

"Nice to meet you as well," she said, "Welcome to our high-functioning dysfunctional family. What did you say your name was again?"

"It's Lado," I said. "I go by Lado. Glad to be a part of it. I hope to make this place even more high-functioning and maybe, if I'm lucky, more dysfunctional as well."

"I'm sure you won't have a problem being lucky here," she said. She looked over at Jennifer, who obviously felt excluded by the turn the conversation was taking. "Is my party set up?" Maria asked her.

"I asked Abdul to do it, but I don't think he has. I would go check and see."

"What time is the reservation?"

"Six thirty. It's for twenty four so you're probably going to need to pull one of the tables from the eighties to make two twelve tops." Maria walked away. I wanted to watch her. I like to watch women walk away. But I sensed Jennifer's eyes on me and I made sure not to stare at Maria. I could already tell Jennifer had been made to feel insignificant by comparison during the exchange.

I looked around. I was impressed by the professionalism of Birch, especially compared to Doraku. I was impressed, too, by how I felt about myself in the uniform, in the space, and part of the team. Birch was about making money. I could feel it. All the servers, all the bussers, the managers, even the hostesses were there to get fat off the Birch cow.

I told Jennifer I should go find George. I said that it wouldn't be good for Clara to see me slacking on my first day, but what I really wanted was to get away from the host stand and maybe flirt with Maria a little bit. Jennifer rolled her eyes at me, and at the time I didn't know what she did that for. Now I know that it's because I was protected from any sort of disciplinary action so long as Jack and Clara were fucking and I was part of team Jack. Clara basically ran the place and Jack, my referrer, was sleeping with her. Did I mention the professionalism of the place?

That's how Jack maintained his power, by banging the most powerful person in the restaurant. His presence in the kitchen was elevated, in a way, to that of the head honcho because he was the boss's favorite. To be sure, he earned that position by being the type of guy he was. He was always fun to be around, and he was magnetic. Not just in a sexual way, either. You wanted him to like you. If he liked you it elevated your social status to a higher level, not quite to Jack's level, but to a level higher than you were at before. I think Clara was attracted to him for that reason. Clara, without a doubt, was very attractive in her own right, and together they made a damn fine pair.

At that time I didn't fully understand the dynamic of the restaurant's social fractions and hierarchies. I had never experienced it before. At Doraku, all the servers were male, and to my knowledge none of them was banging any other one of them. But by the way people talked, even on my first night, I could tell that the Birch crew was an incurably promiscuous cohort.

I found George in the kitchen. He was preparing some coffee for brewing and was yawning. "Is that for you or the customers?" I asked him.

"Both," he replied. "And they're 'guests,' not 'customers.' Don't let any of the managers hear you call them 'customers.' In fact you may as well just eliminate that word from your vocabulary as long as you're here." He reached into his apron and pulled out his book. He unfolded it and pulled out a little one-and-a-half by three-inch piece of laminated paper with small type on it. He asked me whether Clara or anyone had given me one of these before. I held it and read it, and I said, "No, I haven't seen one of these yet." George began to describe what it was. "Basically, it's an outline for how you should approach each table. Obviously sometimes things are going to be a little different. But it's simple things, like, at what point during the meal do you bring out the bread. When do you bring out the bread? Don't look."

I looked up at him. I wasn't sure. "Right after you bring the waters," I said, more so asked.

"No," George said. "You don't want to bring them food before they order anything. I prefer not to bring bread until I have a table's entire order. You don't want them filling up on free stuff and then deciding, 'I think I'll skip a salad tonight.' By that same token, I won't even let the bussers bring out water until I've gotten a chance to offer my guests bottled water or Pellegrino. As servers everything we do is about driving up our PPA. That's how we make our money."

"What's PPA?" I asked him.

"Have you ever worked in a place like this before?" I told him I hadn't. He asked how I got the job. "I'm friends with Jack," I said. George nodded his head as if it immediately made sense to him. "PPA stands for 'Per Person Average.' It's what each guest you wait on spends in here, on average."

What I saw in his eyes appeared to be the expression of a man facing a dilemma. I would come to understand later that George was considered by many to be the best server in the house. He was the best combination of professional, knowledgeable, and likeable. Looking back, I believe that, in that moment, George was measuring me up, considering whether or not I was a threat to his being number one. He wondered how much of his knowledge and skill set he should share with me.

Perhaps I should take a moment to explain why George may have contemplated not training me to the best of his ability. The people who fit in and thrive in the workplace are called "rock stars," and for good reason. The amount of sustained mental focus required to perform at a high level for six to eight—or sometimes, as I would find out, eighteen—hours straight, without a break, is extreme, and that's without even bringing into consideration the physical requirements of the gig. You're on your feet the whole time and constantly moving, carrying things, sometimes running.

Literally, sometimes I ran at Birch, through the kitchen and into dry storage or banquet storage for a new tub of ketchup or a champagne bucket. I can recall times where I was actually out of breath when I was talking to my tables. Not everyone can perform that well physically and mentally for such long periods of time. As for servers, those who perform the best and most efficiently, and who can sell the best, make the most money. The accumulation of a few dollars here and a few dollars there in sales goes a long way to improving your paycheck. That's what George meant about bottled water. If every one of your tables ordered bottled water instead of tap water, at the end of the month you'd have about one hundred dollars in tips that you would not have had if all your guests drank tap. And that's just talking about water.

This brings me to a little thing called "performance-based scheduling." We are talking about competition, after all. Performance-based scheduling is just what it sounds like: scheduling servers' shifts based on how well they perform individually. A modern restaurant keeps track of its servers' performance through the computer system. (Although my experience has led me to believe that sales numbers can be manipulated in order to make some people look better than others, and in a way to reverse-justify certain scheduling decisions because certain servers are on the receiving end of favoritism.) The thing with Jack banging Clara is not at all unusual in a busy restaurant with many different working parts, and if Manager A is getting it on with Server B and Manager A is making the schedule, Manager A will probably give positively unfair treatment to Server B and screw over Servers C-J. That's just the way it goes, and it can drive you crazy if you're not one of the anointed few, so to speak. That's an abuse of managerial power through PBS. The way PBS is supposed to work, which isn't exactly fair in the first place, is the servers who are the best sellers and drive their PPA up the highest gain access to the best shifts and the best sections and eventually make the most money. One reason performance-based scheduling is annoying is because it's not as fair as it sounds. Some restaurants rely on the amount of "upsells" on certain seemingly arbitrarily selected items that people would otherwise either order or not order, i.e. a margarita. You can't sell a margarita to someone who either does not like margaritas or is simply not in the mood for a margarita, and selling a margarita to someone who asks for one isn't exactly a testament to a server's selling ability. I'm getting irritated just thinking about it. And then there's the whole teamwork propaganda that they're always shoving down your throats, which directly contradicts PBS because, as one might imagine, PBS commonly encourages animosity among the staff. The less-favored feel resentful of the more-favored while the more-favored feel superior. I should calm down.

I tended to perform well, so PBS never really screwed me over that badly except for a while after Jack and Clara split and Jack quit and it seemed like Clara hated my guts and wanted to get me fired, which probably would have happened except I wasn't having it and stood up for myself and, basically, threatened her with airing out her dirty laundry for her higher-ups to see. It's all so very political, and politics sometimes interferes with making money. I was always one to think that it didn't quite matter who was screwing whom, or who told whom what, I just wanted to make my money and get on with my life. It's when social politics began to interfere with making money—both for myself, personally, and for the restaurant and the other servers I liked—that I got pissed off.

And by the way I'm talking about food and beverage service. Food, for eating, and beverages, for drinking. We're serving people food and drink. At the end of the day we aren't saving any lives or changing the course of history, just filling people's bellies and getting them drunk. If anything we were cutting their lives shorter, what with all the salt and the butter and the alcohol we were serving up. It's a surprise people don't die in restaurants more often than they do. (Speaking of which I was out to eat at a restaurant not long ago and I made a visit to the bathroom to relieve myself after some beers. While I was pissing I heard the sound of a man vomiting in one of the stalls behind me. It was an awful sound, always is. But it got worse when I heard the sound of his pants unbuckling as well, and of him tugging his pants down. I heard a fart. It was a wet fart into open air, an unmistakable sound, not into pants or underpants but into open air. I turned and looked; I couldn't help but be curious. I could see under the stall that the man was on his knees facing the toilet, and I presumed his head to be in the toilet as he vomited, and his pants were, surely, down to the floor. I saw his body lean back, and he farted again, and then took a shit. I saw it plop onto the floor and pile up in a long, coiling turd. It wasn't even diarrhea, which I would have expected from what appeared to be an uncontrollable bowel movement. I told my server about it when I saw him next. He thought I was joking and he went into the bathroom to see for himself. Poor bastard, he saw what I had seen. Soon management was involved and an ambulance was on the way. That was the closest thing to death I'd ever seen in a restaurant. To this day I won't go back there.)

I didn't take any tables that night, or the next night, or the next. It would be a whole week before I was put on the floor on my own. I trained with George for the first three days, Barry trained me once, and Maria trained me once. I liked all three of them, each for different reasons.

George was meticulous, clean, soft-spoken, and knowledgeable about the food and beverages served at Birch, and he was able to articulate his knowledge well. He was efficient without being hasty.

Barry was a seasoned professional server. He worked at another place in Midtown and pulled a lot of doubles between the two restaurants. He made a nice living from it and he drove a nice car. I never could figure out how old he was in all my time there. He made a point of keeping it a mystery. I would guess he was forty-five, but if he told me he was fifty-five or thirty-five I would have believed him.

Maria was the server most familiar with traditional fine dining. Even though Birch presented a rather casual atmosphere, Maria showed the guests the experience of fine dining. She always served drinks from the right, food from the left; cleared drinks from the right; reset silverware appropriately for the course and protein served; and she was known for her impeccable bottled wine service. A majority of my training shift with Maria was spent learning how to present a bottle of wine to a guest and open it at the table.

Altogether there were just shy of twenty servers who worked there, some of whom worked only breakfast, some worked a combination of breakfast and dinner and weekend brunches, and some worked only dinner. My goal was to be a dinner server exclusively. Doing so would keep my mornings and afternoons free for writing, which was how I liked it. Eventually, I made that happen, but I had to earn my way there by working back-to-back doubles and triples and sometimes sixty-hour weeks.

During my first week there I didn't get much writing done because I was pretty busy studying the menu and getting the food knowledge down. I remember how big of a deal the other servers made the menu test out to be. I had been through college and done my fair share of studying, so I didn't think that studying a food menu would be all that difficult. Still, I got the impression that many servers struggled with it, and they expected me to struggle with it as well, which I did to some degree. There were a lot of French terms and sophisticated culinary techniques that I needed to learn or at least understand, which was difficult, but the chefs helped me to understand them. The hardest part was learning about all the different food allergies and what foods had what allergens and whether or not the cooks were able to substitute those ingredients for something else and, if they were, what substitutions would work and wouldn't bring about a disaster at my table. People expect a server to know that sort of thing when they're paying fifty dollars for a meal.

The first night of training, I hung around in George's shadow until the end of the shift, even while he did his checkout, and I watched him fill out his paperwork and do his tip share. Two percent of total sales went to the bussers, three percent of total alcohol sales minus bottled wine sales went to the bartenders, and two percent of food sales went to the food runners. However, all that was subject to lessening or, in some cases, greatening of percentages based on the bussers', bartenders', and food runners' respective performances. On that particular night, George tipped by the book. I got the feeling he always did, and I would end up modeling him by being good and consistent with my own tip share. On my way out, I got my things from the locker room. I had brought a riding jacket for the cool night. When I said goodbye to the bartender, I was invited to have drinks at a pub called The Rabbit Hole where several other staffers would be hanging out. Jeremy gave me directions to the place. I rode my bike there.

It was a dark, quiet place where the music wasn't too loud and the drinks were inexpensive. It had been described to me as the perfect place to get together after work for those reasons. It was located in Olde Town, and Olde Town was just north of Columbia Avenue. Because it was outside of downtown, the people who got drunk there didn't have to worry so much about the police pulling them over and popping them with a ticket for driving under the influence. Restaurant workers, being experienced, clever drinkers, flocked to The Rabbit Hole.

I would come to like Olde Town a bit. It was more laid back and quiet than downtown. I couldn't imagine the type of person who would want to live in the city center. I would find it to be over stimulating. However, the type of folks who lived in Olde Town weren't exactly my type, either, or I wasn't their type, more like. They were the types of families who had done well during the industrial boom and had been smart with their money, and a lot of that money remained in their family, despite the decline of the industrial economy and decrease in manufacturing in the area. But the houses, which had been built as early as the eighteen nineties and were very sturdy and well-maintained, were in excellent condition and demanded a high price. Even if I wanted to, I could never afford to live there. The people who did were the type who would not allow themselves to be seen at a place like The Rabbit Hole. As it turned out, The Rabbit Hole was in business mostly for quick lunches and industry people like us who got out of work and wanted to tie one on before heading back over to our rental housing in West Valmesta.

I didn't have trouble finding the place. Jeremy had given me good directions. I found a rack to lock my bike and before I walked in I reached into my messenger bag and pulled out my pint of Jameson. I glanced up and down the block. I didn't see anybody. I enjoyed the sound of silence after the windy bike ride and the cool spring night. It was probably midnight. I took a pull of Jameson before I walked in the door.

Inside it was dim, as I had been told it would be. Cigarette smoke filled the stagnant air and I could smell the familiar stench of stale beer and unclean human bodies, which was a comforting thing for me. I spotted some people from Birch. Kitchen workers and servers were sitting at the same long table. I walked up to the table, my bag around my shoulder, feeling a little uneasy because I wanted to sit by Jack, he being the person I knew the best, but there wasn't an available seat next to him. He was sitting between Jennifer and Mike, one of the line cooks. I sat down at an open seat between two people I hadn't met before and across from George, who already had a drink in front of him. George gave me a smile. I lit up a cigarette. People were talking, but quietly. I could tell that this hangout was about unwinding and not partying, although people were not being shy about ordering hard stuff and straight shots. The level of camaraderie among the hourly-paid workers, both front of the house and back, surprised me. A server and a line cook who, two hours prior, had been arguing about who fucked up in what way and who needed to get fucked were getting along swimmingly and appeared to be on friendly terms. I think Maria even bought one of the cooks a beer. Instead of front of the house staff complaining about back of the house staff and vice versa, everyone was instead complaining about the incompetence of their respective managers. Alas, I had not graduated to some higher calling. We servers and bartenders were as working class as they come, in the shits with the cooks and the dishwashers. As the saying goes, servers and bartenders are the aristocrats of the working class; but we were working class nonetheless. Drinking our beer. Talking shit about Management.

I enjoyed it and I was relaxed. They all spent time getting to know me and asked me genuine questions about myself, and I returned the interest with questions of my own. It was becoming evident that it was a very interesting group of people that I had become a part of.

George, after a few drinks, was very friendly towards me, almost to the point of being flirtatious. I played along. I knew he knew I wouldn't actually follow through, so we both enjoyed the playfulness of it. He was in a relationship with a man who was just finishing up his MBA and would soon be earning a nice fat salary. George was just working for a little extra cash in the meantime. He had been a server for many years, and he had made a good living of it. He spoke with a sort of nostalgia, as if he were already through with it. It seemed he was more the passenger than the driver in his relationship, and would be accompanying the MBA man throughout his business career, wherever that would take him. I asked him what he would do with his time and he smiled wide, big white teeth flashing and his eyes squinting from the contraction of his cheek muscles. "Whatever I feel like," he said. I asked would they be married, and I admit I was ignorant in that moment. Of course it was illegal for same-sex couples to get married in our state, at least at that time. George reminded me of this fact and I felt quite bad about asking. He said they would probably move to another state when his boyfriend graduated. I asked George what his boyfriend's name was. Paul was his name.

Jack spent most of the night looking at his phone. I assumed he was texting back and forth with Clara. Clara was the closing manager that night and probably wouldn't leave until twelve thirty or one o'clock a.m. On weeknights, the restaurant closed for dinner service at ten thirty. There was always a closing server whose responsibility it was to make sure everyone did their side work and rolled silverware, and the closing server also took the last few tables to walk into the restaurant. After cashing out the remaining tables and resetting the kitchen and dining room for breakfast service, the closing server finally left the restaurant somewhere between eleven and one o'clock, depending on a variety of factors including how late the tables hung around and how much work there was to do. At that point, the closing manager could do the paperwork and the cash drop and lock up and leave, but that sometimes didn't happen until one or two o'clock. I noticed that Jack kept ordering a shot with his beer, and he was drinking them fast. *He must have ordered a shot and a beer three times now*, I thought, and that was just since I had arrived. He was quiet. Occasionally he would smile at his phone, and eventually he got up to leave. He said goodnight to everyone and walked out the door.

As Jack left, I noticed, out of the corner of my eye, Jennifer's countenance change. Sitting next to Jack she appeared alive and energetic, and in his absence she darkened and grew sullen. Her body language told me she was sad about Jack leaving. I'm guessing she thought of Jack and Clara together, and perhaps she was jealous. I noticed she was sitting across from Maria. As much as I enjoyed mock flirting with George, I wanted to get to know and flirt with Maria. I wanted her badly from the moment I saw her. I got up with my beer and with the cigarette I was smoking and went around the table to sit where Jack had been sitting. Jennifer didn't see that I was coming towards her, but I felt Maria's eyes on me. I slid into the spot and sat down and pulled the chair by the seat to be under me when I sat, close enough to Jennifer to indicate that I came to talk with her but not too close as to make her uncomfortable. Maria was looking at me from across the table. I wanted to make her jealous by ignoring her and feigning interest in Jennifer. Since Jennifer was vulnerable and probably very horny, I could get her interested in me very quickly. She would be laughing and blushing in no time. As long as Maria wasn't overly bright, which I didn't get the impression she was, she would see this and think of me as the charmer and the funny guy. Playing girls is easy if you knew how to do it, and I was shameless about it.

I started a conversation with Jennifer with a cliché, "what are you drinking," or something like that. I can't remember what I said and I can't remember what she was drinking or if she was drinking anything at all. We talked for a while back and forth. I made her laugh. I never looked at Maria, though I knew she was listening and watching. I wondered how close they were as friends. I realized they had been having a light conversation together before I sat down and interrupted, and Maria suddenly found herself with no one to talk to. Out of the corner of my eye, I saw that Maria was sitting between one of the Birch line cooks, who was wearing a tank top and whose armpit hair was visible, and the pantry cook, who had taken a phone call. Mike, on my other side, sat quiet and dumb. Maria looked around and began to fidget uncomfortably, but she was too polite to butt her way into our conversation. At the same time Jennifer turned in her seat to face me and open herself up to me, I looked over at Maria for the first time. I acted like it was the first time I had noticed her since arriving at the bar and I asked her how her night went. It was pretty good timing, I thought.

Soon after I had Maria and Jennifer's full attention. They each wanted equally to be the most desirable. I played them against each other. I sensed that they were usually competitive and not always the best of friends, but that night they at least pretended to be cordial. The night before with Ryan had been a thrill, and I found that after having my appetite satisfied it was far easier to talk to women and to build an attraction with them. There was some sort of causality there. Perhaps it caused a release of sex hormones that secreted through my sweat glands; maybe we humans are much more like apes than we like to think. The more sex a man has the more he is desired by women. Quite possibly by men as well, though that's not the same thing, from a biological standpoint. That night I felt like the alpha-baboon, the silverback. The two young women adjusted their body language again so that all three of us were equally included; everyone else at the table was not. No one else seemed to pay attention to our conversation or to notice that we were talking at all. The world turned as I danced to the beautiful erotic symphony in my own mind. I wanted to see them kiss each other, to see their tongues touching. I thought about it and I imagined it, and the image I conjured excited me. I could see Maria's bra strap peeking out from under her black v-neck shirt on her right collarbone. In my mind I tore it off and kissed her there while she and Jennifer tongued one another's mouth. By that time the conversation had taken on a life of its own, like a good fire. I watched and enjoyed it, and I had to verbally stoke it here and there, but mostly I took pleasure in the simple beauty of it while I fantasized. I hadn't had a threesome since college, where I had a threesome twice, once with two girls and the other time with a girl and another guy. While I had enjoyed the carnal and powerful experience of taking a girl with another guy, for the record, I liked it better with the girls. It was more playful and fun. But both experiences were wonderful.

People began to leave the bar one or two at a time. Some had ridden to work together. Jennifer, Maria, and I stayed and talked until the proprietors turned the lights on. Jennifer seemed suddenly shy in the lighting. Maria looked comfortable and supremely sexy. I wondered what her parents must have looked like in order to produce offspring like her. She and I made eye contact and held each other's gaze for a moment. I was a bit drunk and between the drinking and the fantasizing I had grown quite horny. With my hand under the table I reached and found Jennifer's thigh and gave it a gentle squeeze as I turned to her. "We should go," I said to them. Between my own thighs, a warmth of blood flowed. I looked around. We were the last ones in the bar. The bartender had his eyes up on the television but was leaning against the counter with his arms folded. It was obvious that he had nothing left to do. If we stayed any longer he would start giving us dirty looks. It's not okay for industry people to put other industry people out. You just don't do that.

We three walked out of the bar together. I had my messenger bag with me and I lit up a smoke. They asked me if I drove and I shook my head and indicated my bike, pointing with the index and middle fingers that held my lit cigarette. They asked me where I lived and I said Industrial Park, and they each looked at me with fascination. "You mean, like, the real Industrial Park or just on the West Side?" Jennifer asked me.

"No, Industrial Park. I grew up there," I said, "I like it. You know how home just feels like home." She nodded, her mouth slightly open. Maria was trying not to laugh. She must have thought Jennifer's reaction was silly. "I just moved into a new apartment about a year ago, after I graduated from college," I said.

"Where did you go to school?" Maria asked me.

"State," I said.

"I'm taking classes at VCC," she said, "and then I want to transfer to State. Did you like it there?" I always thought that was a reductive question to ask about another student's college experience, which typically lasts a minimum of four years and for me wasn't an experience devoid of complications. However, for some people, it may be a simple question to answer. I kept my answer simple. I told her I liked it.

"I've been up there to visit a few times," Jennifer said. "You know, to party or whatever. I have friends there."

Everybody had friends there.

"Do you ever go back up there to visit?" she asked me. I couldn't think of any reason why I would go back there just to visit. She said we should drive there to see a football game. I agreed just to be agreeable. I didn't even remember going to see a football game while I was a student there, and I sure as hell didn't want to drive an hour to watch a shitty football game, surrounded by thousands of drunk kids and adults who think they're kids, now that I was no longer a student.

I wanted to get their phone numbers. Well, I really wanted Maria's number, but I thought I should get both of their numbers so that it didn't appear that I was trying to get in Maria's pants. Besides, I wanted to keep alive the fantasy of having a threesome with them.

They both said sure and gave me their numbers, Jennifer quite eagerly and Maria a bit reluctantly, but she gave it. I took out my phone and suggested that each girl pose for a picture somewhere under a streetlamp so that I could save a photo to her number that would appear on my screen when she called. First, I got the picture of Jennifer, who is laughing in the photo. She was laughing and shy and wouldn't look at the camera. There was a breeze that was blowing her slightly stringy strawberry blonde hair, and in the photo she's tucking it behind her ear. Her other arm is folded across her chest and tucked under the elbow of the arm of the hand that is tucking her hair. Maria, in her photo, looks very natural and calm. She has a little smile on her face and the confidence of someone who knows the camera is going to make her look good. Her inky black hair is still in a ponytail from when she put it up at work. Her arms are folded, her long legs crossed. I told her she could be a model. In the picture, her eyes are like little, black, infinitely deep pools of intrigue. Later I would upload the photo to Facebook and tag Maria, and she would use it as her main profile picture for some time. I look at it now and then. I couldn't tell you what she was thinking about in that moment.

I gave them both hugs before they left. Each had driven separately in her own car, but they walked down the street together and turned the corner and they were out of sight. I unsheathed my Jameson and took the last of it down in two big pulls. I found a trash canister to throw the empty glass bottle into. I saddled my bike and rode off. It was late and there was very little traffic. I rode down the middle of the road over the Columbia Avenue Bridge and into West Valmesta. On the bridge's descent I let go of the handlebars and I rode with no hands. I put them out to the side like wings and felt the cool air pass my palms and the underside of my arms, giving me lift. I listened to it. I could hear the wind and when I really tried to I could hear the river. In the middle of the city could be found some of nature's purest representations. Wind and water and darkness throughout an ironclad mountain of civilization. Myriad layers of meaning under the night sky.

I climbed up the steel stairway in back of my apartment and came in through the back porch. Ernie was happy to see me. I let him outside and he peed on the concrete back porch. He came inside and sat with me on the couch as I closed my eyes and felt what it was like to be motionless after a period of prolonged movement. The sensation was heightened by the effect of alcohol in my blood and in my brain. I thought about the girls. I looked at their pictures. I checked my phone calls and text messages, and no one had called. I wondered what my friends were doing. Probably sleeping. I wanted to write some but I decided I was tired and I should go to sleep. Before I could change my mind again, I passed out on the couch with Ernie.

The following weekend, after the aforementioned weeklong training period, I was on the floor at Birch taking tables. Clara gave me a small section, only three tables, so that I wouldn't get "weeded." (Weeded, for those readers who have never worked in a restaurant, is the condition of being overwhelmed by the sheer number of different doings a server or bartender is trying to multi-task at any given time.) I was really eager to make money in the form of tips. Between not working for a spell and then earning training wages for my first week at Birch, I was getting behind on bills and rent. It sucks having to live paycheck to paycheck. Who would disagree with that? I tried to cheer myself up by telling myself I was lucky to have a job in my economically depressed and culturally sad rust-belt city. I guess I truly was lucky.

During my first month or so at Birch I didn't do a whole lot besides continue to study the menu and work on sales tactics so I could make the most money out of the gig. I tried to limit myself to only four or five drinks, and those at night, while I studied, because there was a lot of memorization involved. I continued to find it difficult to make time to write, and I didn't go out all that much, except one night Jack and I had a few drinks at The Rabbit Hole. He was distressed over his relationship with Clara. He told me she was becoming very protective of her phone. For instance, she would leave the screen face-down on the nightstand so that Jack couldn't see who was calling her or texting her, and she would take it into the bathroom with her when she took showers. He was concerned about it and was drinking heavily. He would have two beers and a shot in the time it took me to drink one beer. He thought she was cheating on him.

Cheating on him, though, was a funny way to put it, and Jack admitted it. They weren't officially together. In fact, officially, they did everything they could not to let on that they were together, even though some people knew it, and those who didn't know it suspected as much. It probably would have cost Clara her job if anyone in corporate found out she was sleeping with one of her employees. In the industry, and probably in most industries, it's okay to fuck laterally; that is, get it on with someone who is on the same plane of the hierarchy, i.e. for two servers to give it the old in and out. Obviously there are boundaries, and it's unacceptable to have sex on the clock and it's not okay for your work to be affected by fucking someone you work with, but for the most part it's acceptable and common for servers to fuck servers and cooks to fuck cooks. But a manager fucking a food-runner is a definite conflict of interest and can cause lots of problems and even get the manager fired, or at the very least relocated. Jack was in a tough position because I could tell he truly liked Clara, but he valued having a job, and I think he knew that if push came to shove, Clara would, under the gun, fire Jack to save her own ass.

Since that first night at The Rabbit Hole, I had exchanged texts with Jennifer and with Maria. I fantasized some more about having a threesome with them. Even when I wasn't drunk I thought about it. Jennifer texted me back first. She wanted it. She'd get it, too, if I had the chance to make a threesome happen. Otherwise I wasn't all that interested in her. I suppose I led her on a bit.

I had to initiate contact with Maria. She was the type of girl who was used to being chased. For those types I found it was best to make the first move, but to do so in a way that was entirely non-threatening. It was best to engage her by listening when she talked and picking up on a niche interest of hers or a small part of her personality that not many people knew about, thereby entering her intimate emotional space. If a girl said she liked classic movies, then I would say, "I just saw the scene with Rita Hayworth in *Shawshank Redemption* and it made me think of you." That's a nice thing to say. There's different layers of meaning in that. And she doesn't get the feeling I'm coming on to her. That's what I had to do with Maria. I remembered her dancing in her chair at The Rabbit Hole to a catchy pop song. I texted her and told her I had heard the song again and that it made me think of her. Really, though, I hadn't actually heard the song, only devised a clever plan to let her know I was thinking about her.

My first night on the floor went well. All told, I made about a hundred and twenty five dollars, a hundred and five "on paper" and twenty in cash. Since the majority of dinner guests paid with credit or debit cards we ended up getting most of our tips on those cards, and since we were a corporate-run place we had a corporate auditor who kept tabs on those sorts of things and insisted we employees report our electronic tips. Some servers liked it this way. They preferred getting paychecks. Personally, I preferred cash. We never reported cash tips and, therefore, we never paid our share of income taxes on that money. The way I saw it, if I made cash tips I made about twenty five percent more money. As a citizen and a taxpayer, I could have been conflicted about it, but I wasn't. I was just doing the best I could to make a living for myself.

I considered that good money for my first night, especially considering the amount of work I did. My sales were a little over five hundred on the four tables I took, and the amount of money I made in tips was way over twenty percent. It may have been a coincidence or it may have been that people could tell I was new and wanted to leave me a good tip to be nice. In the beginning, I had a lot of positive energy about working there. I will say that. I was proud to be a part of it and I liked the food and, for the most part, the people I worked with. I remember that there were some rocky moments at first, working in a restaurant like that. At one point the executive chef said to me, very seriously, "This is the big leagues. You guys make a lot of money serving here, and you better hold up your end of the bargain when it comes to representing our food." It's a certain kind of person that succeeds in a restaurant, the kind who responds to those kinds of challenges. It's tough love that prevails as the most effective kind of leadership in a restaurant. People who rise up are the type that aren't easily intimidated and are comfortable with confrontations.

That night we all went out to The Rabbit Hole, as per the usual. Since I started working at Birch I had gone out every night after work for at least one drink, and every time it was The Rabbit Hole we went to. It was a Friday night, so we were fully staffed in the restaurant and the group of us that went out for drinks was extensive. There may have been twenty of us. Maria told me I had done well that night. She was proud of herself, she said, as my principal trainer. I teased her and told her I had learned everything from George, and she pretended to be offended before sipping her vodka tonic. I noticed she was drinking more than I had seen her drink before. I was hoping it wasn't because I was a heavy drinker and she assumed I would like it if she drank a lot. I wasn't so very proud of the fact that I drank a lot. I didn't think it was cool; I just drank because I felt like I had to in order to be myself. It had become a big part of who I was. Besides that, I didn't want her to be trying to impress me. I've never liked a try hard.

Soon I realized that Maria was getting quite drunk, and I decided to try to get her out of the bar. If I can get her to pace herself, I thought, and even change venues I will have a good chance of hooking up with her. I asked her if she wanted to head across the bridge into my side of town. I could tell the idea intrigued her. We finished our drinks and paid our tabs and left.

We walked arm in arm and I maneuvered my bike with my free hand. We were both drunk and we laughed and enjoyed the feeling of being drunk in the streets at night. She had ridden with George to the bar and I told her that I would either call her a cab or walk her to Birch to retrieve her car, depending on how well she sobered up. I didn't like the idea of her driving drunk, but I also didn't like the idea of telling her what to do, so I figured she could drive drunk if she really wanted.

We hit up a few of my favorite, slightly-off-the-beaten-path pubs. Maria acknowledged to me that she had drunk too much in such a short amount of time and that she should drink water, so water was the first thing she ordered. After that she kept on drinking but at a much slower pace than before. In a helpful effort I drank at a slower pace than I normally would drink, so that she wouldn't feel left behind. She talked about her ex-boyfriend and showed me text messages from him. In some of them he called her names, accusing her of being promiscuous, which Maria claimed she was not. I believed her. She asked me about my current relationship status, and I told her I wasn't seeing anyone and that I was enjoying being single. I talked a little about how I had never really been in a serious relationship before, and I had never been with the same person exclusively for more than a few months. Then I told her about Ellery. I don't know why, it just kind of came out.

At closing time the bartender told us we could stay and have one more drink, and I thanked him and we ordered another round. Neither Maria nor I had to work until the following evening. While we finished our drinks I told Maria I had to get home and check on my dog Ernie, and she began asking me about him. "What breed is he? Do you have any pictures?" I told her he was a mixed breed, and I thought he was some kind of cross between a collie and a terrier. I took my phone out of my pocket and began to show her pictures of Ernie. She made the "Aw, how cute!" face for each one of the photos. I asked if she wanted to come over and meet him and have a nightcap with me, and she said yes.

I love the word "yes" coming out of a woman's mouth. Mostly because nine out of ten times I'm trying to manipulate said woman into saying "yes," and to hear her affirmative response to my advances is a sort of positive feedback mechanism that lets me know to keep going. I didn't feel any shame in it at all. In my mind I was just opening Maria up to the things she wanted for herself. Along the way I had to avoid certain obstacles and pitfalls; for example, you can never sound like a creep if you want to get a woman in bed. She can never know there's an endgame. You have to keep your motives to yourself and disguise your actions as spontaneous and in the moment. Keep the game going long enough, and, at some point, being in the moment includes her, whoever she is, coming over to your place, and, at that point, the end game begins.

At my apartment Maria and Ernie got acquainted with each other while I fixed some cocktails. When I asked her what she wanted, she said, "Surprise me." Throughout the night I had seen her drink everything from plain vodka and soda to straight tequila and cheap beer, so I didn't think she would be all that fussy about a cocktail. I made a cocktail in which I muddled lime and fresh oregano with agave syrup and a few dashes of orange bitters, to which I added ice, one part mezcal and one part bourbon for a smoky variation of an old fashioned. I tasted it, and it had exactly the flavor I was looking for. I took a part-empty bottle of club soda out of the fridge and tasted it to make sure it was effervescent enough to add to a drink. It was. I splashed it into the drinks and tasted them again. They were perfect. At least, to me, at that moment, they were perfect. I took out two more glasses and salted the rim on each, and then I poured the cocktails from the non-salted glasses into the salted ones.

I brought the drinks over to the couch where Maria was sitting. Ernie was up on her lap. It made me smile to see them together. Ernie always liked the girls I brought over. I suspected he could smell the chemistry in the room of an attractive, available female human and an eager male like myself. He was an extra-species observer to my endless sexual drama, and things just kept getting more and more interesting. Ernie was the best; he would never rat me out. I could bring home whomever the following night, and Ernie would never spill the beans to them that I had had a different girl over the night before. He would never get jealous, and he would never try to get it in with my girl behind my back. Besides, he was an absolute babe magnet, and he liked the attention he got when girls came over.

I asked Maria whether or not she liked the drink. She told me it was a bit harsh but that she liked it. "Would you like a little more club soda?" I asked her. She declined, saying she liked it and would get used to it. Mezcal, I explained, was made with the agave *piñas* after they had been roasted and infused with wood smoke, giving the liquor a notable smokiness in relation to tequila, which is also made from agave. "In some parts of Oaxaca," I said, "the people drink this stuff for breakfast." She laughed, but I wasn't kidding. It was true. They believed that mezcal was beneficial to their health. "Some people say it's an aphrodisiac," I said.

Maria asked me questions about myself. I guess it was as good a time as any other to have a personal one on one conversation. "I can tell you are intelligent," she said to me, "I can see it. You have an intelligent face." At the time I thought it was a nice compliment, but now I'm not so sure about that. In retrospect, it seems I wasn't behaving intelligently during that period of my life, or not as intelligently as I could have been behaving, and that's why Maria pointed out that I *appeared* intelligent by contrast to how I actually acted, as if I could have played a doctor or a lawyer on TV. Maybe I'm overanalyzing it now. I told her I was a writer, but I didn't say it with much confidence. Sometimes it comes out more easily, or more sincerely, than other times. It has to do with how I identify myself and how I think the other person is going to perceive me when I say it. It's a litmus test of sorts, a way for me to feel out my compatibility with someone. If I say, "I'm a writer" or "I'm working on a book of stories," and the person I'm speaking with gives me a doubtful look, then I lump them into the category of "people-I-don't-need-to-waste-my-time-associating-with." When it comes to writing, I doubt myself enough as it is, especially being a writer in America, where achievement and money-making are paramount values. Therefore, I try not to surround myself with people who are going to doubt my dreams and aspirations, as I myself do.

Unfortunately, it's a lot easier said than done. I've mentioned that money and success are core American values; well, in America, so often success is only considered success if it's the kind of success that makes you money. Even today, as much as we've progressed, it's common for a man to feel pressure to earn money, especially for a straight white man. Being part of the prevailing dominant culture is to feel a lot of pressure to prevail and be dominant. Many women still measure a man's worthiness by his worth, which is why I doubted myself when I told Maria that I was a writer, and probably came off as a total loser. I didn't want her to deem me unworthy as a mate. I wanted to fuck her so bad, and I had come too far to be defeated by the cultural stigma of being a writer, which is a deadbeat, broke, possibly mentally unstable drunkard who puts some words together from time to time when he's not slacking off. I was trying really hard not to let people know that's exactly what I was.

Thankfully, Maria had already made up her mind that she liked me, and she didn't seem to care what I wanted to be when I grew up. It surprised me that she didn't have any overt reaction to it when I told her. Instead she asked me about it, whether I had been published, what I wrote about. She asked me where I worked. I told her it was in my bedroom and that I had a mini library in there as well. She wanted to see it. I took her into my bedroom and left the door open to avoid what I hoped would be the last creep move I would have to avoid before getting her naked—that is, closing the bedroom door behind her. I pointed to the small, espresso-colored coffee table in the corner of the room where I did my writing. There were some books on the table, some rings on the surface where I had left a beverage without a coaster, and an ashtray, along with my laptop, which wasn't open. She walked over and picked up my copy of *The Brothers Karamazov* and began to flip through it. She asked me how to pronounce "Dostoevsky". "It's the book every novelist wishes they could write," I said, "it's a masterpiece." Maria looked toward the back of the room. "Is that a balcony?" she asked. I didn't say anything as she began to walk toward the door. I followed her to the door and she slid it open and stepped outside. I followed behind her.

On the porch I took my cigarettes out of my pocket and asked Maria if she cared for one. She took one from the pack with her thumb and forefinger, her shellacked nails catching the light of a streetlamp. I noticed her nails were painted like leopard skin, and I wondered to myself how the nail stylist would have given them such an intricate pattern. It must have been a special kind of nail paint. I imagined her hands and her fingers with their leopard print nails wrapped around my cock. A woman's hands can be so erotic; they can be used in so many different ways. I think Maria could sense what I was thinking. I lit her cigarette for her, and she commented on how the lingering taste of mezcal and the cigarette smoke made a bold impression on her palate. She liked it, she said. I watched her as she experienced the sensation of taste. I watched her pink tongue as it emerged from between her olive lips and wet her mouth before she raised the cigarette to it. She breathed in, lowered her cigarette and exhaled. Just then I kissed her for the first time. I felt the balminess of her lip-gloss, and I leaned back to look into her eyes. The light of the half moon reflected in them and they showed eagerness and willingness. I kissed her again and this time I licked her lips to taste them, and I felt her tongue touch mine. On the back of my head I felt her hand, the one with the cigarette in it, and what I felt was the base of her palm and her pinky and ring finger caressing me as she made sure not to burn me with the hots. Her free hand clawed at my ribs. With my hands I felt up and down her back and then reached down to grab her ass. As I squeezed it my dick began to swell in my trousers and I pressed it into her hips so she could feel how badly I wanted her. I threw my cigarette off the balcony and into the alley. I'm not sure what Maria did with hers. Still embraced, we made our way back into my bedroom and drunkenly removed each other's clothes. We were laughing at the difficulty of such a simple task in the absence of fine motor skills and delicate balance. Still standing, and still tongue kissing one another, she helped me remove my boxer briefs and I removed her bra. She leaned back to look at my now fully erect penis. I watched her as she put both leopard-manicured hands around it and gently stroked it. I watched her face as she did it. She smiled a little and then bit her lower lip before looking up at me and kissing me strongly. I kneeled and pulled her underwear down to her ankles and she lifted first one foot and then the other foot out of her panties and at that point we were both naked. Naked as God intended, I thought to myself.

I went down and began to kiss her stomach while I caressed her ass. I would reach up and pinch her nipples gently. Then I began to kiss and lick her hips and inner

160

thighs, and she spread her legs ever so slightly and her vagina appeared in full bloom. The amount of desire I felt to see her was sensational. I wanted to see the pink of her like I saw the pink of her tongue just minutes before. I kissed her and tasted her. I was training my palate to appreciate the different flavors of women. I still couldn't see her color so I directed her to the bed. I told her I wanted to see her and I angled her to where the moonlight could bring her colors out, and she spread her legs wide for me. With two fingers I spread her lips, and I could see the pink. It was wet and shiny and reflected the light like a jewel. I put my tongue all the way in to taste and I breathed in the aroma. It was the tiniest bit sweet. I spit a little on her clit and started to rub it with my fingers as I went in and out with my tongue. She writhed with pleasure and told me not to stop. I wanted enormously to put my dick in and fuck her but she kept telling me not to stop licking it. I did the inverse; I licked her clit and then put a finger in her, rubbing up and toward the pelvis where I believed the g-spot to be, and I did that until she came to orgasm. It was only a few minutes. I was surprised at how quickly it happened.

She relaxed and closed her eyes. I pulled away to watch her and she closed her legs and put a hand to her vagina. She quivered slightly. I told her I wanted to fuck her and she said no. I said I would get a condom and she said, "No. Be quiet." I lay down next to her. I didn't talk for some time; I simply lay there with my hard penis sticking up in the air. A minute or so went by before she rolled over to face me. "I'm a virgin," she said. At first I was astounded. I almost blurted out, "How old are you?" but then I thought better of it and I remembered Maria getting checked for ID at the bar. She was at least twenty-one. I looked into her eyes. "I just wanted to tell you that," she said, "because I don't normally do this. And I've never had sex. And I want to keep it that way." I started to lose my hard on.

"Are you waiting until you're married?"

"Well, yea, that's the point," she said. "Or until I'm engaged, I guess. If I was with the person I knew I was going to marry, I would do it. But if men found out I wasn't a virgin they wouldn't want to marry me."

"I can't imagine that being a deciding factor."

"Are you Chaldean?"

"I'm not anything."

"No Chaldean would want to marry me. If you lose your virginity before you're married, you're a slut and no one wants you. Of course some girls do it and manage to keep it a secret, but I would be disrespecting my family if I did."

"So your plan is to marry a Chaldean? For sure?"

"I don't know. I guess. It's definitely, like, expected that I do."

A moment passed and neither Maria nor I said anything.

"I definitely want to marry someone who has the same beliefs as me, and comes from the same background. Even if it's just to avoid going through all that trouble with my family. If my parents found out I was hanging out with you, they'd probably kill me."

I tried not to take that last bit too personally. *I can't believe I'm having this conversation*, I thought. I wondered whether I would ever have a normal hookup again. There I was having a conversation about marriage after I had just drunkenly gone down on a girl I worked with and whom I barely knew, who was basically telling me that she wouldn't ever be able to hangout with me publicly, let alone carry on any sort of a relationship, and that she would never have sex with me and the idea of it alone was shameful. *Have I just been used for oral sex?*

My boner was completely gone, and Maria was putting on her panties, trying to explain to me that I was "lucky" to have gotten that far with her, that she "never does this." She said she liked me, but she didn't think it was a good idea, what we had just done. That it was fun but it should only be a one-time thing. I felt a kind of internal sting. *Should my feelings be hurt?* I wondered. She asked if she could spend the night and I told her it was fine. I waited until she fell asleep. I was looking at her. She was laying on her side in the fetal position with her back to me. She was topless and the covers were up at her hips, which, with Maria on her side, rose up in a hilly curve of smooth skin and tender flesh. I lifted the bed sheet and got a good look at her thonged ass and my dick got hard again. When it was fully hard I began to stroke it, and then I got up and went to the bathroom and jerked off into the sink. It only took a couple of minutes. I thought of Maria at first, of how I'd like to watch Jennifer lick her cunt and her asshole, and then Ryan was there as well, and I thought of all of them together. As I came I thought of coming on Maria's face with her mouth open and her pink tongue protruding. I waited for my boner to subside and avoided looking at myself in the mirror. I rinsed my come down the drain. Then I went back into the bedroom, put some pajama pants on, and got back into bed. As I lay down, Maria turned over and, still asleep, put her arm across my chest. I felt awkward for a moment, but I was tired and drunk and I had just come and I fell asleep quickly.

When I woke up Maria was gone.

ii.

What it is to Serve

The nice thing about being a server is the "commitment optional" nature of it. Usually, neither servers nor their employers expect the relationship to go on for a long time. There are no contracts and rarely any verbal agreements as to the duration of employment, and very few, if any, restaurant servers plan to be restaurant servers forever. All that said it's nice to work a job without the serious commitment that more professional arrangements so often demand. If a server doesn't like the gig, he or she can relocate to another restaurant that's willing to pay them two sixty five an hour with no commitment and hope they've found their way to greener pastures. Granted, if it's a good restaurant with good leadership, the managers will recognize the employees who are beneficial to the operation of the business and do everything in their power to keep them. Granted, also, more serious restaurants can be serious places of business and sometimes they offer real-job benefits. But one never has to fully invest in the place; it's just sell, sell, sell, and kiss ass for less than half of minimum wage, believing all the while that the people who come in to dine and drink are going to tip twenty percent.

It helps to believe in the product, and it helps to be genuine. The best servers are the ones who genuinely care and don't have to fake it. In fact, I've always thought that the best actors were probably some of the best servers before they made it in the movie business. For an actor, to act well is to act truthfully, to convince even himself that the way he is acting is true to the character and real. Serving is like that. To be great at it, one has to truly believe that the guests' needs are as important as the guests themselves believe their needs to be, and to provide genuine emotional feedback in that regard. It's not an easy thing to do. It involves a momentary surrender of the server's own reality as he or she takes on the reality of the guest. It's a very emotionally labor-intensive process, and it requires tremendous focus to maintain that emotional effort for long periods of time.

As a culture, it is important to recognize this. I truly believe that. The twenty percent standard works, if it's honored. Because the wages for servers haven't increased in decades, what was a good tip twenty or thirty years ago—i.e., ten or fifteen percent—is no longer good enough. I've heard people claim that they'll leave a twenty percent tip only if the waitress or waiter is exceptionally fun and engaging, but that's not fair. There should be no expectation to go above and beyond for twenty percent. Anyone who says that is either cheap or ignorant and doesn't deserve the care and attention and, frankly, the hard work that goes into getting food and beverages brought to their table. One should leave twenty percent always, and if the server goes above and beyond what's expected, leave more than twenty percent. Leave thirty, fifty percent, but never less than twenty. That should be a rule. Servers deserve twenty percent, and the people who leave less ought not to dine out and should simply stay home and serve themselves.

Another nice thing about being a server is the pure, Dionysian pleasure perks of the lifestyle. Good servers, who are often interesting, funny, spontaneous, emotionally responsive, and physically attractive, are good because they enjoy the sensuousness of rich food and drink, of mingling and of the night. For me, the perfect way to unwind after every shift was to knock back some suds, make jokes, laugh, and, later, bang a girl's head against my headboard and make her howl at the moon. For a long time I had no thoughts of negative consequence. To be honest, I'm not sure there are any, besides that to live like that is a sort of trap, and I didn't get much of anything else done.

My writing, for example, suffered, or, perhaps more accurately put, didn't happen as often as it should have. I sometimes wonder what I would have written during that time period if I spent more time writing than drinking and trying to get laid. The way I would have written then is different from the way I write now and is different from the way I will write tomorrow. What didn't happen in the past is never to happen in the future, because the timing of a thing is the thing. Oh well, there's nothing to be gained by dwelling on it.

Of course, there are potential negative consequences of living a commitment-free lifestyle. It is not uncommon for servers to experience a sense of aimlessness in their career. As I've said, to be a server is rarely, if ever, the end result of one's aspirations and efforts to achieve. The place in one's life in which one is waiting tables in a restaurant gives way to a feeling of unimportance. Everything about serving people food and drink is of very little consequence in the long run. There is a lack of real purpose, a lack of genuine achievement. There is nowhere else to go but to another restaurant and be a server there, which is a lateral move, both professionally and developmentally as a person. I've read a little on the theory of self-efficacy, which basically suggests that people either believe or don't believe in their own ability to complete difficult tasks and reach their goals, and believing or not believing they usually prove themselves right. It is a profound theory of cognitive science, but I wonder how it would be applied to serving, if it could be applied at all. It would make for an interesting psychological study. At a certain point a server's skill plateaus, and there is only so much more to learn, and then it just becomes a matter of repeating the same process over and over, from table to table and group to group, and earning financial rewards of varying degrees. Sometimes it feels worth it, and sometimes it doesn't.

There can be loneliness. The type of socializing a server specializes in is the dangerous type that can leave a person feeling completely unfulfilled. In relating to guests, it's very difficult to truly empathize with someone who has a completely different set of values and a unique sense of what's important. The effort on a server's part to empathize is rarely returned by the person being served, which, if you think about it, is quite sad. It can be exhausting to give of oneself so tryingly and not to receive the same effort in return. It is, at best, a fleeting connection with the guests, and usually it's only superficial. At worst it can be impossible to even find a common ground, and this can be difficult for a server, especially if their tip suffers.

One can become so physically and mentally exhausted that it is almost impossible to find the energy to do anything else. I'm convinced that, with the stress of dealing with guests and working in such an intense environment, every hour of waiting tables is equivalent to roughly two hours in today's typical job setting; therefore, a thirty-hour workweek in a busy restaurant is about equal to a sixty-hour week in the average workplace, say, selling kitchen utensils at "x"-mart. Of course there are many trying labors, but talk to any server that's been doing it for a long time and they'll tell you what happens. It starts with bunions and leads to back and neck problems and, if unmonitored, will result in more serious health problems. No kidding. Barry had to be hospitalized for a month after years and years of fifty-hour weeks in a restaurant gave him a heart attack.

And that's not factoring in any possible adverse effects related to the lifestyle, such as excessive drinking and the liver and heart problems that go along with that, eating excessively buttery and salty foods on a regular basis, poor skin, baggy eyes, and an overly thin or overly large figure.

Then there are the nightmares. Every server that I've asked about it says they have nightmares. It comes with the stress of working and performing at a high level in a busy restaurant and waiting on people who have very lofty expectations due to the high price of the product being served. (Though I never got nightmares at Doraku. Doraku wasn't that kind of a place.)

I believe I had my first nightmare after about a week of being on the floor waiting tables at Birch. I dreamt it after my first really busy night of having a full section. The nightmare went something like this.

At first it was a night like any other. The pace was at first slow and comfortable, and the tables were seated at a manageable rate. The food came out course by course in a timely fashion, which, as anyone who has worked in a restaurant knows, is a collaborative effort between the kitchen and the server. It is the servers' responsibility to course things out properly on the order tickets and to "fire course two" and "fire course three" at the right time, usually via the computer system. The timing of firing is important. If it's busy, then the courses need to be fired well enough in advance so that the cooks have time to plate the orders among all the other tickets they are working. If it's not busy, then the food is going to come up much more quickly, so the server must wait until the right time to fire the course so that the entrée doesn't come out immediately after the salad. The timing of this is very difficult to master, and requires the server take into account such things as who is working the sauté station and who is working the grill station, and do I need to give, say, Joe on sauté an extra two minutes to work this ticket. The average person would be surprised as to how much this sort of timing affects a guest's dining experience. Some guests want to take their time with their meal. It's a server's job to recognize this and pace accordingly. Other people go out to a restaurant more to eat than to socialize, and they eat their food when it comes and are ready for the next round within a few minutes. The sooner a server can recognize this, the better.

Anyway, the night was going smoothly. The food was coming out on time and it was looking good. I was clipping along at a rapid pace, taking tables as they came in, giving my spiel, bringing drinks and wine. Then, as I was opening a bottle of wine for a table, which, when done properly, takes about two minutes to present, cut the foil, pull the cork, and pour, I sensed someone behind me glaring at me. I turned to glance at them as I began to screw into the cork and I saw four pairs of detestable eyes looking right at me. The four people were sitting at a table in my section and I hadn't seen them before. Immediately I was horrified at the thought that they might have been sitting there for a long time, perhaps five minutes, without my noticing. They were looking at me as if they expect me to stop opening the bottle of wine and come over to their table and give them my undying attention. Of course I've learned that you can't make eye contact with any person at any table other than the one you're talking to. It can only cause trouble. Maybe I learned that by having nightmares about it.

I rushed to get the bottle of wine open and the wine poured, all the while I sensed the hateful eyes on me. By accident I poured some wine on a lady's sweater. That was the beginning of the horrific events of my dream. I panicked and couldn't think of what to do about the spilt wine. I've only heard that red wine stains are permanent. The lady told me in a condescending way that it was fine, and she shooed me off, telling me she would take care of it, to just leave the wine on the table and they would pour the rest of it.

I turned away from the spilt wine table and began to approach the hateful eyes table. Everything else ceased to be important. The gentleman in charge—it was two couples about twice my age—explained to me, with a loathsome drawl and a hissing lisp, that I hadn't even come over to greet them in half an hour. I tried to apologize, but they were not having it. I thought back and tried to recall the last time I saw the table empty, and I decided they couldn't have been sitting for more than five minutes. No matter, they were upset. I had to respect their perception. I tried my best to continue on in a professional manner, talking about the restaurant. They seemed disgusted by my presentation of the menu. They told me they heard such good things about Birch that they didn't expect such poor service. "I have been all over the world," one of the men said, "and I have eaten at many different restaurants in many different hotels, and never have I seen a menu like this. How can you serve *this* to your guests?" he asked, making an unclear indication to the menu.

By then I was sweating. I could feel the heat from the fireplace. My heart was racing and I was having trouble thinking clearly. "How awful they are!" I thought. I had to fight the urge to lash out at them and tell them just how rude I thought they were, how impatient, how unkind. But my position prohibits it. It is part of a server's duty, something every server must learn. I once heard it said that serving is God's work, that Jesus was a servant. In my dream I tried to remind myself of the goodness of this ancient task by recalling a biblical tale of servitude. I was kneeling at the sand-caked feet of a vagabond, and the vagabond was ungrateful. I hastened to clean the sand off of his feet as he scowled. There were others like him, scowling and spitting on me, kicking sand and dirt. How little they understood as I prostrated before them.

Suddenly the spilt wine table was irate. I could hear them talking about me amongst themselves, and then with other guests. When I walked into the dining room from the kitchen, they were jeering me. Some offered sarcastic applause at my reappearance. They said things like, "We thought you were lost!" How rude the sarcasm of those kinds of remarks! The lady with the wine on her sweater failed to camouflage the look of disgust on her face. I tried to be kind.

One of the women at the hateful eyes table said "finally" when I brought over their drink orders. They sucked the booze down as if they were famished, dying of thirst, their spiteful eyes showing a new kind of hateful vigor bolstered by the alcohol. Then their appetizers arrived at the table. They reached at the food with their hands and brought it to their mouths like monkeys. Some of it fell down and landed on their fat bellies. The largest of them inclined himself toward me, expecting me to wipe the food off of him, and I did so.

I realized then that I had forgotten to fire the next course on the spilt wine table. I wanted so badly to walk away from the hateful eyes table and leave the restaurant altogether, but I couldn't. "Is it the sense of duty, the want of money that keeps me here?" I asked myself. I decided it was the money. This could never be anyone's real duty. What a cruel vocation it would be.

Their salad course was delayed. Tables were talking about how awful the service was. I tried to get the hateful eyes table's order but they ignored me, or they couldn't hear my voice over the sound of their own gluttonous gorging. I tried to leave the table when a woman said, with her mouth full of food, "hey, hey, hey wait a second!" and as I looked over crumbs were falling from her mouth. "We're ready to order!" she said, but they weren't ready. It was another five minutes before I finally got their order from them, and the spilt wine table still hadn't received their salads.

I wanted to die. "No, I'd rather just leave than die." But I didn't want to leave, either. "How do I face this crowd? I've never been so ashamed." I began to have an anxiety attack.

I woke up. I was short of breath and my heart was racing, and I realized I was alone in my bed. I had just had the first nightmare I'd had since childhood, and only the second real panic attack of my life. Within seconds, upon realizing it was only a dream, I began to calm down and relief washed over me. The relief came as a shock at first, like a bucket of ice water being dumped over my head on a painfully hot day.

iii.

Love Alters Not

Some weeks later I was at the Industrial Borough Farmers Market, which was held on Thursday mornings and afternoons in Richard Park. It was a nice day, the type of warm sunny afternoon that precedes a cool summer night in the absence of cloud cover. I took Ernie with me. I walked him on the end of a long leash. Ernie liked to explore his surroundings when I took him on walks and I was never one to deny him. What would be his life without getting the chance to sniff about? The desire came from deep within his genetic makeup, a part of his DNA that could be found in identical form in his ancestor the wolf. I liked to watch him express this part of himself. He would sniff at the female dogs we encountered, pee on everything to assert his dominance and claim his territory, pull on the leash in pursuit of a squirrel or a bird, and do all sorts of other things that didn't really have much relevance to his cozy modern dog life.

There were many others who had the same idea as I did that day. There were a lot of people with their dogs at the farmers market. Ernie had a way of strutting and showing off. I had never had him neutered, which I know is fairly uncommon. Most dog owners will have their pets fixed if they have no intention of breeding them. Since Ernie spent most of his time indoors I didn't really see the point. I had him trained well enough and he usually behaved when I was gone from the apartment. Maybe if I had adopted him as a very young pup I would have done it, but since he was a bit older when I got him, I decided not to put him through it.

Ernie was going about his normal business of sniffing basically everything. I was hoping he wouldn't pee on any of the dozens of tables and booths that were set up. Since there weren't any trees or fire hydrants in the market, I didn't think it was likely for Ernie to pee, but one never knew. Whenever he saw a female, Ernie circled around her, which made a mess of the leashes, and the other dog walker and I would make small talk as we tried to untangle the leashes and keep Ernie from humping the lass. It can be interesting to watch the interplay between a male and a female dog and wonder whether they would make good pups. If the female hasn't been spayed, it can be especially fascinating. Dogs are social animals with their own rather complex way of deciding whom to mate with. Interactions between males, while fascinating, can also be nerve-wracking as the two dogs will often engage in dominance displays and even go so far as to try to mount one another. Different strokes, I guess, though we humans aren't much different.

I was feeling some apples, giving each one a gentle squeeze to determine its ripeness. I liked to buy under ripe apples because I liked to eat some of them that way and others I liked to let ripen before eating. Any over-ripe apples would go in the juicer if I didn't get around to eating them in time. I was talking to the farmer, a burly t-shirt and jean wearing man with a mesh baseball cap on his bald head, about how the season had been so far. The season had been good, he said, the weather was as good as you could want it and the crop was robust. His only complaint was that the big orchards were doing just as well. "Not so many customers are gonna come 'round my place knowin' there's a big orchard farm just outside uh town. Farmers market's the only place to share my apples. Organic Empire, that's what you got there, but I guess I ain't exactly certified organic, just have my word on it." I liked Empire apples. I believed the farmer that they were organic; they looked it. There were irregularities in size and color, noticeable blemishes that some people might consider imperfections. I enjoyed eating organic crops. Organically and naturally grown plants were more resilient; they yielded healthier fruit, which made for more healthful eating. I imagined he lost many apples to pests and disease. "Glad folks like you come 'round here. Keeps folks like me earnin' a livin'." I picked out six of the Empire apples and put them in a paper bag. I asked the farmer how much I owed him. "Three dollars," he said. I gave him a five and said, "All set." I looked around. "We appreciate the work you put into providing food for us and bringing it to market." The farmer reached out his hand. "Name's Glen," he said. I took his paw. It was large and plump, as I had always imagined a farmer's hand to be, with dirt stained permanently into the cracks in his leathery skin. "My farm's just west of town. Called Wind Mill Orchard. Come by any time you like. Make a day of it. Bring your pal here," he said, gesturing at Ernie, "he'd have a lot of room to run around." I thanked him for the invite, told him I'd be happy to stop by some time. I thanked him again.

As I started to walk away from Glen's table I felt Ernie pull on the leash. I turned back to look at him. He was standing tall with his tail and his ears erect, looking at something. Or perhaps he picked up on a familiar smell in the air. I followed his line of sight through the small crowd of people. I looked at Glen. "He sees somethin'," he said, and he began to scan the crowd with me. I didn't see anything I recognized. I decided to give him some slack and let him lead. He had his nose up in the air and was tugging the leash, pulling me away from the apple stand. At once he picked up on a trail and put his nose to the pavement, followed it for a moment, and then lost it again. He started to get excited. He was panting now, his tongue out, pulling hard and raising up on his hind legs. I continued to glance up and look through the crowd. People were moving out of our way as they saw us coming. I held on to the bag of apples as I myself began to trot in the direction Ernie pulled. Suddenly Ernie slowed down and put his nose to the pavement again. "What is it, buddy?" I asked him, playing along with his excitement. I didn't expect anything. Moments like these I liked to surrender myself to the whimsy of the dog and follow his lead. Ernie walked in a zigzag for some paces, and then turned and went in between two tables towards the adjacent row of produce stands. The farmers and vendors looked at me strangely. I did a half smile, half nod combo that was sufficient apology for what I thought to be the most minor of offenses. I was just following my dog.

I watched Ernie. Before I had a chance to pull back on the leash he was leaping up to put his paws on a skirted ass. His excitement told me he had found what he was looking for, but I was thoroughly embarrassed. I began to blush as the girl turned around to face me. "I'm sorry," I said, "Damn dog."

As she turned I was expecting just about anything besides what I saw. Standing before me was none other than Ellery Montgomery Jones, wearing a spaghetti-strapped lavender sundress and a derby hat that shaded the appalled look on her face.

I felt my heart sink. I was ashamed. All I could think was how badly I wanted to flee from the situation. The look on Ellery's face turned to anger and then, worse, pity. I would have preferred anything to pity.

I felt like I was living a nightmare. I had resigned myself to the fact that I would never have to experience the feeling of despair that I would feel if I ever talked with Ellery again. Why I did this, I don't know, we lived but miles away from one another. I was bound to run into her sometime. I should have been prepared.

It seemed like a full minute passed, though that can't have been the case. I couldn't think of anything to say. I was paralyzed. When Ellery finally spoke it was softly, with sympathy, as if she understood how and why a shameful man would be willing to insult her in such a heinous way as I had, as if she had convinced herself there was nothing I could say about her to tarnish her image and debase her status. I sensed all these things, and it drove me crazy because I sincerely felt she had betrayed me. I noticed she was with a man. "Hey, stranger," she said to me.

For the record, I don't like when people say, "hey, stranger." It always sounds like an indictment, as if the person being addressed, i.e. myself, Lado, had failed to maintain the level of friendship we had previously attained. As if the first one to say, "hey, stranger," in this case Ellery, had the right to feel ignored, and the other was to feel neglectful. In reality, any time anyone ever said "hey, stranger," it was because neither party was doing a very good job of maintaining friendship.

"I don't remember Ernie being so frisky," she said, bending over to pet him as he jumped up at her with his tongue out. I could tell that she didn't really know what to say. *Should we talk about what happened?* I thought to myself. It could have been an opportunity to make amends. But there were complexities. If I apologized, I would be falling right into her pity trap. And who was the man she was with? She was with a man. I looked at him, and Ellery must have followed my eyes. "My brother," she said. He was talking with a vendor about honey. Ellery made no effort to introduce me to him. I could tell Ellery was growing uncomfortable. Ernie seemed to be enjoying the chance encounter the most out of all of us.

"So, how have you been?" I asked her. She said she was doing "very well." She had taken to exercising regularly, she said. Then she tried to guilt trip me. "I was pretty depressed for a while," she said, "and I found that riding my bike around town and doing yoga made me feel better. I can't believe how long I had gone ignoring important things like strength and flexibility. Do you know how important it is to be flexible?"

"Yea, totally," I said. "I try to do yoga every day. Usually, like, right when I wake up and then sometimes later in the evening, too. It makes me feel so good." I thought back to the last time I had done yoga. *How many months ago was it?* I wondered, distracting myself from the real-life conversation I was having with Ellery. It must have been three months since I had done yoga last, I decided.

"You look pretty good," Ellery said. "Keep doing yoga, you'll just see more and more results." Ah, the dreaded backhanded compliment. I felt it's sting and ache. Just then Ellery's brother walked over to us. He had a jar of honey. He gave Ernie an unkind look and kept his distance. He was obviously not a dog person. "Are you ready to go?" he asked Ellery. "I guess so," she replied, "I was just catching up with an old friend."

"I really wouldn't want to keep you," I said. "Were you just leaving?"

"Yeah, I think we were. It was so good to see you," she said to me. We held eyes for a moment.

"I know, thanks to Ernie here picking up your scent," I said. The words sounded strange as I replayed them in my head. I patted Ernie and forced a smile.

"Well, it was good to see you." As I spoke I realized that, in a way, it really was good to see her. I wondered if I should try to hug her. Ellery giggled awkwardly.

"Hey," she said suddenly, "do you still talk to Manny? I miss him."

I told her I saw him here and there but that I hadn't been socializing much. Just working and writing. "I started working at a restaurant downtown, Birch American Brasserie. I'm a server there." She said she had heard of it, but downtown? She didn't see me as a downtown kind of guy. "I have to feed myself somehow," I said. It felt strange having to explain the need to support myself. As if I had a choice in the matter. I was an aspiring writer with no marketable job skills aside from the restaurant biz, and I had no one else to support me. I had to take whatever I could get. But, as we stood there, I noticed that Ellery appeared impressed by me. The Lado standing in front of her speaking humbly about a real job was not the same Lado that called her a slut to her face and had been so selfish.

Her brother spoke, "I'll be in the car." He walked away and I eyed him. He was tall and quite athletic looking. By the way the situation had transpired I reasoned that he hadn't heard about me, or at least he didn't make the connection, otherwise he may have tried to beat me up. He pulled his phone out of his pocket and looked at it. I turned back to Ellery.

"You guys drove here?" I asked her. "Don't you live pretty close by?"

"Yea, we both do. My brother doesn't like to walk, though."

"That's a shame, it's quite a day for it." I felt more at ease with her brother gone from the scenario. "Anyway, I don't want to keep you. Take care, Ellery." And I made a move to walk away. Ellery stopped me.

"Wait," she said, "aren't you going to say you're sorry?"

"Excuse me?" I said.

"You can't even apologize to my face?"

I was enraged, but I tried not to let on that I was. I thought about punching her. *That would be ridiculous if I punched her*, I thought. *But awesome.* I thought about the near-mythical act of "being the bigger man" versus the legendary act of punching the face of a chick who had it coming. Was being a bigger man even applicable in this situation?

"Listen," I said, in a serious and almost disciplinary tone that surprised even myself, "I'm not going to say I'm sorry because at the time I meant what I said. You would have the right to hate me or be mad at me if it wasn't true. You're the one who, fucking, slept with my neighbor when you and me were basically seeing each other."

"We were not! We never even talked about that. I spent the night at your place once."

"Yea. Like two days before you slept with Kyle."

"It was not two days!"

"Whatever, three maybe. The point is I had feelings for you and you did something that hurt me."

"Come on, man, I didn't do anything wrong," she said.

I, for one, was ready for the argument to be over, but then Ellery continued, "Oh, and just so you know, I fucked him again after that. Many times. Right across the hall from you. And I sucked his dick on the back porch. In broad daylight. The whole time I hoped you would walk out and see me doing it."

"Big surprise there. Finally admitting it. I bet you told everyone I called you a slut but this is the first time you're actually admitting to being one."

"Oh my god! I can't believe you. You need to stop. First of all, I haven't told anyone what transpired between you and me, besides my brother, of course, and my mom and my best friend, because I tell them everything…"

"Your brother? You told your brother. The Cro-Magnon who couldn't figure out how much two jars of honey cost and refuses to walk anywhere?"

"Yeah, and he would kick your ass. He's twice the man you are…"

"Twice the man, yet half a brain…"

"…and he doesn't treat women like shit the way you do. Fuck you, man. You know, I thought you were a halfway decent guy. I really did. I was even starting to like you a little. And you'd be attractive enough if you'd shave that stupid adolescent fuzzy shit off your face and maybe hit the gym once in a while instead of hitting the bar night and day. And from what I've been hearing about you from O'keefe you're pretty reckless about your sexual health. I heard you don't even use condoms! What the fuck, why don't you use condoms? I'm glad I didn't let you have sex with me that night. God, what a mistake that would have been…"

Right then I kissed her. I dropped my bag of apples, let go of Ernie's leash, grabbed Ellery's face with both hands, and kissed her right on the mouth. She was squirming and moaning and trying to push me away, but I held on to her tightly. I heard someone nearby gasp. I managed to put my tongue between her lips and into her mouth, and Ellery promptly bit it hard until it bled, and then I let go of her and pulled away. She spit out a bit of my blood onto the ground and screamed. The look on her face gave me satisfaction. I could feel the blood rushing into my mouth and I spat a mouthful of it into a nearby trashcan as Ellery stormed off.

I decided I should leave before the situation became worse, and I looked up from the garbage can and noticed that a few people had been watching. They looked horrified. I could feel the warm, viscous blood and saliva running down my chin, my blood and water leaving me. "I'm okay," I said with a bit of a gurgle, "thank you. Just a bit of a quarrel. I'll be fine. We'll be fine."

I picked up Ernie's leash and the bag of apples and the two apples that had spilled out onto the pavement, and I rushed home. The whole way back to my apartment I was spitting out blood. When I got inside I walked right into the bathroom and stuck my tongue out and looked at it in the mirror. It didn't look as bad as the blood had made it seem.

Though it was deeply cut, it would heal. But it was a nasty bite from a nasty person and needed to be cleaned out. I pulled a fifth of Jameson from my liquor cabinet and swigged it, swishing it around in my mouth and throughout the wound. A white-hot burning as the alcohol pierced into the cut and I shut my eyes and winced. I spat out into the sink and saw the whisky and the blood and the bits of flesh swirl down the drain.

I poured a tall glass of Jameson, straight up, and I made sure Ernie's bowl had water in it, and I sat down at my desk and began to write.

I submitted five different short stories to five different literary journals. All five of the submissions were for competitions, the winners of which won prize money and were subsequently published, so I tried to submit my best work to the journals that were offering the greatest financial reward. I was making good money at Birch, but it wasn't always consistent, and, besides, how could a little extra money be a bad thing? I had written one story in an inspired, alcohol-fueled frenzy, and the end result, after a few sober revisions, I considered my best work. I didn't want to send it out to every competition because I didn't want to win the least prestigious award with my best story and have to tell the journal offering the most prestigious award that I would be publishing said story and was no longer in contention for their award. In retrospect, I was a bit overconfident because, being a previously unpublished, no-name author, I wasn't likely to get anything published anywhere, even if it was my best work. Like any other industry, "it's all about who you know." Pardon my cliché. And my improper use of the word "who." It should be "whom" you know. I didn't coin the saying.

The deadlines for submission to the writing contests were within three weeks of each other. The rejection letters all came within the same general window of time as I submitted to them, about three weeks. I thought I had mentally prepared myself for the possibility of being rejected by all of the journals, but I wasn't as adequately prepared as I thought. I took the rejection pretty hard. I had been saving my work until I thought it was ready to be released into the world, only to be rejected outright. To me it had been a very difficult step in my career just to send work out. I calculated my moves and expected results, but like I said, I tried to prepare myself for the worst. *There are a lot of good writers out there just like me*, I thought, *and I'm sure these contests are very competitive. Besides, the reading for these awards is entirely subjective. Who knows what these people want to see? There are trends in the literary world just like everything else. How do I know what today's editor, today's reader, wants? I could be behind on the times.*

Or I could be ahead of my time. I had always imagined, for an artist, that to be ahead of one's time was at once both the best possible thing and the worst possible thing. To be ahead of one's time is to lay claim to a level of future prestige that many artists of the day only dream of and never come close to attaining, but, during his life, the artist ahead of his time is never going to be able to appreciate the luxury that accompanies the prestige. Yes, his posterity, if there is any, will reap the benefits of his growing posthumous acclaim, but the artist himself will suffer great anguish during his lifetime. He will be underappreciated and will remain unknown by the masses and he certainly won't make a good living of his art throughout his days. The amount of mental anguish and strain on family life and personal relationships is inexplicable. It is another one of my nightmares.

There is also the very real possibility that my work is simply no good. I want so badly to be good but does that mean that I am good? It does not stand to reason that good work follows definitely from hard work. *I should just try something else*, I think to myself sometimes, *because I will never be as good as I imagine myself to be*. It is these thoughts and feelings that creep up in my subconscious and even into my conscious brain between moments of confidence. It is an unhealthy fluctuation of self-esteem. I am on a bridge to somewhere but the rest of the bridge hasn't been built yet and I don't know if the bridge will even lead me anywhere if I continue to follow it. But every morning I wake up and this is what I ask myself: *What can I write about today?*

I say to myself, and I try to convince myself, that I am right in my aspirations and that my work, one day, will pay off. I can only hope that I will be able to experience the benefit of this firsthand. To speak with an enthusiastic reader of my writing is one of my most precious dreams. *I will not take success, when it comes, for granted!* I shout in my own mind, addressing the cosmological forces that determine things like success. And there I am thinking, perhaps erroneously, that the cosmos reward honesty and integrity. One would like to think so, or else why be honest? Why even try to be good? Yes, I would like to shake the hand of a smiling fan, to read to a crowd, to sign a copy of my little book of unimportant stories.

At the heart of the act of writing is the belief that what one has to say is valuable to someone else, to at least one other person. It is an act of communication. But the process itself has to offer some sort of inherent reward for the writer. Or else why put words together at all?

I'm going to introduce a new term to the language of this composition. It's a simple fusion of two different words that, when put together, take on a more specific meaning than they have as separate words. The term is "artist-writer." "Artist" comes first in the hyphenation because it is primary in the identification of the persona. It suggests many character traits that are associated with artists— contemplative, serious, sensitive, intense, emotional, gifted, creative, tormented, poor, struggling, "starving," and, *ipso facto*, skilled in some artistic endeavor—and, at the same time, with the addition of the word "writer," narrows down the classification by defining the person as one who writes as the principal means of artistic expression. That is the key. The artist-writer feels a need to create, as artists do, and chooses the written word as his means. This is how I have come to view myself, for better or for worse.

The reader may be wondering how this aside pertains to the story it is interrupting. Well, first, I was going on about writing. Writing, and being a writer, or at least being the kind of writer I am, is a large component of my identity. What is characterization but a very detailed kind of identification? It's important to this story how I identify myself, since that determines precisely how the reader will or will not be able to identify with me as the main character. It is, I am sure, obvious at this point that the subject of sex, with its pleasures, its blunders and its miscues, is also an important part of my story. Indeed, I am telling the story of a young, twenty-something man in today's world, who has the sexual appetite of your average bull. To me and to most, sex is as important as breathing.

Therefore, one nice thing I've noticed about possessing the temperament and living the lifestyle of an artist-writer is that there is a certain type of person for whom the artist-writer is an irresistible sex magnet. As the reader is probably very well aware by now, my sexual inclinations lead me toward women. In this case—that is, for picking up women—it helps to be successful as an artist-writer and to have money and/or a high level of fame and respect (not to say that I have those things). The most attractive women of the category that are interested in artist-writers are going to be drawn, as with most other categories, to the alphas. The alpha artist-writer produces great work that is well respected by critics and well received by the masses, and is therefore well compensated from a monetary standpoint. Such an artist-writer will have greater access to teaching jobs at universities and guest lecturing opportunities at home and abroad. Many great male writers come to mind. There are probably a great many artist-writer lovers who would gush over an artist-writer like that. However, success and acclaim mean only so much to a woman if, when it comes right down to the way the artist-writer behaves and interacts in public and in the bedroom, the artist-writer cannot live up to what the woman expects of a man.

Along comes the raw, brutish artist-writer, guided by his instincts and passions, following his own path, making his own decisions. Perhaps excelling at writing to no greater extent than he excelled at wrestling and football when he was in high school, but which extent is fairly great. He has been popular with women and girls from a young age and has a vast pool to pick from, since he is physically developed and probably has a good-sized cock. Having a good-sized cock is important; I don't care what anybody else says. He can win women over with his intrigue, his offbeat demeanor and witticisms as well as with feats of pure, brute strength. He probably likes to drink and sometimes fight other men while he's drunk. To him it's fun, and to women it's sexy for a man like him to succumb to his base desires; it hints at what he's capable of doing, how far he's willing to go to please and protect a woman. If such an artist-writer is able to delicately toe the line between living a life dedicated to the fulfillment of sexual desire and living a life committed to artistic integrity and producing great work, then his work will be read and will be relevant for a long time, and throughout his life he will have many adventures and great pleasure.

There is also the tormented genius artist-writer. Because he feels like there is no one else like him, the tormented genius is solitary, alone, and experiencing mental, emotional, and perhaps physical anguish on a daily basis for the majority of his life. He is perhaps too unsure of himself to ever publish anything or even to try, fearing rejection and ridicule. He is of poor health and hygiene and forgoes personal care for the sake of art. Often he is a drug abuser; he self-medicates as a way to ease his troubled mind. (This is not a judgment. Find one person on Earth who abuses *nothing at all* and you will have found yourself a bore.)

The point of introducing all of these archetypes is to show the reader everything that I am and everything that I am not, because while I am at once all of these things, I am also none of them. I am my own separate beast entirely. At times, I am more victim to the forces of nature than I am an autonomous, thinking human being. While my aspirations are to be fully and greatly human and to support at once the human cause and the cause of all other things that exist, I often fail.

One morning I woke up with most of my clothes on from the night before. I didn't remember getting into bed. I had been up late writing and drinking and had probably been drunk when I decided I must sleep.

I felt a pressure in my bladder and a bit of pain in my kidneys. I got up to take a piss. When my stream weakened and eventually stopped I felt the need to piss some more, but nothing else came, and I tugged and shook my penis to try to get it all out. Eventually the feeling went away. I washed my hands, and I stuck my tongue out and looked at it in the mirror. It was mostly healed, though by the looks of it, I thought, there might be a permanent scar.

Since the incident with Ellery, I had been rather ashamed, enough not to socialize outside the Birch network. It was mostly just to and from work I went.

Things had grown rather awkward between Maria and me. I couldn't exactly determine in what way or why, but they certainly were awkward. I thought she might be afraid that I would tell people what happened between us, which, I knew, could damage her reputation beyond repair. I didn't know whether to be offended by this notion or not. I tried not to let it bother me. We just never really talked about it. But I still sensed that, barring all consequences and cultural differences, she would want to get it on with me and we would have a great chemistry. When we were near to each other and talking, I could feel a force pulling us closer and closer together, and her effort to escape the force was like pulling two magnets apart. I guess sometimes it's necessary.

In a restaurant things change quickly, people are moody, alliances and friendships falter, and faces come and go at a very high rate of turnover—the highest of any industry. Within a month or two of my getting hired onto the Birch staff, George put in his two weeks. He was moving away with his boyfriend and would be pursuing a master's degree full-time. Jack and Clara were having relationship issues, which, between a supervisor and employee, are pretty serious and can cause many disruptions at work, but at the same time can be quite comical from an outsider's perspective. Jack was convinced that Clara was sleeping with someone else. She would go out of town frequently to a cabin in the northern part of the state, saying she just needed to get away from the restaurant for a spell, and she became increasingly protective of her privacy and wouldn't leave her phone out in the open. This all from what Jack told me during the whole debacle. I myself felt bad for Jack more than anything else because he was my friend and he was the reason I had a job there. I think most people, when it came down to it, took Jack's side over Clara's, but that's not to say that Clara didn't have a few supporters. Jennifer seemed to side with Clara, though some time later, while Jack was in a vulnerable state, Jennifer would offer herself to him.

Aside from Jennifer, though, and maybe one or two of the servers, everyone was on board with Team Jack. Barry, who never liked Clara much, was Team Jack all the way. George, right before he left, made it clear that he felt bad for Jack and hoped that he got the better of Clara when it was all said and done. Maria seemed like she didn't want to get involved but she was definitely on Jack's side more than Clara's. And Chef Rob, whom Clara, for her own strange reasons, had been trying to get ousted from his executive chef position on many occasions, absolutely hated Clara, and he was entirely and outspokenly Team Jack and said he would do everything in his power to make sure Clara did not gain the upper-hand over Jack because of her supervisory position. Again, much of this I knew from talking with Jack over beers.

This may seem trivial and petty, but a restaurant operates as a delicately complex interconnection of social relationships, and anything to upset the balance and tip the scale can change things dramatically. The scheduling, the seating, and the allocation of big-money parties are, ultimately, controlled by the front of the house manager. An abuse of power based on personal bias can make working in a restaurant miserable for the people who are on the manager's shit list.

Alas, I began to learn this firsthand. As Jack's close friend and confidante, it was no secret that I was on his side throughout his personal disentanglement with Clara, our boss. It would be hard for an honest person not to be on Jack's side, considering the evidence, which seemed to indicate that Clara was cheating on him. I began to pay attention to the scheduling, which, I admit, favored me when I first started at Birch. I would get nights off when I wanted them and I didn't have to work the waste-of-time shifts or the double shifts that other new servers had to work to earn their stripes. But then I noticed a shift in Clara's favoritism. The new hires, whom Clara had hand-selected and some of whom were Clara's personal friends, were getting special treatment, and more senior servers like Maria and I were getting lousy shifts and were being expected to get to work early and work doubles. The worst was when I noticed that the new hires were getting large private parties with expensive minimums and twenty percent added gratuity—

the types of parties that, alone, make for a three hundred dollar night—and I was getting put in the shitty section.

But there wasn't much I could do about it. Clara was in cahoots with everyone on up in the corporate infrastructure. They all adored her. Who would believe me if I wrote a letter to the higher-ups and asked that the problem be addressed? From a corporate standpoint, I don't think she would be allowed to work in a restaurant while she was sleeping with one of her employees, but, also from a corporate standpoint, I didn't think corporate would take any action against her unless I could provide some valid evidence. It was a difficult conundrum. Jack, for whom working under Clara had become most miserable, would have been able to provide evidence, but he was too good of a guy to be vindictive in that way. I did my best to stay out of it and hoped that I could remain marginally unaffected by it financially. As the reader knows, things weren't going so well for me at that time, and in a way I was clinging to work as a sort of salvation, taking a serious professional approach to a job that I had theretofore considered "in-addition-to" writing.

Things began to look up for me in an unexpected way. After probably two whole months of not hearing from her, Ryan called me one afternoon and told me she needed to see me. She sounded distressed.

"He knows," she said to me when we met up at Manny's. "He called me out." I asked her how Steve discovered that she had cheated on him. "I don't know how he found out. I know for sure he has been looking through my phone recently. I never saved your number because I didn't want any evidence of our affair in my contacts list, but I never went through and deleted our text messages. He must have read the one where I asked you to come meet me, the last time we…" Ryan paused, "…the last time we had sex."

"Is he really good at remembering dates?" I asked her, thinking that no one was *that* good at remembering dates. "Because he maybe could have remembered what day that was." I thought back and tried to remember what the date was when we last fucked. I thought it was about two months ago, but I couldn't be exactly sure of the date. We hadn't even spoken with each other since then.

"Did you deny it?" I asked her. "I mean, how can he really be sure? There isn't much evidence to it."

"I thought about denying it, but then I thought about how I'm not really even happy with him anyway. Like, there isn't even much of a relationship anymore to try and save. So I kind of broke down, and I told him I slept with someone else."

"Did you tell him it was me?"

"No. He doesn't know that. I don't get the feeling he cares to know. I just said that it was somebody I met through somebody at work. The less he actually knows the better. I just want to get this over with."

"Get what over with. The break up?"

"Well, yea, we're going to call the engagement off."

I thought briefly about what it meant to break up an engagement. In quick succession the following images presented themselves in my imagination—a man on a knee, a ring, the faces of anonymous friends and family, presents wrapped in boxes, a church, a cake, a DJ, a beach, Ryan's belly round and plump, a baby, Ryan's bare breast feeding an infant—and I stopped myself there. In a way, I was glad that Ryan wouldn't be marrying him. I didn't like Steve based on what I knew about him, while I did, in fact, like Ryan, or at least I liked having sex with her. I didn't think Steve deserved her. Part of me even wanted her for myself. If I thought about it any more I would start to experience a little adrenaline rush as I sensed the possibility of having to compete with another man to secure what I subconsciously believed to have rightly won.

"So what are you going to do? Are you going to move out?" I asked her.

"Yea, I guess I need to start looking for a new place. I hate moving though! The whole process—deciding what neighborhood I want to live in and figuring out how much I can afford to pay, then finding a place that I can actually afford that isn't going to have a cockroach infestation and give me tuberculosis, because god knows I can't afford much on my own, and then I have to start thinking about, 'Do I need to get a real job?' because waitressing and bartending, even though the money's good, isn't really going to get me anywhere, in the long run, and I'll eventually reach a plateau, career-wise, and have to either accept my fate as a lifetime restaurant worker, maybe find a management job—in a restaurant—and take a temporary pay cut, or I can jump ship as soon as possible and find an entry level job in another field, which is hard as fuck to find in this town lately, and probably also take a pay cut or take an unpaid internship, in which case I certainly can't afford to get my own place right now. And then what do I do? I can't move back in with my parents. They'll probably disown me if they find out I'm breaking off my engagement with a successful, charming man because I cheated on him with..." Ryan trailed off.

"With what?" I asked her. I was interested in what she was going to say, and I was ready to defend myself.

"Well, just somebody that, you know, somebody else that doesn't..."

"A 'writer.' Is that what you were going to say? A deadbeat writer with no money and a lifetime of despair ahead of him. Were you going to say something like that?"

"No, no, what? I think you're great. I was not going to say that. Where is this coming from? I told you, I read your writing, and I liked it."

"Yes, which you should not have done. That stuff is private."

"Well it's good anyway, and you should try to publish it. You should have your name out there."

"But until then I'm a deadbeat and a bum…"

"With lots of talent."

"…and no one in their right mind would approve of their daughter sleeping with a bum…"

"They wouldn't approve of me sleeping with *anyone* besides the person I am engaged to, who happens to be a fucking asshole, mind you, and is probably cheating on me…"

"…because all a parent really wants is to see their children happy and safe, and bums, most definitely, don't make their children happy and safe…"

"…and what's done is done, and I can't change what happened, and I don't regret it, and my parents can go fuck themselves for all I care…"

"…you may as well move in with the cockroaches."

"…because I'd be happier with you anyway."

I had taken to staring down at the table and my drink and not looking at Ryan as I deprecated myself in front of her. I was feeling horrible. There was a reason I hadn't dated much. I knew where I came from, and I knew what it meant to others, in this our American culture that is so focused on success and money and good breeding and clearly delineated life trajectories, when they learned I was an orphan who was once homeless who drank too much and aspired to be a writer. "You mean, like, writing *books*? Well, good luck to you." It was always worse than the words appear to be on paper, because they are universally accompanied by raised eyebrows and an insincere smile, and, sometimes, the person physically *winces*, as if simply the thought of me being a failed writer, and all the suffering that goes along with it, whatever that may be to them, is enough to cause them bodily pain.

"Go fuck yourself," I said to her.

"No," Ryan said.

"You don't know me."

"I want to know you."

"Or where I come from, and what it is I want to do with my life."

"But I believe it when you say it! That's just it, Lado. You don't see it yourself, but some of us do. You're pretty convincing when you say, 'I'm a writer,' and especially since I've read your stuff I know that. It's *really* good. I mean, it could use work, but some of it really shines. But that's the thing; writing is a craft that you can continually develop. You never really peak. You just get better. And you work so hard at it. You've written a lot for someone your age. Granted, you haven't published it, but still, it's a lot."

"Are you some kind of expert? Listen, I felt really humiliated just then by what you said, and it got me thinking about just where do I stand. I mean, maybe I should be thinking like you are, like I need to be thinking about getting the hell out of restaurants and get a decent job so that people will take me seriously, that way I can get on with my life and abandon this stupid pipe dream of being a successful author. Even you, on some level, are aware of it. I mean look at you. You're a beautiful, sexy girl. You could have whoever you want, and on some level you're ashamed of the fact that you slept with me, or that you allowed yourself to be seduced by me, however it is that you look at it, I don't know, and that's in spite of the fact that you actually like my writing and you think it could get me somewhere."

"Stop it. Just stop it, now. Take me home."

"What?"

"Take me home. I want to get out of here. We're arguing and everyone in here is looking at us."

I looked around. It was true that everyone was looking at us, but there weren't that many people in the bar, and I recognized half of them, so I didn't feel so bad. I saw Manny behind the bar with his hands behind his back, bartender proper, looking at me with a shit-eating grin on his face. I turned back to Ryan. "You want me to take you back to your place?"

"I thought I made it pretty clear that I don't have my own place, and Steve's place is not an option," Ryan said, after which we were both silent for a moment. "I want you to take me back to your place."

"Do you really think that's such a good idea?" I asked her. No sooner did the words come out of my mouth than I felt surprised at myself for second-guessing the idea.

"Do we need to pay our tab?" she asked me, and looked over at Manny, who immediately waved her off with a slight shake of his head, as if to say, "Don't worry about it."

"I don't have a car. Did you drive here?" I asked her.

"No, I walked," Ryan said. "Your place isn't that far from here. Let's just walk."

So we walked back to my place. We didn't do much talking. It was as if the argument had evaporated. Despite not having a clear resolution, we simply weren't arguing anymore, and we didn't have anything else to say to each other.

When we got back to my place, I felt something unexpected. It felt like Ryan belonged there. As if I was more at home in my own place with Ryan there. Ernie jumped up at her and woofed, and Ryan grabbed his paws and did a little dance number with him. I asked her whether she wanted anything to drink, and she said no, she was fine. Normally I would reach right for a beer in this situation, upon walking in the door, but I decided I shouldn't.

But then, after a brief internal deliberation, I decided that I would do what I wanted and have a beer. I grabbed one and snapped it open. "Going right for a beer, eh?" Ryan said, in passing. She was flipping through my coffee table book of Spanish food and wine.

I looked at my watch, more for the gesture of it than to know what time it was, and then I looked at Ryan to see how she was reacting. She wasn't really reacting at all. I sat down next to her on the couch and set my beer down on a coaster on the coffee table. I looked at the page she was reading. It was a page with a recipe for *esturión adobado*, a deep-fried sturgeon appetizer with lime mayo sauce and suggested wine pairings, which I had dog-eared.

Some time later, though not much later, Ryan seemed to suddenly have a very urgent matter come to mind. She took out her smart phone and looked at something, I don't know what, and then told me she had almost forgotten that she had to be somewhere. We had been having a relaxing time, or so I thought. I felt at ease with her there. "Will you come back?" I asked her. She said, "Of course, I won't be long." She stood up to leave and I stood and walked with her to the door. "Be right back," she said, and I decided to give her a kiss. I kissed her on the mouth. She put her hands on my face and held them there momentarily, making for a slightly more passionate kiss than I had intended, but I liked it. She left.

I sat back down and opened another beer and began to look through the Spanish cookbook. I wasn't much in the mood for reading so I mostly just flipped through and looked at the pictures while I savored my beverage, felt the sensation of the carbonation on my tongue. I allowed my thoughts to wander. That morning I had slept in until about noon, woken up, and spent a considerable amount of time on the internet, and while Ryan was gone, I went back to the computer with the intention of writing, only to get distracted by web pages. I didn't get anything worthwhile accomplished, just mostly read about trivial things and absorbed useless information. That's the trap of the internet. Using the internet without intention makes for a whole lot of time wasted. Looking for nothing, anything, garbage is found.

My brain felt mushy. A day spent watching porn and reading bullshit makes you feel that way. And the beers seemed to be dimming my neural circuitry. I used to think that, while too much was never a good thing, alcohol helped me function in some ways, arousing the passions and freeing my inhibitions, making me a bit more comfortable to enjoy social situations than I otherwise would without alcohol. But lately I felt that it was only hurting, or at least holding me back from something. I wondered whether the great alcoholic writers experienced these lulls or whether they had some superhuman tolerance to the substance, perhaps a symbiotic relationship among the yeast and the grain and the author and his ink.

About an hour of mushy brain thinking and my door buzz signaled Ryan's return. I buzzed her up and flipped the deadbolt. I opened the door slightly and let it swing open for her to enter. I watched her as she came in, bringing a draft with her that blew her hair up over her face, and she smiled like a little girl. She laughed and she turned on the balls of her feet as she shut the door behind her.

"Sorry, I just had to take care of something," she said right away.

"Is it taken care of, then?" I asked.

"Yes, it's taken care of."

"Can I ask what it was that you had to take care of?"

"Yes, but I'd rather not say, if that's all right."

"That's all right," I said. She couldn't have gone far. She wasn't gone very long. She didn't have anything with her that she had newly acquired. She was dressed the same and appeared to be the same on the surface as when she had left, but there was something perceptibly different about her. The innocence that she had lost in recent months she seemed to have somehow regained, and the brightness of her spirit warmed my living room.

We lay on the couch. I had put on some music and lit candles in the living room and in the kitchen, opened a bottle of wine. An Amarone that, with Jack's encouragement, I had stolen from Clara's office. It was one of the sample bottles from the distributor that servers and bartenders were, ideally, to taste and to sell. She probably didn't even realize it was gone.

Spooning, I had my arm draped over her, my hand resting on the couch. We were speaking in low tones just above the breaking point of a whisper, almost so that I could feel the breath of Ryan's words as much as I could hear the hum of her smallest voice. I put my hand fully on her tits, one and then the other, and I squeezed them gently. "Not tonight," she said, taking my hand by the wrist and setting it just below her breast, on her stomach. I went down further just below her shirt and felt up it, felt the warmth of her soft belly. "I just had my period," she said to me, turning her head to look at me. I craned my head and kissed her.

"Well then you're good to go," I said. She turned away into the couch cushion. By studying the rear profile of her cheek I could tell she was smiling, which was a good sign because, after saying it, I realized that telling a woman when she was and wasn't "good to go" was potentially upsetting.

"I would want you during your period, even. I'm okay with that," I said.

"But it's so messy," she said.

"Only a little. Besides, it's natural. I mean, if you don't want to, it's fine, I'm just saying, if you did still want to, even if you were on your period, I would want you." I was trying to furnish my words with enough romanticism and warm tonality so as to sound like a true gentleman. I guess that's what a gentleman is, a man who is adept at tenderly and genteelly going about the satisfaction of desire, so that he doesn't sound selfish. All the better if he actually believes he is unselfish.

"I just want you to hold me," she said. "I've had a lot going on lately, and it feels good when you hold me."

I held her for a while. I closed my eyes, even began to drift off. My thoughts began to appear in my imagination with the vividness of a dream, the way thoughts do in the in-between of being awake and dreaming, and suddenly I imagined myself tongue kissing Ellery, only this time it was a welcome kiss. She had her hands tied behind her back, and was submitting to me. And then it was not I, but Ryan kissing Ellery, and I was watching from a casual distance. Ellery was on her knees, hands tied behind her still, and Ryan was naked with her nipples erect and pointing and she pressed herself against Ellery's mouth so that Ellery had her tongue deep inside her.

I got hard against Ryan's ass. Evidently she felt it and we both kind of woke up, and she sucked in a quick breath. As she exhaled she half whispered, half moaned my name, "Lado." She reached down and between her legs and felt for me. I felt up her shirt and grabbed at her breasts and touched her neck, and we began to kiss each other. She unbuttoned her jeans and I shoved them down past her ass and took her from behind, right on the couch, both of us still hovering somewhere between full consciousness and sleep.

When it was done we lay on the couch, silently, about ten minutes, until I wanted a cigarette. I asked Ryan if she wanted a cigarette and she said, "No, thanks."

"Well do you want to get some fresh air at least while I go outside and smoke?"

"I guess. Is it cold?"

"I don't think so." I looked out the window and tried to ascertain the temperature visually. The sun was down. It looked comfortable but the last few nights had been cool. I got up and found a blanket. "Here," I said, handing it to Ryan. Her eyes were closed and she opened them sleepily, then sat up and took the blanket. She wrapped it around herself over her shoulders and then crossed her arms across her body and wore it like a cape. She stood up that way; I kissed her and ran my hand over her hair to smooth it down. She left her jeans unbuttoned as we walked through my bedroom and out onto the back porch, where I lit up a cigarette and we leaned against the rail and into the cool summer night, my arm around her, the faint half moon and my cigarette the only light in my little back alley corner of Valmesta.

The following afternoon, at Birch, was one of the first times I realized I sounded like a robot while I was introducing myself to my tables. While I was giving my spiel I fell into the habit of routine and monotony, which, for my guests, makes getting waited on feel more like a trip to the Secretary of State than to a happening restaurant. I noticed it as I talked to my first table of the night. In the months since I had started working at Birch, I learned to avoid any sort of nervousness that would happen as a healthy and natural response to talking to a group of complete and total strangers, but in that particular circumstance I became at once completely self-conscious and almost unaware of what I was saying. It was like an out-of-body experience. There was a sort-of autopilot type of response going on, the likes of which people are probably familiar with as pertaining to everyday tasks like driving a car and grocery shopping, which are simple and don't require much higher-level thinking, so that one can carry on said tasks and simultaneously think about other things. But people are probably not so familiar with that autopilot experience regarding social interaction, and it was very disconcerting. I was speaking from a sense of routine, but I wasn't really aware of what I was saying; I could hear the words that were coming out of my mouth as if I were an observer, but I wasn't really paying attention to them. I was paying more attention to the dangly earrings one of the girls at the table was sporting and the amount of grey in a gentleman's moustache—was his moustache twenty-five percent grey? thirty-five percent?—so that I wasn't really aware of what I was saying. This feeling persisted until the end of my spiel, which, at Birch, was usually around two or three minutes, and at the end of it, I wasn't sure how to gauge the guests' reactions because I didn't quite know what I had said. Did I even ask them if they wanted anything to drink? No one at the table made a move to speak up. They all four just stared at me, the gentleman with the partially grey moustache looked at me with his mouth open, and the girl with the dangly earrings finally swiveled her head around the table and asked, "Do we want anything to drink?" As I watched her earrings dangle about I felt relief for her taking charge of the situation. No one said anything. She swung her head back around to me. "I think we need a few more minutes," she said.

"Take your time," I said, and forced a smile. "If you need anything, my name is Lado," I said as I walked away. The rest of them turned to face me and gave me a strange look. I must have already said my name, I thought. They were as weirded out by my spiel as I was.

I tried to recover from the experience and make the best of it, both for my tip's sake and for the sake of the people dining at my table. But from that moment forth things were different for me at Birch. I realized that the honeymoon was over, that even though, at the start, I enjoyed the job and the learning experience, I had grown tired of it. My inner desire for frequent change—and often drastic change, at that—had manifested itself as a desire to beat feet out of Birch and out of the restaurant industry, especially as certain truths about the way the industry operates had come to light for me. Besides, my feet and back were hurting me from the hours and hours of scuttling around on the hardwood floors, and the psychological stress of working in the industry was taking its toll.

All of this would have been tolerable for me if not for one thing—my writing continued to suffer. I didn't have very much time to write and, when I did, I usually had lots of other things on my mind to contend with, the mundane daily activities that keep my life moving forward, like feeding myself, making sure I had enough rent money, and getting my rocks off. Truth be told, I was doing okay. For instance, I always had just enough money to make rent and pay my bills, I found time to shop for groceries and do my laundry, and, after Ryan officially separated from her douche bag fiancé, she spent a lot of time, and basically lived, at my place. Ergo, I was getting my rocks off on a regular basis with a pretty hot chick that I liked and who actually liked me. What can I say? We clicked.

The reader may be wondering whether I felt any sort of distrust in the relationship because of the fact that Ryan and I had begun to see each other while she was engaged, and, therefore, my first impression of her was that of an unfaithful fiancé. Did I know she had it in her to be unfaithful? Yes. But no, I didn't feel distrustful. And it wasn't just naïveté that kept me from distrust.

During the early stages, trust wasn't a relevant concern. We were just getting to know each other and were enjoying a wellspring of sex and orgasms at a frequency that I had never, and I can't imagine Ryan had ever, experienced before. All during the dog days of a Valmesta summer, which, by the way, was one of the hottest on record in a town that is known for having hot, humid summers to offset its cold, dry winters. Ryan and I were in the beginning stage of a supremely passionate affair, and I think we both knew right away that our physical connection was the bud of a voluptuous romantic blossom, so there was an unspoken understanding that we were doing it exclusively. Even if there was concern that one or the other of us was getting it in with someone else, between work and ravishingly fucking each other's brains out, neither one of us had the time to give anyone else so much as a French kiss or a hand job. No, for us, trust wouldn't become an issue until around the three-month mark, which is the first of many make or break points in a relationship, and Ryan and I simply weren't there yet.

Anyway, I didn't get any good writing done because working full-time hours in food service zapped me of the energy necessary to work, and any and all of my free time was being spent with Ryan. And spending time with Ryan was also costing me money in the form of lunches and dinners and coffee for two and so on and so forth, so in turn I had to work more shifts at Birch in order to afford all that. I became even more tired and worn out from work and less and less motivated to write. It was obvious to me that from an outsider's perspective I was much more of a food and beverage industry professional than a writing professional. That thought repulsed me.

But what could I do? That's America. If I didn't earn a living I would end up homeless again. A homeless college graduate that just can't hack it in the real world, or that the real world simply doesn't have a spot for. And it's so very difficult for an artist to reach such heights as to be supported by the free market and, thus, make a living by making art. As artists we are expected to find ways to support ourselves until we get to that point, and many artists don't.

Then came the day when he showed up at Birch. He was sitting at the bar when I noticed him looking at me. Most of the people sitting at the bar had their eyes on their food or on the television, or they were having a conversation, but he was alone and he was watching me. How did he know which one I was? He probably looked me up on Facebook to get an idea of what I looked like. Even though my photos were for "Friends only," he still could have seen a thumbnail of my profile picture, enough to get the gist of what I looked like.

He didn't order any food. He was drinking beer. A couple of times he got up, presumably to go to the bathroom. He would come back and order another beer and glare at me when I came over to the service end of the bar. Once I looked him right in the eye, and he continued to glare. I held it for a few seconds right up until the point at which it would be inappropriate to stare at someone while I was working, i.e., the point at which my manager, if she saw me, would have just cause to reprimand me for staring at someone. I walked away. The next time I returned to the bar he was gone. I didn't think too much of it.

He must have known the employees' entrance to the restaurant was on the western side of the building. I clocked out at ten seventeen pm and exited through the employee door and descended into the alleyway. It was dark and had been raining lightly. I stopped to let a woman on a motor scooter pass by before I stepped down, and by then I had a cigarette between my lips and I smelled the wetness around me. Wet concrete, wet garbage and wet something else I couldn't quite place. I heard him before I saw him.

"You must be Lado," the man's voice said. The sound of it came from over my right shoulder, against the wall of the adjacent building. I turned to face the voice and saw him step into the middle of the alley where I could see him a little. He was right on me. Now that he was standing up I could tell he was taller than me and he appeared strong enough to manage his height powerfully and skillfully. Probably in his early thirties. I hadn't noticed in the bar earlier, but the man was wearing a white button down shirt and tie, the shirt unbuttoned at the top and the sleeves rolled up to his elbow. He wore slacks and dress shoes. He looked like the kind of guy who played college ball, barely skating by in all of his classes, enjoying a full ride. He was perfect for mid-level management in a corporate setting. Easy for the more intellectually-gifted higher ups to piss on, but a naturally gifted pisser-on himself.

I sensed his anger and unpredictability right away. A look in his eye told me he was high on something, maybe coke. I had no idea what he was capable of. *Was that why he had been disappearing to the bathroom?* I thought he might be high on something else that I wasn't personally familiar with, and, if that were the case, he was even more unpredictable.

"And who are you?" I asked him. I was trying to remain calm. In retrospect I should have been reaching for something blunt or sharp. While, I sensed that he had bad intentions, at the time I thought I could talk my way out of it.

"You don't remember me? I believe we've met before."

I said nothing.

"I'm Steve, nice to meet you." An insane smile.

Should I run? Behind me, the alley leads out into a side street. In the other direction, beyond Steve, is the main thoroughfare where my bike is locked. But I couldn't outrun him, even if I could get past him. Even if I got to my bike on the avenue he would get to me before I could unlock it, mount it, and ride off.

I noticed I still had a cigarette in my mouth. I began checking my pockets one by one, looking for a light. "I got it," Steve said. He was already approaching me. As he lit my cigarette, I awed at the size of his hands and the breadth of his shoulders. After it was lit, I took a step back to try to regain some of my personal space. Steve seemed happy enough to let me have it. He began pacing a little side to side, jittering somewhat. His dress shoes glistened as they reflected the light of a streetlamp.

"I wanted to forgive you," he said. "And I can forgive Ryan. I mean I'm no saint!" He said this with his arms out and his palms open and his torso bent forward. He smiled that crazy smile again. His teeth were unnaturally white. "I fucked around. A lot. I admit it. I guess she had a right to do the same. And honestly, you can fucking have her, her and all of her fucking messed up in the head issues. You can try playing shrink for her and see how you like it. It's fucking exhausting. Exhausting! I hope that works out for you and I hope it works out for you when you find out she's bored with you and she's found another dick to suck."

I wanted to interject. "Honestly, Steve, I only have good intentions." *He said we met before, but when?* My cigarette was halfway gone already.

"Whatever, man, that's fine. Like I said. You can have her. Can I ask, is it good?"

What the fuck kind of question is that? I could tell he wanted me to answer the question. He seemed genuinely interested. "Yeah, it's good."

Steve looked away. "To be honest I could tell right away, because for me it was never really that good to begin with, but the times we were together after that—and yes, there was some overlap—the times we were together after I could tell she was fucking someone else. It was like fucking a dead fish." The man was unraveling in the alleyway. "Do you have a cigarette?" he said. I gave him a cigarette, and he lit it up. "She's fucking mental."

"Look, Steve, the first time it happened, I didn't even know. I never wanted to disrespect you. Man to man. Believe me, I know, it's just not cool to do that with another man's girl."

"Shut up."

I shut up. He took a drag on his smoke.

"I told you, you can have her."

Then why is this conversation not over?

"I forgive you both for that. And if you're going to be with her, you better take good care of her, because she deserves that much, even though she's nuts. But you know what man? You fucking with Ellery? I can't let that go."

My mind went blank.

"She's family," he said. "You're too fucking stupid to make the connection, aren't you?"

And then I remembered the afternoon at the farmer's market, and I remembered him being there. In my mind's eye I could see him walking away to pull the car around for Ellery; right before I pulled the most bonehead stunt of my life and Ellery nearly bit my tongue off. Steve was Ellery's brother *and* Ryan's ex.

"I'm going to hurt you really bad," he said to me, "but look at it this way: You're lucky I don't fucking kill you."

It all happened in a matter of seconds. He was coming at me and I tried to get a firm footing while I put my arms up to try and push him away or block any blows. He didn't waste any time and he threw a haymaker right away that I ducked. I discarded my bag and tried to regain my footing. He came at me again and I threw a right hook, hoping to land it on his nose, but he was fast and my fist grazed the side of his head. I may have gotten his ear a bit.

He got me in a hold not unlike a Muay Thai clinch. He tried to knee me, but I saw it coming and managed to wiggle out of it and push him away as he drove his knee upward. He was off-balance momentarily so I went at him, but he grabbed my shirt at the shoulders and used my momentum to spin me around and throw me. I almost went down but I caught myself with my hands and popped back up, but he already had a wallop coming and socked me in the left eye with that big haymaker. I felt the bones above my eye crack, and for that brief moment that I was falling to the ground, I couldn't see a thing. Just a blinding white light like a bolt of lightning.

"Get up," he said. I got up. I could feel blood gushing from by eyebrow and I was blind in my left eye. At the time I couldn't tell if it was because of the blood or because my eye had been ruined. My glasses were off my face. I glanced around and saw them on the ground a whole ten feet away. To the best of my half-blind, near-sighted ability to ascertain, they appeared broken.

I said something like, "My glasses…"

"Shut up," he said. "You know what? Maybe I will fucking kill you."

While I was pleading with him, "I can't fucking see!" he was coming at me again. I put my hands up in front of my face, feigning total blindness, and he must have fallen for it. He was lackadaisical as he stepped up to me. I gave him a quick right to the mouth, which drew some blood. He stepped back and spat it out. He ran right at me and form-tackled me like a linebacker. I got his head in a grip under my left arm and on the way down I did my best to drive his head into the ground. I felt his head hit the ground first but then it was my back hitting harder than I had anticipated, and it knocked the wind out of me. I panicked, I gasped for air, and, looking up with my good eye, I saw my attacker with a murderous look to him and a big open gash across his forehead. He socked me again on my left cheek, and the pain of it put me out.

I came to briefly in the ambulance. Clara was in the ambulance with me, and so was an EMT. Clara looked nervous. I tried to talk but my mouth was swollen and had gauze in it. The EMT urged me to try to relax. "You've lost some blood," he said, "we're going to get you hooked up to an IV." I looked at Clara and she tried to smile. She shook her head as if to say, "don't try to talk."

"Should I call someone?" she asked. I saw she was holding on to my phone. I nodded. She pulled up a list of recent phone calls, on which list Ryan appeared number one. I nodded again and Clara dialed Ryan. "Hello, may I please speak with Ryan? Oh, this is Ryan. Okay. I'm calling because Lado's been hurt…"

I was in and out of consciousness all the way to the hospital, and they must have drugged me up right away because I don't really remember anything after being carried out of the ambulance and then wheeled in the emergency room on a stretcher.

I would come to find out later, as told to me by Clara and Ryan, who had shown up mid-surgery, that after I blacked out in the alley Steve pummeled my face a bit and cracked two ribs with a heavy stomp to my midsection. Barry and Allison, one of the bartenders at Birch, stepped outside into the alley to have a relaxing smoke break and saw what Barry described as, "Some big ass white boy trying to kill Lado, stomping and screaming like a lunatic." Apparently Steve was so pre-occupied that he couldn't hear Barry running up on him from behind. Barry, who had himself been a linebacker during his college days, tackled Steve and took him down hard while Allison ran inside to get help. According to Barry, Steve seemed "fucked up on something" and was putting up a good struggle, but Barry kept him pinned.

Clara called the cops and Chef Jon and Chef Robert came outside to help keep Steve under control. They brought some very sharp kitchen knives outside with them, though that part wasn't in the official police report. As the story goes, Steve, who after being taken into custody was found to have cocaine and amphetamines in his system, broke down when he saw me lying there bloody and unconscious. He thought he had killed me. He cried like a baby, I'm told.

The cops arrived within minutes and the ambulance shortly thereafter. They took Steve away while the EMTs took my vitals and determined that I was in critical condition, whereupon I remained unconscious throughout most of the EMS ride. I was finally fully coming to as I was being rushed into an operating room at the nearest hospital when suddenly I was put out with a heavy dose of anesthetic.

I underwent a surgical procedure late that night whereby doctors replaced the broken bone pieces of skull above my left eye with a bone graft from a cadaver. Thank you donor, and thank you modern medicine.

I somehow didn't loose any teeth and my ribs would mend themselves, the doctors said. I just had to rest and let my body do the healing. They kept me there for three days. In a way it wasn't so bad getting pampered by the nurses and physician's assistants. Ryan was with me when she didn't have to work. She tried to apologize, but I said it wasn't her fault. I assured her it wasn't worth it to discuss it further. "What an asshole," she said, and it was the last we talked about it. She trailed off, lost focus, and was distant for a time before coming back to the present. She looked at me with a warm smile and tears in her eyes. I hoped we would never have to talk about Steve or even mention his existence ever again.

Clara and Jack visited me together. Clara let me know that even though the incident didn't actually happen on work property, and even though I hadn't been there for a year yet and hadn't had a chance to sign up for health insurance, the company would be taking care of my medical bills. She wasn't sure exactly how yet, but she assured me that I needn't worry. Maybe they wanted to avoid a lawsuit at all costs. Perhaps they were partially liable for having served Steve alcohol? I don't know. I was glad not to have to pay.

Jack stayed for a while after Clara left. He confided in me that their relationship wasn't going so well and that he was tired of working in the kitchen. He said he needed a change.

If I quit though, I'm going to go out in style. I'm going to do something big. I'm going to say, 'Fuck you, fuck you, and fuck you. I'm out,' and I'll have something really badass that I do."

"What are you going to do?" Ryan said.

"I don't know. But it will be epic."

My nurse, Candice, came in and told Jack and Ryan that I needed my rest. I told the nurse I was fine, but she insisted.

"No, really, I'm fine," I said. I wanted to say how much I was enjoying it. Ryan, it seemed, was now officially my girlfriend, and it was nice having Jack around. All my life

I had very few close relationships, and the ones I did have I struggled to maintain. I wanted them to stay with me, to laugh with them. That's the healing I really wanted. I wanted the love of a woman, the love of a friend. Something profound had happened. "I almost died!" I wanted to cry out. I had *almost died*, but I was alive. And can anything else more profoundly change a life? Nothing but the nearness to that which frightens us the most can so positively enact change. That was the first day of my life. And my friend gave me a hug and my girlfriend, a kiss, and together they went to get lunch.

A man came in and introduced himself. "I'm Doctor Nealand. I'm the one who fixed you up the other night.""I saw your name on the paperwork," I said. I held out my hand. "Lado. Nice to meet you."

"I was wondering how you pronounced it." He shook my hand. His hand was cold, soft, smooth, and clean. He wore all blue scrubs and his surgeon's mask was hanging casually around his neck. He wore a sterile cap over what appeared to be a balding scalp. "What is the origin of that name?"

"It's Czech. I was born there actually. In a small village outside Prague."

"I see. How old are you now again?"

"Twenty-four."

"A different place now than it was then. I was there—in Prague—once in the eighties. I was mostly just passing through. I spent the summer before med school traveling Europe. Beautiful castles in Czechoslovakia. And my wife and I visited, let's see, two summers ago now. But politically, my gosh, almost feels like two totally different countries, wouldn't you say?"

"I haven't been back in a long time."

"Uh huh. Your name short for something?"

"Ladislav."

"That's nice. What are you doing these days?"

"I'm a server."

"Where at?"

"A place called Birch American Brasserie."

"Oh, yea, I've been there. Good food."

"Thanks."

By then I noticed the surgeon was examining my face. He was admiring his work, studying the specific region of my face where he had carried out his craft.

"You plan to do that for the rest of your life?"

"Well, I'm a writer."

The surgeon looked in my eyes. "Oh. What do you write?"

"Fiction, mostly, but everything really."

"Good for you. Gotta do what you love."

I wondered to myself whether I really loved writing. I rarely thought about it in relation to that thing, love. I decided I did love it.

"You got roughed up pretty bad, I'd say," said the surgeon.

"Yea, I'd say so."

"Did you know the guy?"

"Sort of. He knew me."

"Money or girl got in between you two?"

"Girl."

"Often the case. The one I've seen coming and going?"

I nodded. "Her name's Ryan."

"At least you get to keep the girl. She must be something special to make a man go chimp style on you like that."

"She really is."

"Rest up. When are you out of here?"

"Tomorrow."

"Best of luck to you."

With that he was gone. Out into the hallway and gliding toward some other room where perhaps a patient in dire need of his special skills was waiting for him.

I always wondered what people like that meant when they said, "best of luck," or "good luck." And by people like that I mean people in a higher-level social status than myself. "Good luck" always carried with it some amount of condescension coming from doctors, businessmen, and other people's parents. It's like saying, "I hope that plan works out for you even though it's dumb as hell," without really saying that. Why is it that certain goals carry with them a negative stigma? I could have told that surgeon, decades ago, while he was traveling throughout Europe and trying to get it in with some strange before committing to a lifetime of medicine, medicine, and more medicine that he was foolish for wanting to be a surgeon. I could have said, "You're crazy for doing that! Do you have any idea how much you're going to be set back in loans? Have you thought about how much malpractice insurance is going to cost you? Besides, you aren't even going to be a real surgeon for like ten more years." But no one says that to someone aspiring to be a surgeon, someone whom society basically considers a hero, which by itself wouldn't infuriate me, but because those types of things are said to me it makes me downright fucking pissed off that people who aspire to high-status positions don't have to put up with this doubt that is imposed on them by individuals and society at large. What the fuck? Is it because a surgeon's work is so *honorable* compared to that of a measly writer? I heard once that surgeons are all hardcore alcoholics. Something about the stress of the job or whatever. I don't know if that's true or not, but if it is, that's not part of the image of being a surgeon. Whereas that is totally one hundred percent the image many people have of writers. Once, when I told someone I wanted to be a writer, he said, "So you're going to drink, drink some more, teach high school English, and maybe write some books until you become depressed and kill yourself. Is that what you're telling me?" I can see the light bulb go off in their head. "Ah, but of course, a tormented and self-destructive soul is the young artist." The reaction often seems just short of turning to a spouse and asking, "Honey, should we give him some money?"

I was going crazy in the hospital. No cigarettes and no booze. When Clara called to check up on me I told her I wanted to get out, but she insisted I follow the doctors' instructions. Since her company was paying my medical bills, I couldn't disagree. I texted Jack and asked him to bring me some Jameson. He and Ryan came back from lunch together and Ryan was already giving me an admonishing glare. They had brought me an order of tacos *al pastor* from the nearby Mexican restaurant—I've always had a soft spot for tacos *al pastor*—and I started digging in.

"You must be feeling better," Ryan said.

"I feel great. I really want to get out of here, but I just talked to Clara and she said I need to follow doctor's orders or I won't be covered."

"Who's the doctor?" Jack asked.

"I don't know. Is it the surgeon?"

"They probably have someone who is officially overseeing your file. I don't think you've met that doctor," Ryan said.

"Have you met him?" I asked

"I think it's a her," she said.

"Is she hot? I dig hot doctors." Jack said.

"Have you met her?" I asked.

"No. Just calm down."

"Well don't you think she should be communicating these things to me?"

"You're not paying the bills," Ryan said.

"But it's my health we're concerned about here,"

"I'll work on Clara, see if I can get you out of here. How are the tacos?"

I nodded voraciously, brows furrowed, digging in. "I don't even want to fucking swallow they're so good," I said. Jack gave a swift glance down the hallway and pulled out from inside a paper bag a pint of something I hadn't seen before. He held it gently as if it were a sacred relic, something precious enough not to even squeeze.

"Jameson is my shit," I said.

"That overseas shit isn't good for shit but polishing your shoes. This here is your new shit."

"Should I take offense to that?" I asked.

"Please. You're American as hell. And it's no offense. Jameson is the best shoe polish there is."

"What is it?"

"You really can't wait until you're out?" Ryan said.

"It's Bulleitt. A true frontier bourbon. Bourbon is where it's at. If you're going to be committed to being an American, you'll drink American whiskey." Jack removed the plastic and the cork, handed me the bottle. "Try it."

I took a sip. All those years I had been drinking Jameson and for what? Jack was right. Bourbon is where it's at. The toffee, the oak, the sweet apricot. I tasted it and then I took another, longer pull. I handed it back to Jack.

Jack took a big swig and flashed his teeth like an ape and said ahh. "It's sweet but you can feel the heat of it." He extended the bottle to Ryan. She rolled her eyes and turned to look at me. "Try it," I said, "it's good."

Ryan looked toward the door but no one was watching. "This is really stupid," she said, "I feel like I'm going to get in trouble."

"If you don't take it and drink it we are going to get in trouble," Jack said. "Here."

Ryan took the pint bottle of Bulleitt, which looked like an oversized glass medicinal container. It had the name of the bourbon raised up on the surface of the glass and you could feel it raised. I had never seen her look so mischievous. She was happy to be so. She could barely drink through her half-moon grin. She coughed a little and held her sleeve to her mouth to wipe at her lips. "It burns," she said and made a face, "but it's really fucking good." We passed the afternoon that way, taking scoops of a pint of bourbon in my hospital room.

After leaving the hospital I mostly just sat around for several days. My ribs hurt when I lay, when I sat, when I stood up, and when I walked or moved in any way. Basically, they hurt all the time. I studied myself in the mirror. I seemed to be getting simultaneously skinnier and fatter with atrophy. Above my left eye was a visible scar that would be there for life. I wondered what my mother would think if she could see her son like this, all these years later.

I took Vicodin, smoked cigarettes, read novels to pass the time. I became fascinated by violence, in awe of it. I was entranced by Cormac McCarthy's *Blood Meridian* for a whole four days, and when I finished I went back and revisited its lurid scenes.

I took naps and sipped on pours from a fifth of Bulleitt I had picked up from the liquor store on the way home from the hospital. Jack and I texted back and forth with regularity, him needing the confidence of a friend amid the deluge of relational and professional bedlam he found himself in. Clara was certainly cheating on him, he said. She had gone "out of town" for the weekend and didn't feel the need to provide Jack with the details of it.

Once he called me drunk and insane. He was going to track her down and slash her tires, kill the man she was with. "Even if you *could* track her down," I began.

"I can," he said.

"How?"

"One time she told me her password for her e-mail account. Don't ask. She wanted me to go in there and send something to her so that she could have it at the office. I just happened to remember it. Turns out, it's the very same password she uses for Facebook, her Apple account, everything."

I asked him what he was getting at.

"Well I have an iPhone, and Clara has an iPhone, and I have the 'Find iPhone' app that shows me the GPS location of exactly where the fucking skank is hiding. I just put in her Apple ID and password." It was an app designed for someone who lost their iPhone; by using the app on another user's iPhone, one could locate their own.

"No fucking way. You know where she is?"

"Damn right." Jack told me where she was. He was surprisingly lucid for being so drunk. "Tell me it's not a good idea to go there and fuck that guy up right now."

"That's a terrible idea, Jack."

"She's fucking probably sucking his dick right now," Jack said.

"You can't think about that or you'll drive yourself crazy. Where are you?"

Jack groaned and hiccupped and swore and told me he had to get off the phone. I called him right back but it went straight to voicemail. When I texted him an hour later he didn't respond.

I met up with Manny at the Juice Joint. He had heard about me getting roughed up outside of Birch. I expected Manny to comment on my appearance, since every person I ran into asked me about the scar or at least looked at it, but he didn't. I should have known he wouldn't. A scar didn't change me, nor was it a reason for a man like Manny to judge me or anybody else. He was more interested in my women troubles, as he called them. Last I had talked with Manny I was in a bad way over my falling out with Ellery, after I called her that detestable word, but before I called her that word again and she nearly bit my tongue off.

"That almost feels like ancient history to me now," I said. "I ran into her once at the farmers market. Actually I saw her with her brother, who is the guy that put me in the hospital."

"Ellery's brother? I heard it was some other girl's fiancé."

"Yea, same guy."

"You mean to tell me you insulted the guy's sister, and then you started doing the rumba with his fiancé?"

I nodded. "Unbeknownst to me at the time,"

Manny laughed. "No wonder he went crazy and tried to kill you," he said. "You're lucky to be alive, amigo."

I was lucky to be alive. I was blessed. I felt the power of life, a sense that something about living is important and meaningful, and one has to cherish life and live well. I felt it for real, not just the idea of it. But unlike an idea, it was difficult to communicate this feeling, especially to a guy like Manny, a musician. He understood music better than words, and he didn't talk much. Even when he and I would have conversations it was mostly I doing the talking. He was a mysterious guy, and I mean that in the truest, most complimentary way. I mean he was on a level that most other people weren't on. His music seemed to come from somewhere else; it was a different language, strange symbols representing alien things. People who heard it couldn't so much understand it as they could interpret it. At the very least you felt where he was coming from.

I think that's where he and I bonded. I felt—I still feel—that I had something to say. I had a message to communicate that was abstract and mystical, but I had chosen words as my medium of conveyance. Words, which are abstractions themselves, in order to signify abstract notions. How was I to handle the paradox? I respected and looked up to Manny as an artist who had sorted this dilemma out in his own way. He had discovered a way to communicate.

Not only was he an expert at his craft, he had also made a good living at it. He found a way to thrive as an artist in the world, which was something I was struggling mightily with. I guess that sort of sums up our talks. He listening, I inquiring, probing, trying to absorb some of his essence. I would talk for a while, and then he would go up and play a set, and I would watch. I had to listen to his music. It was our trade off. I gave him words, and he gave me music.

Manny was a high-status artist. A business owner and a talented musician, he was respected throughout the community. But I knew better than to ask him direct questions about how he achieved the position he had attained. That wasn't how the mentor-mentee relationship worked. It took patience and commitment, and it couldn't be forced. I watched Manny as he licked a cigarette paper and deftly finished the rolling procedure. "What's this new girl's name?" he asked me.

"Ryan," I said. Manny raised his eyebrows and looked away like he was thinking hard about something. He lit his cigarette and got up and walked toward the stage. Looking around I noticed that the dark place had filled up. It was a lively crowd considering everyone was sitting down and quiet. There was a palpable, positive energy. I felt good.

Manny took up his guitar and began picking at the strings and tuning his instrument.

Things at Birch were, at times, frustrating, even though all of the front of the house staff were making good money, myself included. It helped to be part of a hotel, because even on nights where there was very little walk-in business, there were still hotel guests that dined in the restaurant. Many of them were regulars, some of them foreign. I got along with the foreigners very well. Not only am I an immigrant, I am also a curious and open-minded individual who dreams of traveling the world. Meeting people from faraway places is a way to learn about those places and share culture.

Of the foreigners who came in regularly, none was a more loyal patron and none was more liked by our staff than a German engineer named Heilgar. Heilgar once told a bartender at Birch that his name had its Germanic roots in something like "happy," which was funny because Heilgar was as stoic as they come and didn't express very much emotion, positive or negative. He was neither a jolly gentleman nor a sour curmudgeon; he simply didn't have a wide emotional range. He did have a wonderful sense of humor, albeit a very dry one. His jokes were usually of the self-deprecating variety.

Heilgar would be standing outside the door of the restaurant at six thirty am when the opening server unlocked the door. He wouldn't even need to order because he ate the same thing every day, and everyone who worked the breakfast shift knew his order by heart. Smoked salmon lox with a toasted bagel, coffee, and orange juice. He was quiet in the mornings and would be in and out of the restaurant by quarter to seven, when off to work he went. Just the right amount of money would be left on the table, enough to cover the food and drink and a generous tip for the server.

He worked for a German engineering company with an office in Valmesta. What he did for a living involved designing and manufacturing products for automobiles. While much of the industrial business had died down in Valmesta, some survived the market crash, and those businesses that survived sourced their products form German and Japanese companies; ergo, we hosted a lot of German and Japanese businessmen in the hotel.

Heilgar was very skilled with his hands. One night, while he was sitting at the bar at Birch, I saw him transform a foil candy wrapper into a very thin piece of sheet metal in a matter of seconds. When I showed some astonishment he shrugged and said, "This is what I do for a living."

He would stay at the office late and return to the hotel around eight o'clock. He was usually in the restaurant by nine pm. He ate a sausage with potatoes and drank beer until it was time to go to sleep. By eleven he was usually quite drunk, but he never showed it. On weekends he would wait for the employees to finish cleaning, and he would have a drink with us, Heilgar already five or six beers deep. A few times he came out with the staff for an after hours session at The Rabbit Hole. But no matter what, even if he had stayed out with us until three in the morning and passed out blotto, he would be at the door at six thirty for salmon lox.

He was a creature of habit to the extreme, mechanical in his routines. He and I were polar opposites in that regard. I like change. I go to bed and get up at seemingly random hours, I eat random things at random times throughout the day—whenever I feel hungry—and I choose my drink, my vice, and, until I met Ryan, my women by seemingly random measures. Or so they probably appear to be random to a creature of habit like Heilgar. In reality such choices are anything but random. Instead, they are deliberate reflections of my mood, my state of mind and level of curiosity at any given time. I was usually looking for something new and exotic, an unfamiliar flavor, a new drug, a theretofore-unfelt orgasm.

Then again, maybe the only thing that separated Heilgar and me was age. Perhaps when I am his age—Heilgar was almost fifty—I will be more set in my ways than I am now.

Heilgar had been traveling to Valmesta from Germany for extended stays at our hotel for over twenty-seven years. By extended stays I mean eleven out of the twelve months of the year. Therefore it was longer than I had been alive that Heilgar had been living in Valmesta. This seemed to blow both of our minds. He couldn't believe that he had been in Valmesta long enough that people who were born after his arrival were now his drinking buddies, and I couldn't believe that he had spent all those years in a hotel.

I never saw his room. To my knowledge, no one, not even the cleaning staff, ever saw his room. He didn't require housekeeping.

When Heilgar announced his impending departure, everyone was surprised. He had become like a permanent fixture in the grand scheme of the restaurant. Part of the well-oiled machine that we were. He was one of the few dependable routines in our hectic lives. We even had a "Reserved" place card that we would set down at his spot at the bar at eight o'clock sharp because we knew he would be there.

His departure was about two months off when he made the announcement. I speak for the rest of the staff when I say that I had mixed feelings about his leaving. On the one hand I was glad for him, because it was becoming obvious that Heilgar wasn't altogether happy with his situation. Downsizing and poor management decisions at his office were causing him a lot of grief. The operation he had spent all those years working to improve was turning to shit because of greedy owners and incompetent managers. Not only that, Heilgar had been away from his home for the majority of his adult life, and he had never really been able to build a permanent, stable life here because he was working all the time.

On the other hand, I was sad to see a good man like Heilgar leave. While his stay had always been temporary, his leaving, he said, was permanent. And as was to be expected of Heilgar, he didn't discuss his feelings about the situation in the days leading up to his departure. Not even a little bit. It just was.

Nonetheless, when a dozen or so employees got together at Birch on Heilgar's final night in Valmesta, all of us believing that we would never see Heilgar again and might never hear from him again, Heilgar was visibly affected. A few of the staff—myself included—had come in on our night off to give him a proper send-off. When it was time to say goodbye, Heilgar and I hugged each other. We had never hugged before and the embrace was a bit self-conscious at first, neither of us knowing where to put what arm or how long to hold it, but it was a good hug. He made his rounds saying goodbye and made to walk toward the door. We watched him as he walked away. He swayed toward the left in a slightly inebriated effort to avoid the cleaning crew who were mopping the floor. "*Guten abend!*" I called to him as he walked through the door and into the hotel lobby toward his room.

How time passes by. It can be hard to get into a rhythm of the daily motions and the ups and downs of life, and then once you do find rhythm you run the risk of becoming complacent. And I am a firm believer that complacence is never good. It takes all the excitement out of things.

It was the dead heat of summer, the middle of August or so. The heat and humidity is inescapable that time of year in Valmesta. I had been meaning to take Ernie to the groomer for a bath for some time. He was starting to stink. On my way out I checked my mailbox in the lower corridor of my apartment building. Amongst a plentitude of junk mail was a letter from a literary agent I had queried regarding representation. I opened it and read it:

Dear Lado,

We may be passing up something great, but our slush pile is so colossal at this time that even if we were to interleave your collection of literary short fiction into our reading list, we can't guarantee that we would even get to it in the next year, if ever. We simply do not have the manpower to take on any more clients at this time.

Best of luck to you in what is sure to be a bright future. Might I suggest trying your hand at a lengthier work.

Sincerely,
[Agent]

At least he went out of his way to send me a real letter. I folded it neatly and slipped it into the back pocket of my cutoff jean shorts so I could add it to my collection of rejection paraphernalia at a later time.

Stepped outside. Lit a cigarette. The usual. My pupils took a moment to get used to the intensity of the light, and the air was so thick it felt like a steamy washcloth over my entire body. Ernie was already panting. The street was empty and the neighborhood was somewhat quiet for a workday afternoon, perhaps by chance, but more likely because of the strength of the heat. I looked around and found a group of attractive girls in shorts and tank tops. I rolled up my t-shirt sleeves to expose my upper arms and began walking toward the group of girls. I wanted to be near to them, to smell their perfume and the fruity sunscreen on their skin, to hear their voices and feel their energy.

The dog groomer remembered Ernie from the last time he was in, which was probably a year or more ago. My name eluded her, though, and she introduced herself as Emily. "I remember Ernie, he was such a good boy! He didn't like it all that much but he behaved himself, that's for sure."

"He's a pretty well-mannered guy," I said. "Keeps me from getting too down."

"Aren't they the best?"

"When should I come back?"

"Shouldn't be more than an hour. We don't have much going on today."

"I'll be back in an hour then."

"Great," she said. "Come on, Ernie."

Outside again I called Jack. He didn't answer. I scrolled through the apps on my phone hoping for another form of diversion. I opened up an internet browser, but I didn't have a connection. I crossed the street and sat on a park bench. Just as I sat down Jack called me back.

"Wanna get a drink?"

"Yeah."

"I have an hour to kill. Ernie's getting groomed."

"Dude, I wasn't gonna say anything, but he stinks.

"I know. That's why I'm having him groomed."

"Well, you tell me. I have all day."

"You don't have to work today?"

"Nope. I walked out," Jack said.

"What do you mean you walked out?"

"I mean I up and walked out like I said I would if she kept up with her shit."

We met up at Manny's. No matter where you were in West Valmesta you weren't very far from Manny's. We were sitting on the outdoor patio and a young server came up to greet us, one that I didn't recognize. He must have been new. He was perspiring visibly.

"You look like you could use a beer yourself," I said to him right away. He smiled obligatorily. I ordered a farmhouse ale that I knew was good and would be refreshing. Jack ordered the same and a shot of tequila with lime. "Are you going to do a shot with me?" he asked.

"I have to work at five," I said.

"Dude."

"All right. Two shots of tequila with lime."

"You want them chilled?" the server asked.

"What are you, crazy?"

"So, yes?"

"No, that'll just water 'em down. Bring 'em straight."

They came out fast and we put them down right away. Two beers and another shot later and I had the story from Jack. Apparently he found out with certainty that Clara had been having sex with other guys, or at least one other guy. In fact the guy showed up at Birch to surprise Clara with flowers and a CD mix he had made for her. "Who even makes CD mixes anymore?" Jack said. I thought about Ellery.

Clara, who was upset by the surprise visit, sent the man away promptly. Shortly afterward Jack approached Clara in her office and confronted her. "Did you fuck him?" he asked her. "Jack, even if I did, would you really want to know?" Clara was distraught, confused, and vulnerable. Jack then shut the door to Clara's office and locked himself in with her.

Altogether they were in there for about half an hour in the middle of the dinner rush. What exactly happened, Jack wouldn't say. "Honestly, I'd tell you pretty much anything, but it just wouldn't be right to tell you how that went down," he said. "She's leaving that place with pretty much zero integrity intact, and I'm not going to deprive her of the last sliver by talking about what happened between us." It was true. Like I said before, pretty much all the staff, both front and back of the house, respected Jack, and an offense against him was an offense against the whole lot of us. While she may have been in good standing with the high-ups, those below her on the corporate ladder had begun to loathe her.

"And then, I pretty much just took my apron off and walked the fuck out."

"Wait, she's leaving Birch?"

"Yea, she got a GM job somewhere else, at another hotel restaurant."

"In Valmesta?"

"I can't say. She put in her notice though. Like, a week ago"

I thought about it for a spell. "About fucking time," I said. I told Jack I had to pick up Ernie and get ready for work.

"I got the tab," he said. We clanked our glasses together and finished the last of our beers. Half-drunk, I made my way back to the dog groomer to pick up Ernie.

When I got to work I wondered how many people knew about Clara's imminent exodus. I studied each person's face, looking for an indication that they knew what I knew. As a general rule I try to stay out of gossip so long as the subject of the gossip has no bearing on my life. But this most recent tidbit was a cause for all-out celebration, as far as I was concerned. I could hardly contain my ecstasy.

I was the only one who knew, but I didn't get to enjoy being the only one for very long. Towards the end of our pre-shift meeting, Clara made the announcement that she was resigning and would be starting at a different restaurant in a different city at the end of the month. *Good riddance*, I thought to myself. *Good fucking riddance.*

I was surprised to discover that it was raining heavily when I left the building that night, so heavily that my clothes were soaked through within seconds, hundreds of gumball-sized raindrops doing belly flops on my bare arms and neck. I couldn't help but laugh at having to ride my bike home in the storm, which I did less carefully than I probably should have. My bicycle tires had already been ridden through two seasons, and they had a significant amount of wear to them, so I didn't have very good tread in wet conditions, and my glasses were being spattered with the aforementioned raindrops with a frequency that even the most effective windshield wipers would be unable to allay. Without a lamp, it would be impossible for passing cars to even see me on the road, and I wasn't wearing a helmet. The worst part was that I couldn't smoke a cigarette.

Still, I enjoyed the ride. The rain was refreshing, purifying, and not cold. I laughed like a madman and cursed incessantly all the way through downtown. At one point the avenue descended into what had become a pool of water over the pavement, and as I rode into the flood an automobile approached in the opposite lane, and a deluge of street water sloshed over me; I didn't care.

Then, suddenly, I was out of the rain. As I ascended the Columbia Avenue Bridge, I stopped pedaling and turned to see the storm over downtown. Lightning exploded in the distance, followed by a burst of thunder, like a fracture in the city skyline, and I was dripping wet on the dry pavement.

I locked my bicycle and buzzed up to my apartment. Ryan's voice came through the speaker. "Hello?" she said.

"It's me," I said.

"Don't you have your keys?"

"Yeah, I need you to bring me a towel. I'm soaked."

I heard Ryan's footsteps in the stairwell on the other side of the door, and she opened the door and handed me a towel. "You're making a puddle!" she said. She had heard the thunder, but from afar. It hadn't rained on the West side. I toweled off and removed my shirt before coming in. Everything was clean and smelled nice, even the dog. I opened a beer and sat down at my desk to check my e-mail while Ryan lay on the bed and told me the boring and mundane details of her day that somehow seemed interesting coming from her. I stepped outside for a cigarette and Ryan followed with a beer of her own.

We talked and drank. "Can I ask you something?" I said to her, after we had small talked our way deep enough into the conversation to bring it up. "What did you really think of my writing? I mean, when you first read it, in the office, before you knew me."

"I told you I liked it," she said, "you already know that."

"Did you enjoy reading it, or find pleasure in it?"

"Which piece?"

I paused, thinking. "The one…"

"Never mind, yeah, I enjoyed it. I enjoyed everything."

"What is it that you liked about it?"

"This is funny," she said.

"I don't understand."

"It's funny that we're talking about this right now, because I get you through your writing. In a sense I feel like this conversation is unnecessary."

"In that we've already communicated through my writing and your reading of it?"

"Yeah."

"Well, can't we try to have a conversation about it now? Let's do that. A separate communication."

"I'm trying. Let me think." I watched her gather her thoughts. "The thing about it is that it's different from most other pleasures. The pleasure of reading is different. Or, it's everything, or could be everything or anything, but it's also always only reading. I don't think I'm doing a good job of explaining."

"I follow. I like what you're saying. Go on."

"Okay. I guess all I'm trying to say is that, when I read your writing, I feel like I'm reading real writing. Like, you're the real deal."

"Can I really believe that assessment, or do you just like me?"

"I don't know. You asked what I thought."

"You're right, I'm sorry. I just find it really hard to believe it myself."

"I get that, but just try to."

"Did you happen to read the story about the younger brother whose older sister died of cancer, and after her death he went on a quest to find answers to life's greatest questions?"

"Yes! I liked that one. It was very...I don't know how you would say it, *surreal*?"

"Yeah. Or magical realist. I was inspired by magical realism when I wrote that."

"I can see that. It was very moving. I was sad at one point, but by the end of it I felt like the narrator turned a difficult experience into a positive force for himself. And even though he was disappointed in that he didn't find what he was looking for, he still found something. Maybe something even greater."

"By the end he understood that death is the only thing that makes what we have mean anything. That without death nothing in life would be what it is."

"And I feel like the narrator feels at the end like he will always have his sister, even though time seems to progress in a straight line, our experience of it is really more cyclical or nonlinear."

"Like, what happened in the past is still happening now, in a sense."

"Even if it's just in your own mind," she said.

Ryan looked away. I followed her line of sight. In the distance could be seen the old Valmesta Station, a decaying monolith protruding from the earth over a somber cityscape.

"Do you think your writing—that story in particular—has anything to do with your family history?" Ryan said.

"It's really hard to say."

"I know you don't have a sister. Am I right? You just have the one brother."

"Alexei is my only sibling, yes."

"Do you still talk to him?"

"Not really," I said. Ryan sat awaiting further explanation. "I honestly haven't spoken to him in five or so years. The last time I saw him was the summer before I went away to college."

"That's the summer that you lived outside the station."

"In the train car."

"Do you think he's still around?"

I tried to imagine the life Alexei would be leading if he were still living in Valmesta. I couldn't picture it. "I think I would have run into him," I said.

"So where do you think he is?"

"I don't know. Maybe in jail."

"Could he be, you know…"

"Dead?"

"I don't know, could he?"

"He could be."

"That's fucked up. And if he is, then the last time you talked to him…"

"Really, he could be anywhere, doing anything, he probably isn't dead."

"Well if he is, then you're the only one left to pass on the family name."

"Yeah."

"And what happened with your mom and dad?" Ryan said. Her interest in my past surprised me. No one had taken that kind of interest in my history before, not even me.

"I'm not sure exactly. It's hard to know for sure because I only know what was passed down to me from my aunt and uncle. I guess my dad was already in his forties when he had me and Alexei. My mom was younger. They weren't married when they had my brother, which I guess caused trouble in my mom's family and they more or less disowned her."

"What did your dad do?"

"He was a painter. I guess he was always under surveillance because the style he worked in was prohibited at the time."

"Because it was the Soviet Union."

"Exactly."

"I feel like all the arts would have been strictly regulated then."

"They were. And I guess my father didn't really like that very much, he had his own ideas and his own vision for his work. From what I'm told, he kept a private collection of his own work, and made a living on commission doing paintings of, say, Joseph Stalin."

"That's a pretty cool story, man. What happened with his private collection?"

"Don't know."

"Wow. And he died how?"

"He had cancer, I believe of the throat."

"And your mom?"

"Pneumonia. About a year before my dad actually."

"God."

Ryan took the last drink of her bottle. "You want another beer?" she said. I nodded.

"Can you grab my cigarettes, too, please?" I said.

While Ryan was inside, I allowed my gaze to return to that old station. The train car was probably still there somewhere, shrouded by a clump of foliage, never having gone anywhere. And I wondered whether to tell her the thing I had never told anyone else.

Ryan returned with two new beers and my pack of smokes. I lit one up and we sat in silence, and I began my story.

It was that summer, oh, that unforgettable, awful summer, when I wore the same attire day in and day out. That summer when I ate unripe apples and pears that I plucked from the forsaken trees nearby and strolled through grocery stores collecting free samples. That summer I drank from plastic half gallon jugs filled with rum and gin, and slept with a knife in my boot.

In some ways living in the train car was like living in your everyday hippy commune, and there were a lot of other young people doing it. Not all of us were completely down and out; some were doing it for the fun of it. I, for one, was a soon-to-be college boy. Granted, I had no other options. Anyway, see where I'm coming from.

I had really grown to like one of the hobo girls. She was a little younger than I was; she was sixteen at the time. They called her Soupcan Sue, or Soozy. Her hair had been cut short and bleached with peroxide some months prior, and she had grown several inches of dark brown roots to go with it, and she always wore a studded leather sleeveless jacket, showing off the lean-muscled shoulders and triceps that one acquires through complete self-sufficiency.

I'm not sure exactly how it happened, but we started having sex. First in the train car, with some semblance of privacy, and later everywhere around the train car, in the shade of pear trees, during heat waves and thunderstorms and whether the sun or stars shined overhead, not caring who saw or heard or whether there was any divine witness to our heathen exhibitions. There were no laws to observe, no rules to follow, nothing to deter us from doing what we felt like doing. It was a base love, but it was love nonetheless that I felt for her.

Then there was an evening that I returned to the train car from a day's carousing about. I had run into Alexei, and the two of us spent the afternoon drinking and catching up. When I took him to where I had been living, we found Soozy in the train car, sobbing. Sobbing and at the same time distant, like she wasn't even in her own head. When I reached out a hand and touched her shoulder she shuddered and shrieked and buried her head in her arms folded across her knees. I studied her body, her clothes. There were bruises on her skin; her denim shorts were covered in dirt.

"Who did it?" I said.

"Don't."

"Tell me who fucking did this to you."

Nothing, just sobbing.

"How bad is it. Are you hurt bad?"

"I'm not hurt, okay. I'll be fine."

I leaped out of the train car and began searching. Alexei followed. About ten minutes we scoured the area, around back of the station, into the urban wild, moving quietly. In a nearby clearing we came upon two adult men sitting on logs, warming a soup can over a fire, grinning. Alexei and I entered the clearing and made our presence known. The men stood up to face us. They were long time hobos, probably not from Valmesta originally. Maybe on the run. They had done it.

Alexei was on them. Before they could even make a move, he clubbed at one with his fist. The other grabbed Alexei by the collar. I reached into the fire for the can of soup, and the hot metal scalded my palm as I poured the soup over the man's neck and back. He screamed and, turning, tried to remove his shirt, and I started to pound at his head.

They were not good fighters. We beat them nearly dead.

Alexei said, "You need to get your girl to a hospital."

"Yeah, we should get back to the car."

Alexei shook his head. "You go. Let me see your knife."

"Come on. They're done."

"They are not."

"Alexei, you don't have to do this. Soozy is more important."

"Give it to me," he said. What was I to do? I looked at the two men. The one who had been burned lay in a hump in the long grass, trembling, seeming to cry. The other man had gotten to his feet and was wobbling like a proud, punch-drunk boxer, the look of his countenance not much steadier than that of his legs. Alexei made his way to the fire and removed one of the bigger logs and before the beaten man could regain himself Alexei raised the log lengthwise over his head with both hands and brought it down over the hobo's head, ending him.

"You're not going to stop me," he said. "They deserve it. Don't they?" My eyes were moistening and I dabbed them with my shirt so Alexei didn't see. In the way that a young man is true to his elder brother, I didn't disobey him. What he intended to do was just in his eyes, and I could see it. I gave him the knife.

I took Soozy to a small emergency room, where they took her in and treated her right away. Outside of her room, the doctor told me she had been raped and beaten by at least two attackers. I would find out later that Soozy had contracted hepatitis, but that she would be okay. But she was never the same as she was before. I felt so bad I wanted to die. They asked for an address to send the bill to. "I'm sorry?" I said.

"An address," the clerk said. I didn't know what to give them.

"Do you take cash?" I asked.

"We would prefer another method of payment."

"I don't think that will be possible."

The phone rang and the clerk answered.

"Emergency," she said. "Yes, you can have them come on back."

Two police officers entered through the double doors. They asked me questions: Where I lived, what was my relation to the victim, did anyone witness it, and did I know who did it. I told the truth about everything but did I know who did it. I tried to be cool, I knew it would do Alexei proud if I did, but my head was spinning. The memory is fuzzy now, was fuzzy as I recalled it to Ryan.

I remember the doctor wanted to keep Soozy sedated at the hospital for a while, it would be good for her. I talked with the clerk, trying to figure out who to contact and how we would pay for the visit. Soozy didn't have ID. I didn't even know her real last name.

Alexei arrived about an hour after the police left. His clothes were changed and he wore a backpack. When I told him the cops had shown up, he said, "They won't find anything. How is she?"

"She's okay. She's asleep, I think they have her medicated."

"Good." The clerk was studying Alexei. "How much for the treatment?" he asked her, removing his backpack.

"I'm not going to know until her stay is over."

"And when will that be?"

"You'll have to ask the doctor."

Alexei reached out with one arm to hand me the bag. I took it from him. It was heavier than he made it look. "This should cover it," he said. I remember I didn't say anything, didn't know what to say.

Across from me, silhouetted by the little bit of light from the street lamp, Ryan sat in disbelief. "And then he shook my hand and left, and I haven't seen him since."

"Holy shit, man," she said.

"You're the only person I've ever told that story to," I said. Ryan's mandible hung from her cheeks like some gruesome pendant. "You asked about my family," I said.

It was a few days later that I found myself in the liquor room with Maria. The bartenders on duty asked me if I could go back into the liquor room and grab a case of beer that they had run out of at the bar. It was toward the beginning of my shift and I wasn't busy yet, so I didn't mind helping out. I asked if they had the keys and they said no, ask Clara. I asked Clara if she had the keys to the liquor room and whether I could borrow them to grab some beer for the bartenders, who were busy at the moment. She was on her cell phone, texting, and she didn't look up to answer me. "Maria's back there doing inventory," she said. Why Maria was doing a manager's job I didn't know. Probably because it was one of Clara's last days.

So I went down the hallway and through dry storage and I saw that the door to the liquor room was closed, but in the crack under the door I could see the light shining through. I knocked. The door opened and Maria stood looking at me with a clipboard in her hand. "I just need to grab some beer for the bar," I said. Maria stepped aside and let me in.

Maria was taking inventory of the liquor in the main liquor room. Neither of us said anything. I walked into the beer cooler. I watched the steam of my breath. It took me a moment to find the beer that I was looking for, since I had never stocked the bar before and I wasn't familiar with the layout of the beer room. When I found the case I was looking for I picked it up and walked out of the cooler. My nipples were hard from the cold and my glasses fogged up and I couldn't really see much, but I could tell that the door was closed and I sensed Maria behind me. She giggled at my glasses being fogged up. I asked her if she could get the door for me, but instead she came around the front of me and set the clipboard down, grabbed the case of beer out of my hands, and placed the case on the shelf.

"What's up?" I said.

"Haven't you always wanted to do this?" she asked me in a little girl's voice. She was looking at me the same way she looked at me when she spent the night at my place. She was a hungry girl. She flipped the light switch off, and it was completely dark in the liquor room.

"I don't know if this is a good idea," I said. "Clara would fire us on the spot," though I was really more concerned with the fact that I had, for all intents and purposes, a girlfriend. I just thought that the prospect of getting fired would be more of a deterrent for Maria, and perhaps even more of a deterrent for myself, than the fact that I was seeing someone.

"I didn't think you were such a square," Maria whispered in the dark. I felt her hand on my thigh as she felt for my crotch. I pulled away a little bit and I said, "Maria, really," but she kept her grip on my package with one hand and with the other hand she squeezed my cheeks firmly and scrunched up my lips into a pudgy baby face and shushed me right before she kissed me. "You'll love it," she said. By then my boner was already at seventy-five percent or so, and my capacity to resist was, as mathematics would have it, down to about twenty-five percent.

"What exactly is it that I'm going to love so much?" I asked her in a tone that was somewhere between innocent curiosity and submissive dirty talk. I was putting forth the effort not to reciprocate, and Maria sensed it and knew it and it turned her on even more. She reached her hand into my pants and underneath my boxer briefs. Her hand felt cold at first but only for a few seconds, as it warmed up around me and I became hard as a rock. She let out an erotic gasp and we kissed hard.

Of course we didn't have sex for the same reason that we didn't have sex the first time we hooked up. Instead Maria gave me one of the most memorable blowjobs of my entire life. Memorable because it was complete darkness in the liquor room and I had absolutely zero visual cues, just the physical sensation of her warm, wet mouth and the friction of her tongue and the little bit of suction. Once for a spell she took it out of her mouth and held it over her head in her hand and licked my balls, licked from the base of my cock and all the way up to the tip slowly, squeezed my bare ass and put her fingernails into my skin. She smacked herself in the cheek with it a few times and I heard and felt the dull smack of it against her buttery smooth skin before she sucked it again. She rubbed it against her cheek, the wetness of her saliva lubricating her skin, and the way she laughed brought me closer and closer to orgasm. When she put it back in her mouth it was maybe another thirty seconds of it until I came. As I began to moan and my muscles tensed up with the pleasure of it, I could hear her asking for it, "Mmm hmm," she said. I felt the vibration of her voice box. When I came I came a lot and for a long time, probably ten consecutive shots of it into the back of her throat, and she took it like a champ and swallowed all of it. I leaned back into it and tipped my head up to the ceiling, my mouth agape. I nearly fell over it was so good. She kept sucking at it until I was empty.

Afterward I could hear Maria wiping, presumably, the saliva off of her face. She stood up and kissed my cheek. "Did that feel good, baby?" she asked me. I made a face at her calling me "baby," but in the dark she couldn't tell. I already felt ashamed. I told her it did feel good. She turned the light on and we looked at each other. Maria was smiling. I stood there with my dick out. She looked beautiful. He skin was radiant, her posture sound. It was like she had just taken a B12 shot. Her clothes were in order; her hair was in a perfect little bun.

"Come on," she said.

"If you wanted me to come on you should have said so," I said. Maria smiled briefly but it waned into an all-business face. "Let's go. We need to get out of her before someone catches on."

I gestured toward my still erect penis. "I'm going to need a minute before I can put this thing away," I said.

"Okay. Turn the light off and lock the door behind you," she said, and she turned, pushed open the door, and walked out into the dry storage room. She closed the door. A few seconds later, I heard her in the hallway speaking to Clara, who was probably still in her office texting. "Here are the keys," Maria said. Clara said thank you and asked if I had gotten the beer that the bar needed, and Maria said that I had.

I let my boner go down before I tried to stuff it back into my jeans. Any guy will tell you how uncomfortable it can be to have a boner in the pants. I looked around at all the liquor and saw an open bottle of Bulleitt on the top shelf. I pulled it down from the shelf and uncorked it and took a big swig, and then another, and I corked it and put it back. The surface of the whiskey was significantly lower than the line indicated by the mark drawn on the outside of the glass, but I didn't care. I let the bourbon settle in my stomach, the warmth of it radiating throughout my abdomen. I grabbed the beer for the bar and turned the light off and walked out, closing the door behind me.

That night I rode my bike home from The Rabbit Hole with a few beers in me, and when I arrived at my apartment Ryan was there kneeling on the floor surrounded by boxes full of her things that she was unpacking and putting away. There was music playing and there were candles lit, and my apartment smelled even better than it had all those times before. It was the candles that made the spicy smell. It was warm, but it wasn't hot, and there was the smell and I felt like I had just arrived at a place truly worthy of the title *Home*. I looked around and saw that it was clean.

Ryan and Ernie were coming towards me, six legs trotting energetically, Ryan's two bare and smooth and thin and utterly sexy. She had on a very short pair of navy trousers and a loose-fitting, sleeveless shirt. She held her arms wide and leapt up for me to catch her and she wrapped her legs around my waist and I held her up with her ass in my hands. Ernie barked twice.

I held Ryan up and I kissed her and as I did so the shame of what I had done earlier that night, or of what I had allowed to happen, overwhelmed me and I laughed and then I almost started to cry because of how bad I felt. I didn't expect to feel so bad. Until that moment I hadn't planned on telling Ryan what happened but when that moment came I realized I had to tell her and there was no way around it. I stopped myself from crying. "What's the matter, baby?" is what she said.

"I did something tonight and I feel really bad about it," I said.

Ryan's demeanor quickly changed from concerned to confused and then defensive. She crossed her arms. "What happened?"

"Well, I never really told you about it because it wasn't important and you and I weren't exclusive and I didn't think we would get to this point we're at now..."

"Just tell me what happened, Lado."

"Well, there is a girl I work with, her name is Maria, and she and I hooked up. Just once. A couple of months back," I said. As I said it I saw the gears turning in Ryan's head, doing the calculations.

"Did you fuck her?" she asked me.

"What? No, not tonight. I mean, not then, either. We've never fucked, actually. It's against her religion."

"Her religion?"

"I know."

"So what happened tonight?"

"She gave me a blowjob in the liquor room."

"At Birch?"

"At Birch."

"What a slut," Ryan said. She paused, took a deep breath. "So it's against her religion to have sex but she's allowed to go down on you in the liquor room?"

"Ryan, I'm sorry."

"You're an asshole."

"I'm not perfect, and I'm sorry, and I feel bad because I really like you."

"Do you? Really?" She was gathering her purse and sweater and appeared ready to walk out. "Were you thinking

242

of how much you like me while some work slut gave you a
blow job?"

"Actually, yeah, the lights were off, and…"

"Ew, okay. Enough. Stop talking."

I stopped talking. I reached out toward Ryan, but she
turned away and told me not to touch her. Some time passed
and I studied her. Even with her purse flung over her
shoulder, I knew she didn't want to leave.

"You do know that's not at all okay, right?" she said.

"Yes. Yes! I know. I'm sorry. I want to be with you,
and I'm an idiot for not realizing that sooner and for fucking
up, but I mean that."

"I want to be with you, too," she said, softening, "but
I'm not going to waste my time with a cheater. I've been
down that road."

"I know." I felt more ashamed at that moment than
ever before or since, and I was afraid of losing her. I began to
cry. "I've just never really been with anyone."

"Well, this is the 'we are exclusive' conversation. An
unusual one."

"That's what I want. You're it."

"That means that from this point forth there's no
fucking around."

"Absolutely zero fucking around," I said.

"I've made my share of mistakes," she said. "We all
make mistakes. Just don't make any more of those kind,
okay?"

I nodded and she kissed me, and then pulled away
abruptly.

"You didn't return the favor, did you?" she asked.

Dare I jest? "I knew I forgot to mention something,"
I said, and Ryan laughed.

We had sex that night on the floor of our warm,
candlelit apartment amid a bouquet of cinnamon and clove.
"Oh, my God," she said, again and again, in whispers and
moans. "I love you," I said.